I0647864

The Rebounders

By
Patrick James Brown

© 2018

ALSO BY
PATRICK JAMES BROWN

The Mick

Pirate Captain Rotten Rudolph
And The Very Rotten Rescue Voyage
With Illustrations by Jack Thor

The People Celebrate:
A Report on North Dakota's Centennial

The Rebounders

A Novel by
Patrick James Brown

This is a work of fiction. However, it is based on the loves and losses, places and times of my life. I have never lived in New York but have toured the city many times when I visited my daughter Sara, a feisty Midwesterner who took to the City like a native, much to her mother's chagrin. I have worked for several advertising agencies, have been the client of others, and have worked as a freelancer. While I have drawn on my experience, any resemblance to any one person, living or dead, is an unintended coincidence.

Copyright © 2018 by Patrick James Brown

All rights reserved. No part of this novel may be used, except for excerpts for critical reviews and commentary, without the express written permission of the author.

Cover design and page layout by Mike Lacher, Gray Dog Design, Fargo, North Dakota.

Library of Congress Cataloging-in-Publication Data

Brown, Patrick James.

The Rebounders: a novel/by Patrick James Brown. — First Edition

ISBN 978-0-9963068-2-9

PRINTED IN THE UNITED STATES OF AMERICA

First Edition: November 2018

ACKNOWLEDGEMENTS

I am forever grateful to my friend and editor, Greg Lauser, who has improving the quality of my writing his only goal. I cannot ask more. Thanks, too, to my son-in-law Mark Trokan, for ensuring the accuracy of my New York settings. And I can't forget Mike Lacher, a talented and skilled graphic artist, and patient and forgiving friend.

In addition, thank you to Timothy Olson, JCL, Collegiate Judge and Ponens with The Catholic Diocese of Fargo (ND) for his detailed explanation of the process of charging and investigating a priest for divulging what he hears in the confessional.

Readers of my first drafts offered encouragement and constructive criticism, and for that I need to thank Linda Pederson, Jill Landry, Katherine Tweed, and Lindsay Landry. And finally, thanks to Paula Swanson, who read my final manuscript for clarity and said she didn't hate it.

I must also thank the many advertising and public relations clients who allowed me to communicate and promote their organizations. Many times they acted on faith that I could do what I said I could, which always drove me to write, create, and direct better. They deserve much credit for my skills.

— - —

For Susan, my eternal love, the ending and the beginning.

— - —

Prologue

In the end, she must have simply exhaled her last breath. Through dry, cracked lips. Over a thick, swollen tongue. Alone. Well, not counting the angels and our two French Bulldogs, Sigmund and Freud.

I had gone for my morning run before the private nurse arrived and I had to get ready for work. So, I was out running through Central Park when she died. I didn't really enjoy running through Central Park alone, but it was close to our brownstone and I could go at a good clip and not have to worry about getting hit by a taxi or a bike messenger. Besides, even at 50, I was also too fast for any muggers, whom, I'm convinced, smoked like chimneys, which meant they couldn't run more than 10 feet without getting winded and turning their attention to an elderly man or woman out for a stroll at 6:00 AM.

Why was I out running when Missy was obviously so close to death? "You've got to take care of yourself," the private nurse admonished me. Yeah, I know, exercise, eat right, and take Geritol. I'm "in" advertising, so sometimes I think in slogans. "You can't help her if you're exhausted and sick," she explained. Really?

Well, I've got news for you, lady. I've been exhausted and sick ever since numerous neurologists had diagnosed, confirmed, and reconfirmed that Michelle Clarke-Sullivan, M.D., my beautiful wife and brilliant psychiatrist, had ALS, short for amyotrophic lateral sclerosis, which in polite circles is euphemistically referred to as Lou Gehrig's disease.

"You'll live a long life," one of the docs had told her, upon confirming her diagnosis. A week later, following yet another painful needle probe inside Michelle's elbows, her best friend, the head of the neurology department, had told us, with unprofessional tears in her eyes, "I'm afraid, my dearest friend, your case is very advanced. Your journey will be much shorter than we had originally thought."

On the drive home, I had gripped the steering wheel of our five-year-old Volvo and started to sob. "Why are you crying?" Missy had said, "I'm the one who's dying!"

Gallows humor being what it is, we both laughed.

Progress rapidly it did. Not every ALS patient spends years in a specially designed wheelchair. Missy went from walking holding onto my arm, to walking only with a "granny walker," to falling when she got out of bed, to refusing to stay in bed so she wouldn't fall, to having to stay in bed because her legs refused to obey any commands, to ... Well, you get the picture.

Oh, and her lips and tongue were dry and cracked when she died because she couldn't swallow. Hadn't been able to for two weeks, and had a healthcare directive in which, with the blessing of my older brother, the family priest, she had declared that she was not to have a feeding tube, or IV, or ventilator, or any other present or future life-sustaining technology. So, quit thinking I'm a horrible person for not taking better care of her. I did my best.

The funeral was a lovely Irish Catholic/German Protestant affair. My brother, Fr. Terrence gave a wonderful canned homily, with a few personal things thrown in, a joke or two, and a salute to Missy's Lutheran family and friends.

That's how, at age 50, I became a widower with two semi-grown daughters, Katherine and Abigail. Well okay, Kate and Abby.

And how, you may ask, am I, at age 54, lying next to this gorgeous blonde 53-year-old woman on an immaculate white sand beach in the Caribbean? That, friend, is our story.

Chapter 1
Jack

After the funeral, my daughters, Missy's parents, my parents, and I positioned ourselves near the community room front door, like in a wedding reception line, but more of a downer. I was the last in the line, so I got to hear all the condolences the others received. By the time folks got to me, about the only thing left to do was hug and shake my hand. So it went for close to an hour as doctors, nurses, a few of Missy's former patients, my co-workers, friends of both our families, and people I had never seen, filed by. When it was time to go, the girls and I started to help with the clean-up, but we were shooed away by an elderly nun wearing an apron over her modern habit, as she handed us three large plastic bags of sandwiches.

"Eat the egg salad ones first. Don't want you coming down with food poisoning," she admonished. Sigmund and Freud were going to eat egg salad sandwiches, we decided on the limo ride home.

Both sets of parents came to the brownstone and we visited quietly until, exhausted by Missy's final days, the funeral preparations, and the actual funeral, and burial and reception, I experienced an exhaustion that I had not known since my days in Marine Corps boot camp. I yawned, my eyes closed and the next thing I knew, it was dark as our daughters shook me gently by both shoulders.

"You're snoring," Kate said. "Everyone's gone. They said to tell you they love you and will talk soon."

"I need to walk Sigmund and Freud."

"Abbey already did, so let's all go upstairs and go bed."

"Okay, and thanks, Abbey."

"No problem, Pops."

Off to bed we went – two half-orphaned teens, two French Bull Dogs, and one newly minted widower.

As we have every Saturday for the two months since Missy's funeral, my little brother, Bobby, my friend, Lew, and I, play a wicked game of two-on-two basketball on Central Park's asphalt courts. None of our other friends will play with us because they know they could end up in traction. We always grab the first tough-looking guy who shows up to team up with Bobby. That guy never shows up again.

Lew, however, is nuts. Justifiably so. He's a former Navy SEAL. And at six-three, with properly muscled arms and legs and a demeanor that would scare an NFL linebacker, he's always my teammate. Funny how that seems to work out.

Lew grew up in Dothan, Alabama, the son of a high school math teacher and a high school football coach and civics teacher. Not only had he always been big, but he was smart, scoring so high on his SATs that both U.S. senators wanted to appoint him to the Naval Academy. His parents had marched with Martin Luther King, Jr, so they knew how their son might be treated in a school filled with privileged white boys. They had traveled to Washington, D.C., and questioned both senators about why each wanted to appoint a black boy to the academy. Both had said because he was smart and would serve his country well, and both had mentioned that appointees to all military academies are from all walks of life and all colors and creeds. However, one had said that Lewis Washington would make his parents and his community proud, so he got the honor.

That senator was right. Lewis had made his parents proud. He had excelled in varsity football and had been a Midshipman company commander when he graduated. He also had turned down the NFL draft to try out for the Navy's SEa, Air and Land (SEAL) Team, more grueling than an NFL try-out camp. He graduated at the top of his class, but it had come at a price. It earned him the same dangerous deployments as all other SEALs. He told his parents he had every right to expect danger because he wanted those assignments, but they could never ask where he was and he could never tell them what he did or where.

Eight years later, Lt. Cmdr. Lewis Washington handed in his Trident without explanation, became a private security guard and, at times, a mercenary. I met him when he had come along with his security company's owner to our agency for a quick direct-mail campaign aimed at vulnerable international companies. My boss had pushed them off on me. I had directed most of my questions at Lew, which he appreciated. We went to lunch and we just became fast friends. I admired his background, his accomplishments, and his knowledge. He admired my sense of humor and lack of bullshit. It was a friendship made in heaven.

Ten minutes into this week's game, Bobby huffed as he tried to drive around me for a lay-up. Bobby huffs at the slightest exertion because our mother always spoiled him. While the rest of the neighborhood kids walked the seven blocks to St. Patrick's Elementary, Mom made sure Bobby got a ride from one of the neighbors. Or a taxi. Now, he's a semi-in-shape computer geek who supervises 15 others at an entire company of computer geeks. The perfect fit, except Bobby works hard to maintain his pudgy, yet not obese, physique.

"Don't you think it's time?" he puffed.

I stuck my left knee in his way. "For you to make a basket...snag a rebound?" I grunted. The ball sailed out of bounds and bounced against the chain-link fence.

"No, asshole," he yelled over his shoulder as he trotted over to where the ball rested, "for you to start dating."

"Shut up," I said, immaturely. We generally resort to our younger selves when we're together. Missy used to call it 'birth order bullshit.'

Bobby dribbled the ball back to the sideline without looking down. He likes showing off that way. Just to irritate me he stood off court, just bouncing the damn ball. "How long's it been?" he said looking straight at me, still dribbling. I was getting pissed off for two reasons.

"Not long enough," I replied, "and throw in the damn ball." I knew exactly what he was referring to. He and a few others think my love life, or lack thereof, is their business. It isn't, and I'll get back in circulation when I know I won't feel as if I'm cheating on Missy.

"I ain't talking about your tool, fool," Bobby joked, crude as always.

I looked down into his eyes. Lew sensed a conflict and walked over. That could have been because I'm three inches taller than Bobby, my face was red and my tightly fists were white.

"It's only been 14 months, two weeks, and ..." Lew grabbed my elbow so I would know he was there to keep me from taking a swing at my irritating little brother. When a Navy SEAL grabs your elbow, it has a calming, frightening effect, even if he's a good friend. And I needed that because Bobby wouldn't let it go.

"That's over a year, Jack," he pointed out. "You have to move on." Lew let go so I grabbed the ball and started to dribble.

"And YOU should learn defense," I taunted Bobby as I drove to the basket. The ball bounced around the rim and dropped through the chain net for two! Lew grabbed the ball, but I took it from him with every intention of bouncing it off Bobby's thick skull. Thinking that Lew would protect him, Bobby just kept at it.

"You're in denial...Shit, you didn't even cry at her funeral," he had the gall to say. I'd finally had enough. I can't keep my temper when I'm angry AND hurt. So, before Lew could get to me, I threw the ball at Bobby's head. He ducked so I missed, which pissed me off even more.

"Fuck you, Bobby, just fuck you!" I got in his face, my fists clenched. "I cried ... Missy and I cried together...plenty. When they gave her that goddamn death sentence...when she couldn't walk or feel her legs...when she couldn't swallow...We cried."

I turned away before I did something stupid, like pull Bobby's ears down around his shoulders, and I stormed off the court.

Bobby yelled after me. "It's time, Jack...you need to start dating...at least get laid, for Christ's sake." Always has to have the last word.

It isn't actually a word, but I flipped him the finger as I walked away. "Lunch Thursday, Bro?" I heard him yell.

Chapter 2
Jack

The third Saturday of every month is my day to go to Confession. I don't always make it, but it's a goal. Besides, the priest I confess to is my brother. I figure that gives me a whole heap of forgiveness and a straight line to somewhere good when I die.

Confessionals are like cocoons, dark and soundproofed, because when you're in tenth grade you don't want a Mary Katherine McClanahan in line behind you hearing the gory details of your transgressions and then entertaining her friends with your attempts to look up Sister Mary Louise's habit when she sits in the stands and cheers for the girls' basketball team. So, confessionals are soundproofed.

After all these years, I've learned how to project my voice in a stage whisper through the confessional screen so only the priest can hear. It's a talent many Catholics perfect.

"...for these and all my sins I am heartily sorry," I finished up with Fr. Terrance. I always pronounce "heartily" perfectly so it doesn't come out "hardly." Another Catholic hang-up.

"Hearing your Confession is like being stoned to death with cotton balls," my brother said, quite blasphemously I thought. "For your penance, say three Our Fathers, three Hail Mary's, and volunteer in the parish for one hour. And now, make ..."

"I am NOT filing your correspondence again," I interrupted him.

"Okay, then clean the kitchen AND the bathrooms at the parish homeless shelter," he whispered loud enough so Cardinal Dolan could hear him.

"Let's take this outside, pilgrim," I whispered in my best imitation of John Wayne.

"Say your Act of Contrition and wait for your absolution!"

After he did his forgiveness routine, I got off the kneeler and parted the curtain just as Terry came out of his cubicle. We walked passed two fidgeting pudgy adolescents and a rotund woman who appeared to be their mother because she held the boys by both shoulders so they couldn't make a break for the exit.

"I'll be right back," Terry smiled and said to the woman, who scowled at him as if to say getting her boys to Confession was hard enough without a goddamned delay.

"I'm through doing your shit jobs, Terry." We were standing on the top step of the massive front steps of St. Patrick's Cathedral. I admit, Terry looks saintly in his priest's apparel. And his salt and red-pepper hair, ruddy complexion, and straight, thin nose make him look like the statue of a saint of yore. We're the same height, so it's easy to look each other in the eye when we "discuss," like we're doing now.

"It's all the Lord's work...have you started... dating, yet?" he asked slyly. Talk about being blindsided. You'd think a guy with a doctorate in theology would be subtler.

"What's with you people?!" I exclaimed. "I'm still grieving; don't you get it?"

"Even the Holy Catholic Church says marriage is only until death, Jack," Terry said in his most officious voice. "You can still mourn Missy's passing, but it's time to move on."

"I'll decide when it's time...and neither of my brothers is going to push me into something I'm not ready for..."

At that, I stormed down the steps. Over my shoulder, I said, "I declare this is still Confession, priest ...You can't tell Ma."

"Who do you think asked us to nag you?" he said, much too loudly because every tourist mounting the steps into New York's famous cathedral, and most of the pedestrians streaming by, looked at him. I just looked back, exasperated and frustrated with my entire family of third-generation Irish immigrants.

"I know a choir member who thinks you're hot," Fr. Terrence yelled, inappropriately, and again, too damn loudly.

"I'm not listening!"

"Start dating, Bro! She's gone...You're officially parted." Now everyone on the steps had frozen in their tracks and was staring at us, following our "discussion" back and forth like a Rod Laver tennis match. I wasn't thinking about my brother the priest, just my older, nagging brother when I turned around and flipped him the bird, which I shouldn't have done, at least not in front of St. Patrick's with hordes of tourists flowing in an out.

Terry solemnly shook his head from side to side and raised his right arm and slowly blessed me and then the crowd on the steps. Nice touch.

The woman grunted slightly as she opened one of the massive wood doors and slid sideways out of the church just as Fr. Terrence yelled to the other man that he was going to tell someone what the man had just confessed, maybe even what she had confessed! When she recognized the priest from the back of his head, she quickly pulled her Pashmina over her custom-dyed silver hair. She knew she was a rather attractive 60-year-old petite woman that no man should reject, so she couldn't believe her good luck in overhearing that this man, this priest, was going to divulge what he had heard in the sanctity of the confessional. As a lay member of the Society of Christ Scourged, she was appalled. As a woman scorned by him in high school after two whole years of wanting to give him her virginity, though, she was delighted. Her testimony would most certainly force the archbishop to remove this holier-than-thou priest. Karma's a bitch, she muttered into the folds of her scarf, and you, Terry the Almighty, made me one.

Chapter 3
Jack

You can smell my mother's Sunday family dinners two blocks away. Lots of onion and garlic. I'm sure she asks the produce manager at Trader Joe's for the strongest, most pungent bulbs in the store. I know he always sets them aside for her because she's a sweet little Irish woman with a wicked temper, and he's afraid of her. Has been for the past 18 years, ever since the day she demanded fresh Yukon potatoes for her Irish stew and he mistakenly gave her one with an eye. He and customers within 50 feet of the potato bin heard about that for the next month, until Ma figured she'd punished him enough. Of course, a free five-pound "sample" bag of small new red potatoes didn't hurt his cause any.

On this Sunday, the inviting aroma of pot roast greeted me as soon as I got out of the Volvo. I knew it was pot roast because that's what's up in the weekly rotation. Irish stew, then leg of lamb, then roast chicken followed by pot roast. I don't always make it to these Sunday dinners. Sometimes I'm on a photo shoot outside the city, but when I'm in the city, I'm there even if they aren't as much fun anymore since, well, you know.

I'm dreading today because of my asshole brothers and the probable confrontation with my mother about my complete lack of a social life. She's a little hard to figure about that. See, she and Missy were very close. Since I don't have any sisters, you might say they had a loving mother-daughter relationship. Why she's encouraging me to get back in circulation after the death of her quasi-daughter is a little baffling.

I walked up the steps, took a deep breath, gritted my teeth and pursed my lips into a tight smile as I opened the door.

"There you are my sweet boy!"

"Hi, Ma," I said lovingly as I reached down and hugged her.

"You're so gaunt," she teased.

"Now, Ma, you know I work out a lot."

"I know, but you gotta eat. Come in and sit down. Everyone's already here."

Arm in arm, we entered the dining room. Around the table, already stuffing their faces with fresh-baked sourdough biscuits, are my ever-ravenous and always-dieting college daughters, Kate and Abby, Fr. Terrence, Bobby, and Sandy, Bobby's saintly wife. My father, all six-foot-two of him, is at the head of the table, which is closest to the kitchen door so he gets the full benefit of the kitchen aromas and first shot at hot food when Ma walks it to the table.

My father is one of those hard-working guys who occupy every middle-class neighborhood in America. He enlisted in the Air Force during the Korean War because, he proudly explained, in the Air Force the only ones who do the fighting are the officers. So, he became an airplane mechanic, a skill he used as a civilian to become a diesel mechanic on Long Island. He is still a good-looking guy at 76, with a full head of white hair, freckles across his bulbous nose, and muscular arms. His scarred knuckles signify the many slipped wrenches he endured on the job.

We're good friends now, but it wasn't always so. From my fourteenth year until I headed to college to become a writer, my father and I hardly spoke, unless I was correcting his grammar or he was yelling at me to turn down my damn stereo. Today we laugh at the same jokes, root together for the Mets and the Jets and the Rangers, and have heart-to-hearts over a couple of glasses of Jameson. I'm thankful that we survived my teen years to become friends.

"Hi, Dad!" my girls said in unison as their grandmother and I came into the dining room. Sandy smiled up at me with baleful eyes as if to say 'Oh, you poor man.' Her husband mumbled a greeting through a mouthful of biscuit.

Out of the public eye, the priest waved to me with the middle finger of his left hand, which, fortunately, neither of our parents saw.

I took my usual place to my father's right. "Hello, Jonathan," my father said warmly. Mom brought out the pot roast, already carved, surrounded by carrots, potatoes, and strong onions. She sat and immediately Fr. Terrance lead us in prayer (St. Hypocrite) before we passed the food and began eating.

When the food made its way around to her, my dear mother started in on me ... after politely wiping the corners of her mouth. "I just don't understand you, Jonathan. You're still a young man. Fifty-one is young these days."

"Oh, right, Grandma," smirked Kate. "Fifty-one is 'real' young."

"I don't want my Dad dating," Abby interjected. "He still misses Mom. Don't you, Daddy?"

"Of course I do, Sweets. Every day in every way."

"It still wouldn't hurt you to have coffee with a woman once in a while, Jack," Bobby piped up between a bite of roast and a gulp of wine.

"Remember what I told you after Confession yesterday, Jack," Terry just had to say.

"What did he confess? Any good shit?" Bobby asked, in all seriousness. "Robert O'Malley Sullivan," Pop glared at Bobby, "don't use that language at the dinner table."

"Or anywhere!" Ma added.

"Sorry..." Bobby said lacking an ounce of sincerity. Then he leaned over to Terry. "Really, Bro, any juicy shit?"

"I confessed my eternal loathing for my baby brother. Pass the roast, asshole."

"Boys!" Ma said. "That's enough!"

After an uncomfortable silence, Abby asked, "Why do you think he should start seeing other women, Grams?"

"Because he's all alone. You two are at that college. I just worry about him being lonesome at night. It isn't right."

"Everyone! Leave Jonathan alone. The longer he's single, the better my chances that he'll give up advertising and join a monastery," my father said, helpfully.

"Thanks, Pops," I said. "Some choice. I like advertising. I'm good at it, and as a wise ad man once said, it's the most fun you can have with your clothes on."

"Maybe you should try something where you take off your clothes," said Bobby, ever the classy nerd.

"Ewwwwe. That is so gross, Uncle Bobby!" said Abby.

I stared off, my fork and knife poised to cut a chunk of roast on my plate. The words "clothes off" triggered a daydream in which I'm making love to a faceless woman with blonde, then auburn, then black hair. Then I heard her voice.

"Are you okay, Dad?"

Instant reality. I dropped my fork and heard it clatter against the rim of Ma's Sunday-best-dishes plate. "Huh? Oh, sure, Katie."

Bobby snorted wine out his nose, then his wife, my hero, smacked him hard on the arm with the knuckles of her left hand.

"What?!" he yelped.

No one else seemed to care about my momentary lapse in consciousness, so we finished our meal in interesting blather about the Jets, the Yankees, and the latest hockey players from North Dakota and Manitoba to have signed with the Rangers. After dessert, a way too rich Guinness cake, we all cleared dishes and the guys did dishes until Ma came into the kitchen and chased us out because she doesn't want her dishes chipped. We could be careful, but my mother is a control freak, so we abandoned the dishes and the kitchen. Time to leave anyway.

I walked my girls out to the car they share at college. When we got to the front bumper of the 1996 Nissan Something, I hugged them both.

"Study hard, don't drink or do drugs. And no fighting!"

"We're good, Pops," Katie said, smiling up at me.

I don't really care to be called "Pops" by a 20-year-old college kid, but there're worse monikers, so I always ignore it. I looked over at Abby, who was pouting.

"She hogs the frickin' car," Abby said.

"Please don't swear, Abby, and you share the car, Katie."

"As much as I can," Katie said too quickly as she hopped into the driver's seat. After starting the car, she leaned down and craned her neck so she could look around Abby at me through the passenger window. "Bye, Pops. Love you!" Abby just stared forward and then turned her head and blew me a kiss. I saw tears welling up in her eyes. They drove off too quickly, radio blaring.

Katie reached over to the radio and spun the volume control counterclockwise. "Hey! I was listening to that!" Abby yelled.

"We need to talk," Katie said. "Dad's doing the best he can."

"Katie, he doesn't listen like Mom used to. I could always call her and she knew exactly what to say."

"Jesus, Ab, he's a guy who isn't a psychiatrist. Give him a friggin' break."

"I miss her."

"We all do."

At that, Abby reached over and turned up the volume louder than it was before.

Chapter 4
Jack

On the drive home, my mind wandered from fond memories of family times to loneliness – thoughts of Missy and our good times and some of our standard disagreements – and work that my team needs to do for our clients.

I lucked out and pulled into a parking place on the street only 20 feet from the steps to my brownstone. My neighborhood is quiet, the sidewalks are lined with 30-year-old ash trees, their trunks surrounded by small wrought iron fences, and there's hardly any litter. That's because we have a neighborhood organization whose members pick up litter, a different person or family every day. I love it here and get along with my neighbors.

As I unlocked the door, Darby got up and looked at me pleadingly. When I'm gone, he always lays by the door and waits for me. Today he wanted another walk, so before doing anything else, I grabbed his leash off the coat hook behind the door and we walked several blocks. Back home, I fed him and poured myself a "few" fingers of Jameson, neat.

I felt sorry for myself, so I plopped down on my leather couch and grabbed the photo album that I keep on the coffee table. As I looked through the photos of our early marriage, I managed to consume most of my drink. Oddly enough, the woman in the photos is the same woman in my daydream. She's standing naked in front of me and then jumps on the couch.

"This empty nesting is more fun than it should be," she says, throatily.

"We've waited twenty-five years for this much fun," I whisper into her ear, which is quite hairy. The woman licks my cheek. I struggle to open my eyes. There, beside me, is Darby, his nose two inches from mine.

"Off the couch, Darby Science Diet breath. It's time for bed."

I got Darby from an Irish Wolfhound rescue organization in Connecticut 14 months after Missy died. Sigmund and Freud had been her babies, French Bulldogs we also rescued so we would have company after the girls went away to college. The two dogs had become so despondent after Missy's funeral that they both died of broken hearts, or so the Vet diagnosed. My heart was broken, too, so a few weeks later I came across a YouTube video of two Irish Wolfhounds sitting on a couch licking the face of an elderly woman who giggled as she tried to make them stop. Below the video was an ad for a rescue organization. The next day I called and was invited to fill out an application and visit with the dogs. Two days later I drove up and filled out the lengthy application in a cramped office. Then I went out to the yard, which was actually a field, and one of the dogs, a male whose head reached my shoulder, trotted over and nuzzled my right hand until I scratched behind his left ear. He'd already been named Darby. Two weeks later, after a dog-adoption psychiatrist had approved me as his "Dad," Darby came home with me.

And so tonight, as he did every night, Darby snorted and ran up the steps to my bedroom, where he promptly jumped on the bed. I got undressed, brushed my teeth and crawled into bed. Darby barely raised his head to look at me, so I pushed my feet under him, which annoyed him enough that he jumped down. I pushed my head into the pillow and stared at the ceiling.

"Maybe it's time, Missy. Maybe it's time to move on," I muttered before drifting off to sleep listening to the rhythmic sounds of a 150-pound snoring behemoth.

Chapter 5
Suzanne

I was on a week-long modeling job on St. Kitts when my life blew apart. The photographer was shooting, cooing and cajoling me to undulate a gauze-like scarf, the size of a twin bed sheet, over my head rhythmically to highlight my breasts within the low-top swimsuit I wore for a fashion magazine piece about swimsuits for Baby Boomers.

Our wardrobe consultant had finally stopped adjusting the straps so they tugged ever so slightly on my nipples, which stood straight out thanks to the cold water I was standing in and the gale from the portable wind-tunnel fan ten feet to my right. The makeup artist, a friend I always asked to work on my modeling jobs, had just brushed blush on my chest. The lighting guy was struggling to keep the reflector in just the right position so the shots would make every woman who looked at them want to rush to an exclusive shop on Fifth Avenue or Rodeo Drive to capture her very own $450 cut-out suit.

"Don't fuss over her so much," the photographer yelled above the fan, "we'll just Photoshop her."

The crew cringed as he said it. They knew my feelings about having my body digitally enhanced and they knew what was coming.

Storming out of the water, I stood toe-to-toe with him. "You do and I'll sue your ass and then I'll own the magazine," I yelled, my fists balled up and turning white. "I work my ass off to look this good, so you're going to use me as you see me. Got it?"

Out of the corner of my eye, I saw Jimmy, our assistant editor, running across the beach. As he got closer I could see the troubled look on his face. I turned away from the photographer who had just mumbled into his camera lens, "I think we got what we need anyway, bitch."

I ignored his snipe and waited for Jimmy to say what was on his mind.

"Suzanne, let's talk over there," he said, pointing to a cart we used for bottled water and fruit.

"What is it, Jimmy? Has the shoot been canceled?" I asked.

He started to cry. "No, Suzanne, it's Rick. He's had a heart attack."

"What!!! That's impossible. He runs marathons. I just talked to him last night."

Jimmy took both of my hands in his and looked at me with tears in his baby blue eyes. "I'm so, so sorry, Suzanne. Rick's dead."

My knees gave out and I collapsed onto the sand, Jimmy still holding my hands. The crew surrounded us, and Paulette, my friendly makeup artist, knelt beside me and threw a protective arm around my shoulders.

"What is it, Suzy, what's wrong?"

The blood had left my brain, but I still managed to choke out the words. "Rick's dead. He had a heart attack. Rick had a heart attack. He's dead."

"Oh, God, oh God," Paulette moaned and hugged me tighter. We rocked back and forth on that beach for what seemed like hours. I remember crew members squeezing my shoulder before they began packing up. I think the photographer even apologized for his crass remark and kept his hand on my shoulder for a minute.

I don't remember much after that. Paulette and I caught a seaplane to Nassau and got a flight home. I shook so hard on the flight to LaGuardia that I had to run to the coffin-like bathroom. I squeezed through the door just in time to vomit in the sink. I stood looking at my distorted reflection while I rinsed out the sink by pushing down the stupid faucet over and over and over and over until the pain in my wrist brought me out of my daze and I stopped.

Another passenger was trying to get in, even though the Occupied indicator was showing. I slunk out past the irritated guy in a Beautiful Bahamas T-shirt and wobbled back to my seat to find Paulette talking to the flight attendant in hushed tones.

The flight attendant quickly stood up, gave me a sorrowful smile, and then retreated to her little galley. She returned in a few minutes with a Bloody Mary, which I gulped down, and a beer. I fell asleep after the beer and woke up when the wheels touched the runway.

We got our bags and I walked zombie-like passed the gypsy cabbies, through the doors and into a waiting limo that someone had ordered for us.

I wanted to go to the morgue to see Rick for myself, to believe it was real, to caress his face, kiss his lips. Paulette called someone, I don't know who, and told the driver the address of the funeral home where Rick had been taken after an expedited autopsy that I learned after the funeral was a professional courtesy. The coroner had been Rick's med school classmate. Tough duty.

As we rode on several expressways, the sun shone brightly in a picture-perfect blue sky. How rude, I thought, dark clouds should cover it like the thunder-head that had suddenly descended over my life. Rude, too, were the people going about their business as if my Richard hadn't died and was still doing rounds at the hospital. Didn't they know I was grief-stricken and that they should be, too? I began to sob again.

At the funeral home, Paulette put her arm through mine and we did a slow shuffle to the doors. You run into a hospital if a loved one is hurt, you take your own sweet time walking into a funeral home. No hurry. No Code Blue. No paddles. What's done is done.

Understandably, Richard was in a drawer. The funeral director, an overly solicitous woman dressed in a tailored blue suit over black pumps and, strangely, a white button-down shirt and a red power tie, told me in a near whisper that after I spent time with my loved one, I could pick out a casket worthy of his position in the community, which, of course, meant top-of-the-line. I asked Paulette to make that decision and select a modest model. My God, what a grieving widow remembers!

We sat at the end of a long mahogany table in a barn-red velvet-curtained room behind the viewing area so I could answer the funeral director's questions about Richard's life for his obituary ... Long Island ... undergraduate Harvard magna cum laude ... Harvard Medical ... skilled heart surgeon ... and on. When we got to the family questions, something snapped. I shivered slightly, straightened my back, leaned forward, put my forearms on the table, and assumed control. I suppose it was finally the reality of Richard's death when I responded that he leaves three sons, Richard Jr., Mark, and James; Suzanne, his wife of 26 years ... A Mass of Christian Celebration would be held Tuesday at St. Patrick's Cathedral ...

They would be happy to write the obit, she said, but I took a copy of the form to give to a magazine writer friend who I knew would do Richard's life justice. And yes, she'll email you a copy for your memorial program in time so you can print it for the funeral.

The sun was still shining in a blue sky when we left the funeral home. I paused just outside the doors and inhaled deeply. What the fuck, I said to myself. He was in perfect health, ran marathons, ate the AMA's recommended heart-healthy diet. He was supposed to live to a hundred, not die of a massive coronary when he was on a training run, for God's sake. And speaking of God, how could he take this wonderful man so soon.

I looked up at the sky. It isn't fair, you bastard. Then I stood still as a rock, closed my eyes, inhaled deeply through my nose, and was immediately struck by lightning. Not really, but I thought it would happen because I was furious with God and had the audacity to tell Him so.

Chapter 6
Suzanne

Richard's funeral was lovely, I think. What I remember vividly were hundreds of flowers – so many that I was embarrassed. Arrangements from colleagues, former patients, the medical school, the hospitals, friends of his, friends of mine, both of our families. Richard, Mark, and James escorting me to the front pew ... a moving homily from a Fr. Terrence Sullivan, who hadn't known Richard, and kind remarks from him at the rosary and memorial service the night before, and at the gravesite.

The boys and I had picked out the readings and music several days before at the funeral home, me still in shock and hugging myself; the boys taking charge in a matter-of-fact way. That would have been funny to anyone else who knew they had stopped attending church after their Confirmations. As a result, Richard had told them that he and I had done our duty and they were now adults in the Roman Catholic Church who were responsible for their own eternal damnation. A little sanctimonious, I had thought, but I saw the corner of his mouth turn up slightly in a half-assed smile when he said it. So much for instilling the fear of God.

At the "lunch" back at St. Patrick's, everyone remarked how meaningful the readings were, how lovely the service was and "don't you think she could have afforded a nicer casket." Talk about a buzz kill!

We stayed until the church ladies began to clean up, signaling the end of this part of the funeral. The boys and I started to help, but one of the ladies shooed us out and we left after hugging each of them.

I had asked the funeral home to bring me some of the plants and a few bouquets of flowers, but I asked them to leave most of the plants for the church and to take the remaining flowers to several homeless shelters. It seemed like the right thing to do.

Back at our brownstone, Richard, Mark, James, and I sat in the living room. "What's next, Mom," Richard asked as we settled in, each with a beer.

"I've already told my agent that I'll take a few weeks off to let this all sink in.

I need to meet with the insurance guy and our attorney, go through your dad's clothes and books ... and decide what to donate. So, you'll want to go through it all and take what you want," I said. "Then it's back to work in exotic locales, like the coast of Maine, modeling jackets and hiking boots for L.L. Bean ... I hope."

"They wouldn't dare turn down an attractive widow lady," James said. "Just tell your agent to play that up."

We laughed. Then we cried. And cried. And held hands. Their mother is a widow... I'm a widow. Reality reared its ugly head.

The boys stayed in their old rooms that night. We went to bed after a few more beers and no dinner because we weren't hungry after the funeral lunch in our grief-stricken stomachs.

I know it's a bit of a cliché in every movie about a woman who loses the love of her life, but that night and every night for the next month I wore one of Richard's t-shirts to bed. I dug through the laundry basket and found one of his favorites that he had worn running the week before. It smelled of sweat. It smelled of him.

My sons spent the next day helping me go through Richard's clothes. They divided his running outfits by playing rock, paper, scissors, winner got to pick half of the pile. None of them wanted any of their father's clothes. We have our own style, Mom, they had said. I saved two of Richard's Harvard Med sweatshirts, which I had always worn anyway. The rest we bagged up for Goodwill.

And the books could wait.

Chapter 7
Jack

Monday. I never understood the whole 'Mondays Suck' attitude. I fill my weekends with exercise, brunch with friends, family dinners, playing fetch with Darby, reading a biography or the latest James Patterson novel, and daydreaming. Lots of daydreaming – about Missy, the early years, the middle years, and not so much about the last few months. I recharge the battery.

I like my career, so Mondays give me the start of another week doing what I love – working with creative people and crafting damn good ad campaigns. I don't enjoy office politics, so I stay above the fray most of the time. Sometimes it's unavoidable, like this morning.

Instead of driving to the office, on Mondays I like to take the bus so I can get an eyeful of the large billboards that dominate the Manhattan landscape. We design some of the more strikingly effective car boards, the ones with the gorgeous blonde and her stunningly handsome boy toy riding out of the board, her scarf billowing out in the wind. Of course, that's all smoke and mirrors, but the client loves it because it's caused a few minor fender benders when limo drivers get distracted by the scarf.

I find myself staring blankly out the bus window after 15 blocks and what seems like 30 stops. Memories of Missy and the kids rise up at the oddest times. They always come in reverse chronological order, eventually ending up with when I met the good doctor.

It all began when Cindy, or Cynthia as she wanted everyone to call her, had worked for months to land the account of the city's largest healthcare center. Always dressed impeccably in the latest business attire, and usually wearing a low-cut blouse like the ones lady television cops and female FBI agents wear under their Armani suit coats, Cindy had impressed the hospital's CEO and department heads with samples of our campaigns for a nationally known cancer treatment chain, and a promise that we would make the public love their staff, blah, blah, blah ...

Two days after her presentation, she got the call from the CEO's administrative assistant, a no-nonsense guy with an accounting degree. She was to come over and have lunch with all the medical department heads, who would come and go due to their busy schedules and vastly more important responsibilities than spending their high-priced time with the center's ad agency rep.

Two days later, our creative director, Bill Reynolds, an extremely smart 44-year-old journalism school graduate with an MBA, three junior copywriters, me included, our art director, Ronnie Peters, and Cindy, er... Cynthia, climbed into the agency stretch limo, and headed to the main hospital. During the ride through New York's mid-morning traffic, an obviously nervous and egocentric Cynthia and our creative boss, talked in hushed, conspiratorial tones before she raised her head, looked each of us in the eye, and, in a tone that would melt granite, told us in no uncertain terms that we were not to say anything to any doctor, nurse, cook, or orderly. Either she or Bill would introduce us and ask all the questions. We four were to nod, take notes, and 'shut-the-fuck-up', as she so eloquently phrased it.

We arrived, too stunned to say anything to anyone, and were led into a large conference room where box lunches sat on an enormous u-shaped table in front of each plush leather swivel office-type chair. As I approached one chair near the front, Cynthia glared at me, so I moved toward the back. After I passed the middle, she gave me a quick nod and I, followed by the other three underlings, grabbed a spot. We traded box lunches so that each of us had what we wanted. Fortunately, none included a tofu and non-dairy cheese substitute, so I was more than happy with my lean beef and Swiss and carrot sticks, although I would have preferred potato chips.

We proceeded to eat as the CEO's administrative guy told us the CEO was attending a fundraiser at Peter Luger's and probably would be unable to join us, but would try, time permitting.

Doctors came, waved after being introduced, sorted through box lunches that were stacked on a table near the doors, and departed, presumably to chew out interns and berate residents, with the occasional patient visit thrown in for good measure.

After lunch and an exhaustive parade of middle-aged and should-have-retired-years-ago physicians, Cynthia and Bill led us on our pre-arranged tour. The rest of us were taking notes feverishly as we marched through the departments and into elevators, where Cynthia reminded us that copywriters, like children, should be seen and not heard.

The final stop on our four-hour tour was the Psychiatry and Mental Health Section on the seventh floor. It was designed to comfort patients and visitors, with walls painted in muted beiges and browns, some tasteful sculptures, without any points or sharp edges that, upon close inspection, were bolted to the floor. Yep, I notice those kinds of details. It's a curse.

Our psychiatry tour guide was third-year resident Melissa Clark, M.D. She was tall, about five-ten, had a lustrous Maureen-O'Hara-red ponytail and the most beautiful green eyes on the planet, which accented her high cheekbones and sculptured jaw. Her nose was Celestial and slightly turned up. I didn't dare notice anything lower than her shoulders, which appeared to be softly squared off, like a yoga instructor's, beneath her white coat. I was absolutely stunned at her appearance.

When we shook hands, our eyes met and I'm almost certain my jaw dropped, or maybe it just felt like it. We held our hands together and I stared into her eyes, completely smitten until Cynthia ruined our moment with a dry cough. I broke my gaze and turned to see our scowling account executive giving me a look that said my job and my life were in jeopardy. I didn't care. Before I joined the others, I asked Dr. Clark for her phone number. She reached into her coat pocket, pulled out a business card, and quickly wrote something on the back. Then she put it back in her pocket! Crap, I thought, she changed her mind. After she gave us a tour of the ward and explained all the latest medicines and therapies, she accompanied us to the elevator. As we waited for the elevator, she stood next to me at the rear of the pack and slipped her card into my hand unseen by the others, thankfully, and gave it a slight squeeze.

Over the next three weeks, I reported to the medical center at 8:50 each morning to do my in-depth research. Cindy had arranged my daily schedule with little personal time, but every chance we had, Missy and I met for coffee or lunch in one of the medical center's cafeterias, or, just at least once every day, we managed to sneak in a few minutes together, just to say hi.

Missy told me a lot about her family and growing up in Farmington, Connecticut, where she excelled in swimming and science. Her dad was a successful insurance agent and her mom devoted her time to gardening, serving meals at one of the local women's shelters and guiding her only child through puberty and high school.

Missy had been a science geek, but no one teased her about it because her male and female friends relied on her for help with their chemistry, physics, and advanced algebra homework. And, she told me she'd played on the high school's varsity lacrosse team since eighth grade, so she could kick their asses.

I told her about my goofy Irish clan, my hard-working dad, my great mom, and my wonderful brother, the priest.

"Is that all of them," she asked smiling sweetly and coyly.

"Well, I do have a younger brother." That's all I said.

"I'm sure I'll get to know them all."

What?! Whoa, this was complicated because we hadn't even gone on a real date yet.

There was a moment of silence as I flipped through my notes to hide the fact that I was working up the courage to ask her on an actual date. I feared rejection, even though the day before she had stood on her tiptoes to kiss my cheek when we parted. I had been stunned then, too, because her gesture was so sweet and so unexpected.

My last serious girlfriend in college had broken my heart senior year telling me she had a "friend," and after graduation they were going to head to California where they were going to open a surf shop with money his daddy had given him.

Well, fuck you and the horse you rode in on, I choked into the Princess phone before I hung up and bawled like a baby with severe diaper rash. Rejection like that wounds a man, especially when delivered by the girl you had thought you would spend the rest of your life with.

Several "Good-time Charlene" girls had helped me heal, but either they irritated me, or my cavalier treatment irritated them. I vividly recall a raven-haired secretary who yelled while gathering up her clothes from my bedroom floor that my avoidance of any topic that was even remotely connected to the word "commitment" was a major buzz kill and a complete downer during pillow talk after sex, which she judged to be surprisingly "adequate."

When I met Missy, I hadn't had any relationship in more than 13 months, two weeks, and four days. No, seriously, I had kept track because my dear mother kept a calendar. Recently she had berated me for having to carry over my dating history onto her new church calendar. "If you don't find someone soon," she had yelled from the kitchen, "you'll end up in a casket at this nice Catholic funeral home that always sponsors the calendars."

My father admonished her to shush because he wanted two priests in the family so the angels would take him and ma directly to heaven with no time in Purgatory. A lofty goal, Da, but it ain't gonna happen during this lifetime, so I guess just Ma will bypass Purgatory. I always tell my parents, I'm going to spend one day less than eternity in Purgatory. That always cracks my dad up and gets a derisive snort from Ma.

Anyway, even though Missy was sending signals that would cause a better man to jump at the chance to ask her on a date, I stared down at my notebook and finally cleared my throat. I looked up at her and blurted out something akin to "I don't suppose you'd ever consider going to Erminia, my favorite Italian restaurant, and then riding the horse-drawn carriage through Central Park, would you?" I don't remember exactly what I said, but I do clearly remember her response.

"That sounds like a lovely evening. What took you so long?"

Oh, I don't know, a terminal fear of rejection, maybe. My heart was pounding and my palms were sweating when she said she would let me know her first 48-hours break in time to make reservations. We got up from the cafeteria table and I wiped my right hand on my khakis and took her left hand.

"There are meditations you can do so you're not so nervous around me," she had said, and she smiled ever so sweetly as I looked first into her gorgeous green eyes and quickly down at my feet.

"I hope there are!"

"I'll give you a booklet a colleague and I wrote. I hope you can practice the techniques before our date. I'll mail it to you so you're prepared for our first night together."

"Right," I swallowed hard in surprise and anticipation, "I hope so, too." We looked around and, seeing an empty hall, shared our first kiss as the elevator doors opened.

We met at the restaurant 11 days later, which was the first evening she was free. My interviews with pre-selected nurses, therapists, and more than a few doctors at the hospital had been completed. So, unable to meet for coffee or lunch, Missy and I talked on the phone nearly every day. She usually called me when she had a minute to talk, and she usually told me about something funny that happened on morning rounds, or an obscure fact about the history of psychiatry. Sometimes when she called I was in a creative staff meeting, but I always called her back so she knew I wasn't just avoiding her. Why would I? I was in love.

Our date was one of those picture-perfect evenings screenwriters put into romantic comedies. I had asked the maître de for a table near the back away from the kitchen, so we weren't surrounded by clatter but felt like we were dining alone. The meal was perfect. Missy had salad and one piece of bread, no butter or olive oil. I scarfed down salad and lasagna. In between bites I asked her more questions about her family. Finally, after I had requested a complete description of the family dog, she had had enough.

"Jack, I feel like you're a police detective and I'm under suspicion for murder," she had said after gently putting down her salad fork and peering into my eyes with her gorgeous green eyes through narrow lids. "Take a deep breath through your nose, for gawdsake! Did you even try the relaxation exercises? They really do work."

She had paused then, her lips turned up in the slightest smile, her eyes widened to normal. "I'm not going to bite you ... hard. I promise you'll enjoy it."

Jaysus, Mary, and Joseph! How the hell was I supposed to relax now? As I reached for my wine glass with my right hand, she glided her right hand across the white tablecloth and placed it on my left hand.

Okay, I thought, she's just playing mind games and is now going to say something like, 'You're a great guy, Jack, but you're just not great enough for me,' or something to that effect. I took a breath to steel myself for the inevitable dumping. I was not expecting the words that came next as she leaned slightly in and squeezed my hand.

"I've fallen in love, Jack."

Here comes 'with someone else.'

"I'm in love with you, Jack."

Huh? What did she just say? My heart started to pound and my head felt like it was spinning around like the demon-possessed girl in "The Exorcist."

"You're smart, talented, you listen to me with your eyes, and you are a great person, Jack. I love you. You make me laugh, my heart skips a beat when you answer the phone and the first time you kissed me, butterflies fluttered in my stomach."

I was in shock, but then I just smiled. "My God, Missy, I am so in love with you, too."

Later that night in bed after an insatiable Missy had nibbled on my right nipple and asked me for the third time, 'Think we can do that again?', I lay exhausted but lucid enough to tell her that I had fallen in love when she slipped me her business card that first day at the elevator. And, as we got to know each other, I came to admire her intelligence, her sense of humor, and even her quirks – Quirks! What quirks? She demanded – I also admitted that the fact that she was beautiful didn't hurt.

She raised up on her left elbow, rolled on top of me with her breasts tight against my chest, jabbed her right elbow into my sternum, and once more demanded, "What quirks?"

"Well, like when you're thinking, you put the knuckle of your right hand in your cheek and chew on your lip. And then, when you're really deep in thought, you twirl a strand of your hair with your left hand so you can write a note."

"Hmmm, you may be right," she purred, and then kissed my lips, long and soft, and said, "We need to sleep. You'll need your strength in the morning!"

After we had dated for six months and laughed and talked for hours on end, I felt right about asking her to marry me, which I did on one knee during dessert at Erminia, to rousing applause from the other diners. She said yes, and called her family and mine, and told them and me, that ours was literally love at first sight that day at the hospital. It can, and does, happen.

Those were my memories as I rode the bus this Monday.

The bus lurched to a stop, and the driver, Mario, who knows me well enough to yell back that this was my stop, opened the doors so I and three other riders could get off.

The first things you notice as you walk through Manhattan are the smells. There are diesel exhaust, the dank, fetid sewer odor at every corner grate, garbage, restaurant kitchens, expensive fragrances, and of course, food carts. Two other things even city dwellers notice are the insidious scaffoldings that tower over the sidewalks and the chewing gum on those same sidewalks.

I try to keep my head up to avoid anyone with head down texting on their phone. How they avoid a paralyzing headbutt with the scaffolding is a miracle, but I haven't heard of any fatalities. Yet.

Rarely does any passerby make eye contact. It's just not something New Yorkers do, as a rule. If you make eye contact, you might have to smile at the woman you recognize from the gym, or the guy who parks your car at a restaurant, or one of the hundreds of lawyers – and who wants to take the chance of smiling at a lawyer?

Chapter 8
Jack

My office is a block from the bus stop. Our agency occupies three floors near the top of a tony high rise on Madison Avenue. It's some of the highest-priced real estate in a part of town well known for high rents, so my staff is under tremendous pressure to produce great campaigns for national and international markets. I'm under pressure to keep them working smoothly as a team, with each member using his or her talents to the best of their ability. You might say I'm their coach, but even a coach can get blindsided by a player. That's what happened this morning as I got off the elevator and was accosted by one of my best artists.

"Jack, can you look at this copy...I can't seem to get it right. Oh, and good morning."

"Good morning, Lester."

We walked past the receptionist, who handed me a stack of messages as I smiled at her, my first smile of the morning.

"You can't seem to get it right, Les," I said over my shoulder as I glanced down at the pink telephone message slips and quickly scanned each one, pausing on one from Paul Jacobs, our best copywriter. Call about Lester, the receptionist had written in her economical script. Paul had called me through her rather than leaving me a voicemail, so I knew he didn't want me to hear how upset he was until he'd had a chance to calm down. Office politics!

"You're an artist, Les, you're not supposed to write copy. What are the copywriters going to do if you write the copy for them?"

I quickly walked into my office and to my office chair, with Les right behind me. I nearly sat on his hand that he had thrust in my face.

"But they're always giving me graphics ideas," he whined. "Why can't I give them copy ideas, Jack?"

"First, Lester, please don't shove paper in my face."

"Sorry."

"And second," I started to explain for the millionth time, "when they write copy, they have visuals in mind and ..."

Laurie, my personal assistant, burst through the doorway, announcing breathlessly, "Langston just called a creative management meeting. He's pissed, you should know, because you weren't here to get his call, and for other reasons."

"Thanks, Laurie...Les, stop writing copy," I said gathering up my portfolio and pen. "You're too good a designer to waste your talent on copy."

"You're so full of shit."

"True," I said, "but I need to calm the beast. Be a team player, Les... Seriously. Work with the copywriters and stop trying to take their jobs. We're a team, and right now, you're one of our star graphic designers."

Leave 'em smiling, is my motto.

As I walked down the hall to the conference room, I noticed everyone going in had a hang-dog look. I politely waited for an opening before I walked through the door. The creative staff had slunk in and slid into chairs near the back of the room, while the account executives, our so-called rainmakers, sat at the front with their backs toward the plate-glass windows, smug expressions on their faces. I quietly took my place in the open chair on Langston Fletcher's immediate right.

Langston Fletcher had worked his way up the ladder at another large ad agency before he approached our former CEO about buying into the agency. Instead, he had been offered double his salary to join us, but said he preferred to work straight commission. That was all the incentive he needed to bring in more business than we could handle. He was so successful that we had had to hire more creatives for his clients, and we recruited the best.

After two years and landing several large national clients, including an auto manufacturer, Langston Fletcher borrowed money from his mother, who owned a successful dairy operation in Wisconsin. She took out a mortgage on her long-ago paid for land, to stake her boy in the cut-throat business of advertising.

And so, with his mother's money and his own savings, he bought himself an ad agency, which, to his credit, he turned into a powerhouse. Keeping it churning apparently was what today's meeting was about.

Langston was in mid-sentence when I took my chair and laid my portfolio on the table top. The table had been specially crafted from wood that had lain at the bottom of Lake Superior. The boards alone had cost more than the GNP of Canada. They were brought up 27 floors through the stairwell because they wouldn't fit in the elevator. I remember thinking that all our employees could have received a large year-end bonus with what that alone had cost.

It wasn't like the new table replaced card tables held together with duct tape. We'd had had a majestic, curvy glass and chrome table designed by Andy Warhol, but Langston's fourth wife didn't want him peering through the glass up the skirts of female staffers. She hadn't realized that they all substituted pantsuits for miniskirts for that very reason. Too late, though. She had seen an article about the resurrected wood and suggested to Langston very loudly in his office that if he ever wanted anything remotely resembling sex at home, he would approve the purchase.

"...and you ALL had better start billing out more time. Jesus H. Christ, people! Is it so damn difficult?!" he yelled as he slapped his right hand on the table. That was my cue.

I said, quite possibly too forcefully, "We're all putting down our time...As much as is ethic..."

He interrupted me, as always when he was on a tear.

"Don't give me that crap, Jack. Our billings are off 20 percent. What am I supposed to tell the partners?"

"You should tell them that they should spend more time courting clients and less time courting their secretaries." Oops. Did I really say that out loud?

"I'm serious, Jack," he said, venom dripping from his fangs. "We're running for the tape, here. We don't even have 10 days left to bill this month."

I had gone this far. I might as well take it to the next level, I thought. The account executives had changed their smug expressions to evil grins.

"I'm serious, too, Langston. It's not our job to bring in clients," I said looking pointedly at the smiling hyenas across the table, in full support of my creatives, who all may have been thinking the same thing.

"Then maybe I need to get people who are serious about their jobs, Jack," Langston barked in a threatening tone.

"These are top creatives, Langston," I said calmly. "Threats aren't conducive to good ideas. Bring in more clients. We'll do on-target creative for them. We always have."

Langston slammed shut his alligator-skin portfolio, scarfed it up from the table, and walked around me toward the door. He paused halfway there and smiled at his account executives and said to me while looking out the floor to ceiling windows at the New York skyline.

"Oh, we'll bring in new clients, Jack," his voice filled with derision. "Your people had better damn well create award-winning campaigns." And with that inspirational snipe, he puffed out his chest, turned and marched out, his account executives in lock step behind him.

"You know we will," I said more to my staff than to him.

Everyone in the room started to talk to me at once. I got out of my chair and held up both of my hands, like Moses parting the Red Sea. "Enough! Show's over. Let's get creatin', folks."

I gathered up my own portfolio, cell phone, and notes that my team had written me during the meeting. I'd read them later in the quiet of my office and respond by phone or in person to any that needed a response.

As I scooped up my belongings, I reflected on Langston's tenor. Sometimes, he would bark at me in these meetings about something over which I had no control, but in this meeting, he had come across as downright contemptuous. That made him look bad in the eyes of the staff, well, except for his account executive sycophants. They looked as if they had watched a lion drag down a water buffalo by the nose. I briefly thought that our professional relationship had taken a sharp turn toward my being on the 'you'd better update your resume' list. I shook off that thought. Paranoia strikes deep and into my heart it did creep.

I had left the conference room deep in thought about the work being done for several clients, when Laurie caught up to me and grabbed my elbow, a gesture that usually signaled that a shit storm was headed my way. Not this time, though.

"I don't know how you can talk to him that way, Jack," she whispered as we walked past the cubicles of the copywriters trying to be the next David Ogilvy. "Aren't you afraid he'll fire you?"

"I'm too old to fire, Lorz," I assured her ... and myself. "And too good," I added with a self-deprecating grin. "Besides, the guy loves me. He just has a tough time showing it."

"We all love you, Jack," she laughed, batting her eyelids exaggeratedly and smiling at me.

"Show me some lovin', baby," I responded grabbing for her hand on my elbow.

"Harassment!!! Somebody call human resources," she giggled, as I spun her around in a pirouette.

Chapter 9
Jack

I can count on one hand the number of times I've visited Missy's grave since her funeral. I went three times the year after she died – her birthday, the first anniversary of her death, and our wedding anniversary. Since then I just visit on our wedding anniversary. Still, I have my brother say a Mass for her every year on her birthday and the anniversary of her death.

So here I was at her grave, roses in hand. It was raining and the wet grass had enveloped my Bass Weejuns Kiltie Loafers, darkening the soles and sides. I reached down with my free right hand and brushed the wet grass clippings off Missy's cement gravestone base. I stood up and looked down at the white marble gravestone with the simple inscription – her name, dates of birth and death, and the words "Wife, Mother, Daughter, Physician." I held the bouquet in both hands and looked around to make sure I wouldn't disturb anyone, but, really, so no one could hear what I was about to say over the tops of the roses.

"The girls are back at school...arguing about the car...still. I don't know how you reffed their fights so well all the time," I said, choking back tears. "I hate being the mom, too. Damn it, Missy! Why did you have to get sick and die?"

I cleared my throat and wiped my eyes with the heel of my right hand. "Anyway, I'm going to start dating. I just wanted you to be the first to know. But don't worry...just dating...nothing serious. Promise. I'll always love you, Babe." I laid the flowers at the gravestone base, put my left hand on the ground for several seconds, straightened up, and turned to walk back to my car.

Then, booph, she came out of nowhere and I nearly knocked her over when we collided. "God, I am so sorry," I blurted.

"It's okay, I should have paid closer attention to where I was walking."

I quickly scanned her and noticed her Burberry raincoat and matching broad-brimmed hat. She carried a dozen or so red roses with matching shoes that were shiny red underneath green grass clippings. When our eyes met, I noticed her high cheekbones, perfect makeup, stunning blue eyes, and sensual lips under a slightly upturned nose, all framed by shiny blonde hair and her floppy rain hat.

Don't judge me for my seemingly sexist powers of observation. When you sit with an art director to pick a certain type of model for a photo shoot or commercial, you learn to notice details like this so you can rapidly whisk the candidates through the process.

She turned abruptly and hurried away and I smiled at the encounter. Trying not to step on top of any of the dearly departed, I walked to my car without turning around, which took a great deal of self-discipline because I desperately wanted to watch her walk through the wet grass in high heels.

Chapter 10
Suzanne

Now THAT was embarrassing, I thought looking at the guy's back as he picked his way around gravestones. Then, if bumping into him wasn't embarrassing enough, the heel of my left foot caught in the turf, causing my feet to twist together like a pretzel and I unceremoniously tumbled onto the wet grass, dropping my bouquet in the process.

I scrambled to my feet, slowly looked around, and thankfully neither the guy nor anyone else had witnessed my clumsy performance. I smoothed my raincoat, picked up the flowers, and walked on.

When I got to Rick's grave, I laid the disheveled bouquet on top of the gravestone and stood close.

"I know I promised to love only you, Rick," I said quietly. "But it's been two years of grieving ... and getting used to living alone ... and grocery shopping by myself. Oh, and cooking for one ... do you know how damned ridiculous that is? And did I mention fending off the personal trainers at the gym? And your buddies! Have you heard the disgusting things they say to your grief-stricken widow? Of course not, or you'd haunt their sorry asses. Some friends!"

Leo the Lech

"Hi, Suze, it's Leo, Richard's favorite anesthesiologist."

I had been sorting through Richard's winter clothes when the phone rang. I had hoped it would just stop ringing so I could stay immersed in my three-weeks-to-the-day-since-the-funeral grief, but the damn thing was relentless.

"Hello, Leo," I spoke softly. "How have you been? I don't know if I thanked you enough for helping out by being one of the pallbearers."

"Hey, no problem," he replied. "But you can thank me by going out to dinner tomorrow. Molly's away at a conference in Boston for big-shot actuaries and you and I could use the company and a good meal.

How about I pick you up at seven?"

"I just don't know, Leo," I said, sadly, "It's only been three weeks since the funeral."

"You need to dress up and get out of your house for one evening, Suze. It's just one night ... er, evening."

I hate being called 'Suze' by acquaintances, and I caught his Freudian Slip, even though he corrected himself in half a heartbeat.

"I wouldn't be very good company, Leo," I said, giving him a reason to bow out gracefully. "My mind would still be on Richard and not even on a polite conversation."

"I won't take 'No' for an answer because you just gave me the best reason to take your mind off Richard for a couple of hours," he said, persistently. "Tell you what, we'll go to Peter Luger's, where I've already made reservations, and split the best Porterhouse on the Eastern Seaboard, have some wine, and I'll try to make you laugh at the jokes the surgical team tells while patients are under. Okay?"

He was wearing me down, and he probably had me at wine, but I didn't want him to know that, so I said again, "Let me think about it, Leo, and call you in the morning."

"Can't, Suze," he said. "I'm in brain surgery all morning, and probably well into the afternoon. Please just say 'yes' now, so you can spend your day getting ready for a fun night with the best-looking anesthesiologist in North America."

I sighed at his insistent use of the familiar nickname, his persistence, and his assumption of what I needed to pull me out of my grief.

"Oh, all right," I said without any enthusiasm. I hoped he caught on, but I doubted it. "But I'll meet you at the restaurant at seven-thirty, Leo. No sense paying for a taxi to pick me up and then head out to Brooklyn."

"That's great, Suze! See you tomorrow."

I hung up without saying goodbye. I felt manipulated and unfaithful to Richard. And angry that this misogynistic egomaniac thought it would take me a full day to get ready.

I went back to sorting Richard's winter clothes, donate here or donate there, and before I went to bed I picked out my most modest blue suit, crème blouse, and black pumps. I would look like a modern nun, but that was the look I was going for.

Next morning, I bounced around the apartment, drank too much coffee, had no appetite for anything else, loaded Richard's clothes into garbage bags, called two charities for pick-ups, tried unsuccessfully to read some novel about a grieving widow a friend had given me, made more coffee, threw it out, went for a long walk, had a light lunch of what I don't remember, took a restless nap, took a long shower, scrubbed my head until I thought my hair would fall out, got dressed, applied a minimum amount of makeup, no cologne, pale pink lipstick, called for a taxi, looked in the floor-length mirror and decided that I looked modest enough to turn off the most determined Lothario.

The taxi ride to Luger's was, thankfully, without incident. I spent the entire ride staring out the window asking God, Jesus, Mary, Saints Matthew, Mark, Luke, and John just why in the hell Richard had to die. It left me and my three sons without this wonderful man in our lives, while so many assholes are allowed to walk the earth. And I had the sinking feeling that I was about to have dinner with one of them.

Leo was waiting in the bar when I walked through the doors. He was, I had to admit, somewhat entitled to be full of himself. He had the ruddy good looks of a privileged kid who had played Lacrosse in his private high school and had been the captain of his Ivy League team. He'd graduated from Harvard Medical where he met Richard and did his anesthesia residency at Mayo. Plus, all the surgeons wanted him in their OR because he had nerves of steel and could calculate anesthesia doses in his head before the nurse anesthetist could do it on the computer. And he knew he was the complete, irresistible package, especially now, dressed in his Armani Navy blazer, grey slacks, no socks, and God-only-knows-what-brand of alligator tassel loafers. But, he hadn't counted on running afoul of the Bad-Tempered Widow!

There was a Cosmo sitting in front of the empty high-backed bar stool next to Leo. At least he had done his research. Start me off with the sweet hard stuff, then progress to red wine, forget about steak, pour me into a taxi, slip me between the sheets ... I knew where he hoped this was going. I also knew I was four moves ahead of this arrogant asshole – the Bad-Tempered Widow was still horribly grieving and had a sixth sense about assholes. I took two sips of the Cosmo, "Let's eat, Leo," I suggested, a little too strongly, I suppose, if Dr. Phil had been standing behind us. "I'm hangry, if you get my drift."

"I'll see if our table is ready," said Dr. Wonderful-In-His-Own-Mind, as he twisted off his stool and frowned down at my drink as

he pivoted. Minutes later he returned and offered me is left arm. I squiggled out of my stool, left the drink, took his arm and we proceeded into the very crowded dining room.

"Aren't you going to take your Cosmo?" he asked, all hurt like.

"No, I'll just drink water and Peter's best Cab with that delicious Porterhouse we're going to share," I said, ever so seductively. He's not getting by cheaply, I thought. Let him think what he wants to think. His temptations are going to cost him plenty. I took three small bites of the very rare delicious steak, three sips of wine, a couple bites of the creamed spinach, wiped the corners of my mouth and pronounced myself ready for Chocolate Mousse and coffee.

Leo, who was chewing on a large piece of steak and bread slathered with softened butter, gave me a stunned look, but summoned Larry, our waiter. I smiled sweetly up at Larry and ordered dessert. He asked Leo if he wanted any, who just motioned to the half a steer remaining on the platter and waved him away.

I hoped Leo was getting at least peeved when he saw me take three small bites of the mousse and two loud slurps of coffee, but the snake had a one-track mind. Nothing I had done so far could dissuade him from his lecherous goal.

In the taxi, he slithered his right arm around my shoulder, but I gently removed it and firmly planted his hand on his right knee. Bad move. He then sneaked his hand on my exposed knee and tried to slide it up higher. I grabbed it and gently put it back on his own knee, where it stayed the rest of the ride to my building.

When he helped me out of the taxi after paying the driver, Leo claimed two things: First, sex was good for grief, and second, I at least owed him a blowjob for what he had spent on drinks, dinner, wine, and the taxi.

My rage was almost more than I could handle, but I did my best. "Leo," I hissed, on the verge of a stroke, "I don't owe you a damned thing since this was your sordid attempt to get me in the sack. Second," I was getting warmed up, "you're married to a wonderful, smart woman, who doesn't deserve you. And third," I slugged him in the stomach with my left fist and then slapped him hard across his handsome face with the flat of my right as he doubled over, "if I ever see you or hear from you again, I will tell Molly about our little date and your demands."

Then I spun on my sensible heels before he could grab me, and got inside the security door where I looked back and saw him straighten up and flip me the bird. I flipped it back and then noticed that the palm of my right hand was covered in spray-on tan.

I held in my anger in the elevator, but inside the apartment, I slammed the door, fastened all the locks, leaned my back against the door and started to sob, angry at myself for going. Sliding down the door to the floor, I was angrier at Leo the Lech for thinking I was so easy, and finally, sitting on the floor, I was furious with Richard for dying and leaving me to the wolves. Oh, and let's not forget God, who arranged this whole fucking mess of a life that was mine from now on.

The pain in my butt and legs woke me up, and I shed my clothes as I walked through the apartment to the stairs and up to my bedroom. As I climbed into bed, the clock informed me that I had cried myself to sleep on the floor for five hours. My sore butt agreed.

Ashford the Asshole

"Maybe you can get her in the sack, Ash," Leo said to Ashford Stanley, his squash partner, as they dressed after their twice-weekly match at the Harvard Club. Today's had been against a couple of skilled hedge fund guys who had given the two physicians a good workout, and the match had been close, but in the end, a couple of ruthless smashes had taken the final game, the match, and their money.

"For one thing," Leo explained, "you're single."

"Yeah, but I'm a divorced Jew and she's a Catholic widow," Ash responded, pulling on his grey slacks.

"You don't need to marry her, for Christ's sake," Leo stage-whispered, peering around the end of the lockers and buttoning his Armani silk shirt, "just have sex a few times, and then dump her."

"You had great luck with that, didn't you?"

"I wasn't at the top of my game," Leo said, "besides, it was only three weeks after the funeral. She's had two more weeks to get horny."

"You really are a pig, Leo," Ashford said into his locker, "and coming from a Jew, that's a huge insult."

"Just schmooze her into the sack and then you can call me all the names you want," Leo said. "Now, let's have lunch. You've made me hungry for a stacked ham and Swiss cheese on Jewish Rye."

Like I said, Leo, you're such a Khazer."
"A what?"
"Never mind."
"Here's her cell number. Just call her, screw her, and give me all the lurid details."

I didn't recognize the phone number, but I had been getting calls from Richard's former patients and co-workers to express their sympathy and ask what they could do to help me (Oh, I don't know, maybe take me out for coffee, go for a walk, go to Mass and brunch afterward, or, how about lunch? You know, something specific, instead of me having to suggest an activity.). So I answered hoping against hope it would be a cardiology nurse practitioner offering to take me to a movie. Anything!

"Hello, Suzanne," the male voice I didn't recognize said. "It's Ashford Stanley, the radiologist who always sat in with Richard and his team when they did angiograms."

I had never met Ashford Stanley.

"Uh, hello, Doctor Stanley."

"I'm sorry I didn't have a chance to extend my sympathies at Richard's funeral. Tragic loss."

"Yes, it was. Thanks for calling."

"Anyway, I was hoping we could have dinner and I could share some memories of working with Richard and hanging out with him after surgery and such."

My shit-detector radar went wild. I knew Richard never hung out with the other team members after surgery. He always, always visited with families immediately afterward and then went on rounds with his residents and any interns who were brave enough to wrangle an invitation. I smelled a rat and he smelled like Leo.

"Well, Ashford, I think you were hoping to share more than memories of Richard's work, but if you remember, he never hung out with the team after letting a resident close, if it was an open-heart procedure, so he could visit with the families and go on rounds."

"Well, Suzanne, maybe after dinner, we could come to my place and ..."

"That's absolutely all I want to hear, DOCTOR Stanley!"

"But, Suze, studies have shown that sex eases grief ..."

"You tell that asshole friend of yours that I've had it up to my eyeballs with you pricks, and if one more of you calls me ... and don't call me 'Suze'... I'm going to file an ethics complaint against you and Leo and every fucking doctor at that goddam hospital! Do you understand me?"

"Loud and clear, you cold bit...!"

Gratefully, Leo and his asshole buddies got the message. No more calls from lecherous jerks.

That was my frame of mind when I bumped into that guy at the cemetery, I was riled up thinking about those tawdry come-ons. On fire! I waved my hands in the air and stomped my feet. My heels dug into the soft, wet ground, and I had to pull them out like I was stuck in a damn bog. After I did that, rather clumsily since I lost one shoe to the turf and the other hung on my toes, I looked around embarrassed. But no one was watching my performance, thank God.

Regaining my composure, I continued talking to the gravestone. "I need someone to love me, Rick. Maybe, just maybe, there's a nice guy out there. I'll never know if I don't look. But not right away, so don't turn over down there."

I looked around again to make sure no one could overhear me. But I realized that the rain would muffle anything I might say.

"Do you remember me telling you about that guy who broke my heart a few years before we met? And it turned out I was his rebound girlfriend? So, here's my plan...Before I get serious about someone, I'm going to save a few girls from the pain of being the rebound relationship."

I was refining the plan as I spoke to the wet grass. "I'll date guys who have recently been dumped by the love of their lives. Then, after a while, I'll make sure I irritate or disgust them, I haven't decided which, maybe both. Then they'll dump me and move on to their serious, 'live happily ever after' relationship. No one gets hurt...well, maybe one of them a little, but not me since I'm in it to break up.

"That's the plan, Rick. I wanted you to be the first to know."

I took a deep breath and waited, staring at the headstone. Did I expect a comment, some feedback? No, just a sign that he approved. Except for a flock of pigeons that always flew over parks and cemeteries in New York, none was forthcoming, so I removed my shoes and walked through the wet grass back to my car, grateful to see that the guy I had bumped into was gone.

Chapter 11
Suzanne's Plan

The initial numbness had worn off after eight months and I began to feel human again. I still had my moments of bone-crushing, curl-up-in-the-fetal-position grief, but those were coming at longer intervals, as were the times I walked through life in a daze.

Even the produce aisle in the grocery brought back stupid arguments Richard and I would have about Romaine or Iceberg. More than once I found myself staring and laughing until I noticed either the 45-year-old produce manager or elderly ladies pushing their carts staring at me. Then I'd picked up a head of Iceberg and moved on to buy Blue Cheese and bacon for my favorite salad.

Almost a year to the day after Richard's funeral I dropped by Monique Delaquarte's office to discuss an investment. We've been friends ever since she began managing the hospital's trust funds, and Richard had sat on that board among others. We had attended a few boring functions, had discovered we hated them, and laughed at the same jokes, so we always sought each other out.

"Just meet us for coffee," she pleaded. "What could it hurt? He's the CEO of a large pharma company, divorced six months ago, and his wife only got their home in Barbados because she was having an affair with her doubles partner."

"I don't know, Monique, it's too soon."

"It's been a year, Hon."

"For him, I mean."

"Have coffee, maybe lunch next week, the opera, a few dinners, you both need to get out."

"You have our lives all planned out, don't you?"

"Saturday, nine-thirty, Dunkin Donuts, Thirty Rockefeller Center. Wear something nice ... for a change."

After our fifth date, a wonderful evening at the Lookout Tavern in Martha's Vineyard, Andrew Page, CEO of the sixth largest pharmaceutical company in the entire world, took both of my hands in his, looked into my eyes, and with a tear running down his left cheek, told me he had fallen in love with his personal assistant, a man he had known for 22 years, and could I please forgive him for wasting my time.

Knock me over with a feather! Now THAT was going to be difficult to keep out of Page Six! The limo ride and the private jet flight were uncomfortably silent. I didn't want to ask any uncomfortable questions, and I was pretty sure Andrew didn't want to offer any more information.

"Well, how did that latest go? Martha's Vineyard? Fancy schmancy! Are you guys dating, or what?" Monique pried.

"No, he broke it off," I said, trying to sound sad. "I told you it was too soon for him, but I think he found someone else already. Turns out, I was his rebound, er, girl."

"I can find you someone else. Just give me a few days."

"Monique, I don't want you to find me someone else."

"Sure you do, Hon. Got to get back in the saddle, so to speak. Now that you've put yourself out there, it would be a shame to withdraw back into your old widow's shell."

"What if I like my widow's shell?"

"Nonsense! Next thing, you'll have 24 cats and an apartment full of old newspapers."

"You're so full of shit."

"Get out of here so I can go through my contacts. I'll call you soon with my top candidates."

Three days later the phone rang with "Money, Money, Money" by ABBA, Monique's ringtone. "Found four guys in need of some lovin'."

"I'm just dating, not loving, remember."

"Right. Here's the first guy, Shannon O'Toole, a widowed lawyer. He's going to call you tomorrow for drinks and apps at some Irish joint. Be nice."

"I'm always ni..." she rang off. "...nice."

When Shannon called, I was just back from a long run, so I was sweaty and breathless and damn glad no one could see me. I had added him to my contacts so I wouldn't be caught off guard again like I was with "Ashford the Ash-Hole."

Admittedly, we had a more than pleasant time. Shannon and I met in front of Molly's. He didn't appear to be a successful NYC lawyer. His black hair was unkempt, he hadn't shaved in a few days, and he wore a Guinness sweatshirt over sloppy cords and untied leather tennies. Had he not stuck out his hand to introduce himself, I wouldn't have gone near him, let alone gone into Molly's with him.

I picked at the deep-fried appetizers and he gobbled his and my share; I sipped my pint of Smithwick's while he downed three pints of Guinness. We shared our similar experiences with grief and family and well-meaning friends. While I just didn't see this going anywhere, I agreed to see him the following week for a matinee and lunch, which turned out to be a street vendor hot dog.

During our slow walk after seeing "La La Land", not the best movie for a couple of recently widowed people, I discovered that Shannon was in such a deep funk that it was hurting his law practice. He was, he admitted, short with his legal secretary, wasn't sleeping at night, couldn't eat (except greasy food and Irish beer, Shannon), and was gaining weight.

"See a grief counselor, Shannon," I urged him. "Soon!"

Two weeks later, he called me. I cringed before I answered, but I answered. "Great news, Suzanne! I'm in love!"

"I hope not with the grief counselor," I blurted.

"Hell no! With her receptionist. It was love at first sight! Well, not exactly. I handled her divorce three years ago and was attracted to her then, but of course, I was married, but now, well, you know..."

"That's wonderful, Shannon, just wonderful. I'm so happy for you." (I really was.)

"I owe it all to you, Suzanne! If you hadn't recommended grief counseling, I never would have called this particular counselor because I remembered her name from my old client's divorce. What a coincidence?!"

"I'm glad I could be there between your wife's passing and your newfound love, Shannon."

"Me, too, Suzanne. You're a lifesaver. Hope the same happens to you soon. G'bye."

"Bye, Shannon."

This in-between dating game was turning into a pattern.

Monique called the next day to arrange brunch, but before she could say a word, I told her, "Enough blind dates, Monique, for now, anyway. I want to discuss a plan and get your thoughts. It will sound better after we have a few mimosas tomorrow."

The next day at brunch, Monique was impatient.

"So, want to tell me why you don't want to date any of the eager beavers I've got lined up for you?" Monique demanded over our first mimosa.

"Patience, doll," I said. "I told you I'd explain everything after several of these delicious drinks. Now, let's go through the buffet line before all the watermelon is gone."

Watermelon never disappears at Penelope, but it was our standard joke to get in line.

After our second trip through the buffet line and fourth mimosa, I launched into "The Plan."

"So, Monique, you know how the guys you've been lining me up with are all recently widowed or divorced?"

"Yeah, I guess so."

"I seem to be helping them get over their lost love so they can move on and find their next forever love, or at least for-a-long-while love."

"Hmmm," she kind of slurred into her French toast. "I see your point. I guess."

"Don't talk, just listen. So, it's not easy on me, but I'm okay with being the in-between relationship because I'm not looking for love. Not yet, anyway."

"Wellllll, I guess I ..."

"Just listen, Mone. It would be painful for a woman thinking these types of guys are ready for a permanent relationship when they're not, so I can be the woman who dates them when they've just lost their love, either through divorce, death, or breakup. I can get them ready to move on. Get it? I can be the in-between girl who dates them on the rebound."

"Won't you get hurt, sweetie?"

"No, and that's the beauty of it! I'll know what I'm getting into, or rather not getting into, from the get-go."

"I'll haf ta hear this again completely sober, so let's have another mimosa and keep this buzz agoin'!"

"Two good ideas."

"But juss ta make sure yur on da riite trak," she slurred, "you'll absholutle luv my personal trainer."

"No, I won't."

"Yessss, you will when you see his fabulous boudy on Tuesday!"

"Monique! I said no more!"

"Jusss this one more, pleeeezeee!"

"You are incorrigible."

"But you love me and you'll love him!"

I had to admit, Paulo Chavez carried himself like the Latin models I had worked with in Cabo and Ipanema. Tall, with dark, not black hair, and olive skin, he had the perfectly lithe build of a long-distance runner who lifted weights as a hobby. When we met for refreshments at his health club, he wore the most beautiful Tommy Bahama tropical shirt, white linen slacks, and huaraches. He looked to be about 40, but age is hard to discern in a personal trainer, especially one from South America.

Turned out, he had modeled quite a bit, but his girlfriends all tired of his constant travel and long absences. The latest one was the most tolerant but had finally broken off their engagement after hearing him on the phone at 3:00 a.m. talking about a child support payment that would be in the mail the next morning.

"You have a child?" I asked, over our smoothie.

"A misunderstanding," he claimed. "My brother's child, but he got caught in a drug smuggling sting in Columbia, a most unfortunate event. After the trial, I promised him I would take care of the child and her mother until he was released in five years. My woman, she would not listen to the story and, well, she threw herself out of our apartment. I am heart-wrenched."

"Broken," I said. "You're 'heart-broken'."

"Yes, if you say so."

"Would you like to have dinner?" I asked.

"Very much so," he smiled, as we shook hands outside the health club. "Maybe it will help me heal my wrenched heart."

Over dinner at a Cuban restaurant the following week, Paulo and I laughed and shared stories about our modeling experiences in Ipanema, especially fending off kids on the beaches begging for anything and everything, despite the military guards.

Over the next few weeks, we mostly talked about his family, how he and his brothers were different. His two younger brothers became engineers, while the youngest took what he thought was the easy way, and became a mule for one of the cartels until the inevitable happened. His baby brother's closest friend turned DEA informant and they were both lucky to be taken alive.

I began to feel something akin to a deep liking for Paulo when, one afternoon, over a late lunch at our Cuban restaurant, Paulo, looking off in the distance, cleared his throat, and said to the street, "You are a wonderful older woman, Suzanne, but I have fallen in love with the mother of my brother's child. I'm flying to Brazil to spend the rest of my life with her."

This is absolutely NOT happening again, I thought, choking on my spicy fries.

Chapter 12
Jack

My visit to Missy's gravesite had been on Sunday afternoon, after Mass and before family dinner, which was delicious, as usual; and irritating because of Bobby's crude comments, also usual.

After a frustrating discussion with Bobby about which was better, Windows 10 or Mac OS, I had driven home and found Darby with his leash in his mouth demanding a walk.

We walked through the neighborhood. I thought more about my plan to be the rebound guy and pondered the details: How I would find the women, how long we would date before I convinced them to break up with me, how I would convince them to break up with me, where I would take them for the break-up date. So much to do before I start.

I'm old fashioned, so I began my Rebound Guy education at the library. I like going to the library where the shelves of books dampen sounds of the city and everyone seems more polite. I decided to research what women don't like about men in women's magazines. I took along my laptop to take notes, which I saved right before the battery died. That also meant my research time was up. At home, I would review my notes and create different personas for myself, best suited to bring each relationship to an end – at the woman's insistence, of course.

First was **Mr. Wishy-Washy**, the guy who never had a strong opinion and could never decide what to do on a date. You know the type: "I don't know. What do you want to do?"

At the opposite end of the spectrum, is **Mr. Full of Himself**, who doesn't care about what the woman wants to do, it's all about his wishes, his plans. Of course, some women like decisiveness, so I would have to make it over the top and throw in some misogynistic words and phrases.

I also decided on the **Mama's Boy** still clinging to his mother's apron strings who would need to call mother during a date to make sure she wasn't lonely on a Saturday night. That would be easy to accomplish. I would just call my home phone and pretend to have a clingy conversation with dear, sweet mom.

Of course, I could act like a combination of two by being a **Wishy-Washy Mama's Boy**. Throw in some misogyny and you've got a guy no women would want to have a long-term relationship with, or so I hoped.

In my research, I discovered that the one type of guy women love to hate the most is a domineering jerk. Closely related to that is an arrogant jerk. I'd need to rehearse those and alert the maître d' at Erminia to inform the wait staff that it was all an act, that I didn't really mean to treat them like slaves. I loved the place because it was where I proposed to Missy. They loved me, probably because I was respectful and polite to the staff, but more likely because I always tip 25 percent. And naturally, it would be easy to cross the line from informative to arrogant about all my award-winning ad campaigns and catchy slogans, like the one for the Bronx Zoo's spring membership campaign: See What's Gnu in Our World!

My challenges would be ferreting out each woman's relationship turn-offs and transforming myself into that guy by the third or fourth date. My goal would be to have the woman decline another date. Better still would be a very public scene with her telling me off and possibly throwing water in my face. If that happened, I'd need to leave a bigger tip, of course.

Chapter 13

The woman was in a hurry, marching intently down the sidewalk. She grasped a large manila envelope in her left hand, her right hand and arm swinging in step, like a soldier on parade.

She had dressed in her finest navy blue dress with white piping and small brass buttons from neckline to hem, with a red scarf tied loosely around her neck. She wore sensible navy shoes with low heels, the kind you find at an outlet store that you still pay too much for because the goods are not any cheaper, the chain stores just like you to believe they are.

Last night, she had rewritten her allegation about the priest seven times, each time violently crossing out weak words – replacing them with stronger, more damning and descriptive words. She wanted to be precise about the appalling conversation she had seen and overheard on the steps of St. Patrick's Cathedral. Her old manual portable typewriter had made revisions painstakingly slow. She had to retype the entire three-page document each time. She didn't mind, though. By the seventh and final version, she had it memorized. She was going to show that bastard priest she was not a woman to be scorned or trifled with … twice!

Satisfied at last, she had signed her name at the bottom of the third page, put the pages in order, and smiled wickedly as she reread her damning accusation. So much adrenalin coursed through her bloodstream that her hands shook as she slid the pages into the manila envelope on which she had scrawled the archbishop's full and proper name in her flowery script. Laying it on the table by her front door, she also had placed her keys and small purse on it and had turned back down the hall to her small bedroom.

She had gone to her closet, flipped through the dresses on hangers until she found just the proper one. Her red scarf would be a fitting accent. Then she bent down and pulled the navy shoes from the neat row. Satisfied, she had undressed, put on her favorite nightgown, and slipped sideways into her minuscule bathroom where she performed her nightly bedtime ritual of flossing, brushing her teeth so hard that her gums often bled, and sitting on the toilet so she wouldn't need to get up during the night.

She'd thrown back the covers on her bed, the top one being a threadbare quilt her grandmother had given her when she graduated from high school, where she had fallen deeply in love with the kid who dumped her for God. Sleep avoided her. She tried breathing through her nose to quiet the voices, but the adrenaline gave them courage to pester her brain, causing her to shake her head on the pillow in an attempt to rid her consciousness of the demons. Sleep finally came at four, just in time for her alarm to go off four hours later.

A trip to the corner bodega that served the strongest, blackest coffee, the kind she needed this glorious Monday, and she had quickly downed two cups, which had pulled her out of her only-four-hours-of-sleep fog and given her the chemical courage a voice had told her that she so desperately needed.

'No, by God, I don't need courage,' she thought. 'I just need energy!'

Her subway and bus rides had brought her to within two blocks of the archbishop's official residence and offices. She had thought she had recognized one of the other bus passengers, a handsome middle-aged man dressed casually, but well. His head was turned toward the window, so all she saw was the side and back of his head, so she wasn't sure, but that was unimportant considering her mission. Anyway, he wouldn't look at you twice, said Arlene – voice number three.

She arrived at the archbishop's official residence precisely at 9:30, her predetermined time. She marched up the wide, well-worn grey marble steps, and stood at the massive innately carved wood doors, with their relief sculptures of Christ's Resurrection on the right door and his Passion on the left door. She paused, took a deep breath, threw back her shoulders, and reached for the doorbell pushing hard. Once. Twice. Four times.

Finally, the massive right door swung open so she could see the carved left hand of Christ with its nail hole vaguely visible. A priest looked down on her from the raised floor. He was young, but his cassock had red striping, which she knew meant he was a monsignor, one of many who worked for the archbishop.

"Good morning," he said smiling at her. "You must be Elaine McGuire. Please come in. The archbishop is expecting you."

He led her along a hallway and through a heavy mahogany door into the archbishop's outer office, where a much younger priest sat behind a computer. He looked up from the screen.

"Ah, Miss McGuire. You're right on time. The archbishop appreciates punctuality. Can I get you anything, a bottle of water perhaps, a cup of coffee?

We serve great coffee. One of the perks. No pun intended."

"No, thank you. I'm highly caffeinated already."

Both priests laughed politely.

"It will just be a second. He's just finishing up a call to his holiness."

"The pope? Really?"

"Yes, they discuss a list of things every other Monday. His holiness likes to stay current with the church in America, and the archbishop is always eager to tell him about church progress. Okay, he just hung up. The monsignor will introduce you. Please follow him."

"This is a very serious allegation, Miss McGuire," the archbishop had said after reading her account of the incident she had witnessed.

"We take very seriously the possibility of one of our priests disclosing anything he hears in the confessional, even if it involves a family member. But unfortunately, your allegation is what we call hearsay. Father Sullivan would need to divulge something he heard directly and not be overheard."

"I know what I heard, and I'm sure your Father Sullivan threatened to divulge what the other man told him in the confessional. He could have been talking about me, too, you know. I had just gone to confession, so maybe he was going to tell his whole family about what I confessed, too. That's not hearsay, is it?"

"No, if he divulged what you confessed, that's a serious sin, but you don't know for sure that he did?"

"He sounded pretty goddamned serious! Oh, sorry, your Excellency."

"No problem, Miss McGuire. If you're that convinced, we'll consider the matter. Someone will let you know what we discover. In the meantime, leave your contact information with my secretary. And Miss McGuire, please pray for us."

She had left her name, address, and telephone number with the priest at the computer, and the monsignor escorted her out of the office, down the hall, and out the massive doors, which, she noted with disdain, were plain on the inside, though highly polished. Guess they want to impress visitors before they come in and not when they leave, she thought.

Chapter 14
Jack

That Friday morning, after the usual round of team meetings to gauge progress on client campaigns, the creatives finished updating their résumés and then settled down to working for our clients. I spent the balance of the day planning my work for Monday and Tuesday morning satisfied with our campaigns and my Things To Do list for Monday. I cleared my desk at 5:30 and walked from my office intent on starting my weekend. As I passed Lester's cubicle, I stuck my head in to say good night. He was shuffling a stack of index cards and mumbling to himself.

"Hey, Les...how're you com..." I did a double take, almost like Curly in the old Three Stooges movies.

"Les, what are you doing?"

Startled by my appearance at the opening to his cubicle, Lester quickly shoved the cards into his middle desk drawer.

"Nothing, Jack. Nothing to see here."

"Lester, if you have to hide them from me, then they're definitely something I'd like to see, so hand 'em over...please?"

Reaching into the drawer, he pulled out the stack and shoved them at me. "Oh, all right, mister snoopy pants. Here! I have a blind date tonight and I'm rehearsing what I'm going to say to him."

I looked through the cards and whistled softly. These would absolutely not come out of the mouth of the Lester I knew. They were crude to the point of being embarrassing.

"Where did you get these?"

"Online."

"Why don't you just be yourself? You know, a whiny, insecure ..."

"Exactly! If I'm myself, he probably won't like me."

"I was joking, Les. You're funny, charming, and extremely gay. He'll love you."

I handed the cards back. Lester smiled sweetly. "I'll keep rehearsing. I don't need dating advice from a breeder!" Like I said...charming.

I walked to the elevator, stopping along the way to wish people well and urging them to have some fun that weekend. I was alone in the elevator. The doors closed and I thought about Lester.

"Here's some dating advice, Les," I said to the closed doors. "Don't get attached."

Chapter 15
Suzanne

When I'm in the city on Friday, I get together with Jennie, Louise, and Charlene, my few close friends, at our favorite upscale Manhattan bar. It was a tradition we started as single women, pre-Richard and kids.

They're like sisters, only closer because we had never fought growing up in a house with one tiny bathroom and a washer and dryer two floors down in the scary basement. Not having that history together worked in their favor. I trusted them with my deepest, darkest secrets, and knew they'd be honest about my plan to become a rebound relationship specialist.

I leaned over my Cosmo as I started to talk. They all leaned in, too. We looked like a flock of pigeons pecking at the same pile of cracked corn.

"Well, let me tell you guys about some of the disastrous dates I had after Richard passed away...

"You remember that kind of guy we all dated and wasted time on, the one who had broken up with his high school sweetheart after six years of dating?"

"I married my high school sweetheart," Jennie piped in, "and we're very happy, thank you very much!"

"We know, Jennie, we know," chided Charlene.

Good for you, Jennie, and thank you for reminding us of your marital bliss," I continued. "Anyway, the point I'm making is that for those of us who didn't marry the lacrosse captain, we had our hearts broken by a guy who never intended to stay with us. That guy was only using us to heal his poor broken heart."

"Been there," said Charlene, "one too many times."

"Okay, so you get it," I said as I looked each of them in the eyes, "except for you, Jennie, but you can be more objective, so that's good. Right?"

"I guess so," Jennie said petulantly.

"Okay, so what if a person never had to experience the rebound relationship?" I asked, rhetorically. "Because ..."

"Because," Louise said, "some other woman would have already been that person."

"That's absolutely right, Lou," I grinned, congratulating her. "And that's why you make the big bucks as a stock market analyst. You're just so damn perceptive!"

"Here's my plan," we all leaned closer, almost knocking over our drinks. "What if I became the rebound person, make the guy dump ME, and then he would be ready for a forever relationship, or at least one that would last for a few years?"

"I don't know," Jennie said. "What if the guy, or guys, fall in love with you? Won't they get hurt?"

"Not a chance," I smiled confidently. "By the second or third date, I'll have found out what irritates them. You know, like that movie "How to Lose a Guy in 10 Days," starring, "er, what's her name?"

"Kate Hudson," said Jennie, "and Matthew McConaughey."

"Right! So, that's the plan. What do you all think?"

"How are you going to find these brokenhearted souls?" asked Charlene.

"I haven't thought that through just yet," I replied, "maybe through word-of-mouth ... And, Oh My God. It's him!"

I was facing the bar and the guy from the cemetery had just walked in! He must come here often because the bartender just nodded at him, pulled out a pint glass, and filled it with Guinness. I ducked below the table.

The girls all turned around to glance at where I was looking.

"Don't look, don't look," I hissed.

"Who? Who? For Chrissake, Suzanne, WHO," Jennie hissed right back at me.

"The guy I bumped into at the cemetery last Sunday!"

"You bumped into him? Did you say anything?" Jennie asked in a stage whisper.

"Gawd, it was horrible," I said, coming up from beneath the table top and leaning further into the table. "I dropped the flowers and then I tripped on my damn heel and fell. I prayed he didn't see me."

"So what!" Louise piped in. "You thought you'd never see him again."

"And, yet, here he is!"

"Really? Where?" three voices asked in chorus.

"At the bar. The one drinking Guinness."

Then I saw Charlene sneak a peek, more like an hour-long stare, then out of the corner of her mouth, she said, "Uhm...him? Ooohh, he's kind of hunky...

For an older guy."

Giggles all around.

"He looks solid," I said in admiration. "Bet he works out... a lot."

"Yeah," Charlene said, "on his walker."

More laughter, until I coughed a dry "shut-up" cough, just before cemetery guy waved to some people near the window and walked by our table. He looked directly at me and smiled, without a hint of recognition, then scanned my friends. I'm sure he checked out their chests, but I was too embarrassed to make sure. When a girl wears a scoop top with a pushup bra, you're inviting looks, I thought as I looked at Charlene. But then, I was a little upset with the guy for NOT recognizing me. Jerk! I'm a model, for crying out loud. Then I remembered the slouch hat and that he wouldn't have been able to see my eyes, so I forgave him.

"Hello, girls," he said without a hint of sexism. Maybe he called every gaggle of giggling women 'girls.' I returned his smile. He looked at me again, closer this time. I thought I saw a glint of recognition in his eyes, but he turned away and walked over to the group he had waved at. I watched his back until he sat down.

"Well," Charlene Scoop Top said, "that was rude! Did you see him checking out my girls?"

"Charlene!" we all said and laughed.

"If you didn't want guys to look, you'd wear a turtleneck," Jennie said to her. "Hells Bells, I even checked out your girls when you joined us." Jennie winked at Charlene and blew her a kiss. Charlene blushed.

"Can't a girl flaunt her assets," she said. "Even a little?"

I looked her right in the chest. "Baby, they're no 'little bit' of your flaunting."

Everyone laughed in agreement.

"Let's talk about something important, like where we're having brunch on Sunday," I said. Deciding where to go for brunch seemed like a United Nations General Assembly argument between the Russians and every other country. It took just about as long, too. I finally had enough, so I said, "I'm going to our fave place in the West Village. Show of hands who wants to join me."

They all raised their hands, keeping their elbows on the table.

"Good, I'll make reservations for four at 10:30."

With that, we talked about kids and how we're too young for any grandkids, so our kids better use protection or we'd kill them, and Derek Jeter, the Yankees, Mets, and Jets. During our varied conversation, I glanced at the back of cemetery guy's head. How dare he not look at me, even once!

Chapter 16
Jack

Several Fridays a month a group of us head to Bobby Flay's Bar Americain for drinks and to unwind. Lew, my Navy SEAL buddy, usually joins us, and a few work friends always show up as regulars. Lew sips his beer, while the rest of us take big swallows of our first round, but we aren't on the lookout for the Taliban like Lew is – a holdover from his years in Afghanistan. He had assured me he's not suffering from PTSD when I had mentioned to him that his habit of surveilling was a little unnerving. He said he just got in the habit of sipping beer and watching for suspicious characters in Kandahar, which serves him well as a security consultant.

This particular Friday my longing for Missy was pronounced, so I needed some laughs with good friends to lift me out of what could easily become a pity party of one. Besides, it was a hot, humid afternoon, and I wanted a Guinness.

Sweat was running down my spine as I walked, dodging construction scaffolding – does remodeling never end – and was very thirsty when I opened the big glass door of Bar Americain. Luke, the evening bartender, saw me open the door, and immediately started the Guinness pour, so by the time I was at the bar, he was scraping off the tan foam. It pays to be a regular and to leave big tips.

I picked up the pint, turned, and waved to Lew, who was sitting with a couple of our basketball buddies. That's when I saw her.

The stunned and stunning woman from the cemetery had just ducked her head under the table where she was sitting with three very attractive women, all of whom appeared to be younger than her. I didn't want to embarrass her, so as I walked by their table, I didn't make eye contact for long, which was easy because one of the women had on a very low-cut blouse and, I imagined, one of those bras designed to elicit lustful stares from Methodist ministers.

In fact, diverting my eyes away from the round, firm ... never mind. Suffice it to say, it was a challenge to look away and look ahead.

I did smile briefly at the woman from the cemetery as I passed by their table, and said, in my most upbeat tone, "Hello, girls!" I was referring to both the four women and the one woman's chest, but they didn't know that. I smiled at my clever double entendre that only I knew.

I walked over to Lew, we did a fist bump because I learned a year or so ago that shaking hands with a SEAL could be a painful experience. He had apologized, but ever since, we always fist bumped.

They had saved me a chair facing the window because they knew I liked to people watch while we joked around and talked about the goofy shit that happened at work. Today, though, the thought struck me that this would be my life. No meeting my best friend, my wife, for a drink and dinner. No warm glow when I saw her smile at me from across a crowded room. Just a bunch of friends I truly liked, daughters I loved with my whole heart, and living parents who are still part of my life. It could be worse. They could all be like my brothers, one a saint, the other a pain in the ass.

One benefit of facing a window in Bar Americain is you get to watch what's going on behind you in the reflection. Once or twice I saw Cemetery Woman look our way, then quickly turn back to her friends. You know the feeling you sometimes get, right, like you're being watched? I thought she was checking out Lew, but I just felt like she was looking at the back of my head.

Then, after I heard and glanced at them laugh, Lew made a remark about a well-known CEO he was guarding, and I was drawn back into our conversation. A few minutes later, a server came over to bring us another round, and I turned toward the rest of the room and saw the four women were gone, being replaced by a bunch of rich-looking women wearing far too much jewelry and makeup. Oh, well, I thought, I'll never see her again.

Chapter 17

"This is a very serious allegation, Terrence," the archbishop said, his face grim, head still bent down looking at the document. He raised his head. His eyes burned into Fr. Terrence Sullivan's eyes, which held steady like a convicted killer who accepted the hangman's noose as his only option. According to policy, even though the archbishop had not thought the woman was credible, she was certainly adamant, so he was bound to report the incident to the Vatican, where it was reviewed and, much to everyone's dismay, the pope had appointed the monsignor the lead investigator.

Based on the Vatican's rules, Fr. Sullivan had been suspended from his duties for a month already, to the anger and dismay of his parishioners who had been told that Fr. Terrence was away on a retreat. Trouble was, anytime a priest went on a retreat, he announced it from the pulpit the Sunday before. In fact, Fr. Terrence had been staying in another parish rectory so he could continue to say daily Mass until he was either cleared or defrocked for desecrating the sanctity of the confessional.

"With all due respect, Excellency," Fr. Terrence said, "you and the monsignor have made that abundantly clear."

"What do you have to say in your defense?" the monsignor asked.

"Bill, please, I'll ask the questions," the archbishop said to his assistant.

"Sorry, Excellency."

"Now, then, Terrence, why don't you tell us your version of the story this woman tells in great detail. Leave nothing out."

Fr. Terrence told the two clergy about joking with his brother on the steps of St. Patrick's after confession.

"I never said I would tell our mother what my brother or anyone else had told me in the confessional, Excellency. You know me. I would never divulge anything to anyone, not even my own mother!"

"Not even by accident?" asked the monsignor.

"Bill," the archbishop chided.

The monsignor bowed his head slightly in supplication.

"Let's say I believe your side of the story. Why would this woman claim that you broke your vows?"

Fr. Terrence had been waiting for this moment. He opened his black leather messenger bag, a birthday present from the brother in question on the 20th anniversary of his ordination. It looked expensive, smelled rich, and he had tried to return it for those reasons. Jack had insisted he keep it and said if he didn't use it, he would regret it for the rest of his miserable, celibate life. Terrence had thanked him, promised he would cherish and use the expensive gift. Then, in a sincere voice, had told his brother that his celibacy had been a choice, one with which he was completely happy.

The priest reached into the messenger bag and pulled out a leather journal. He held it in both hands while he told the archbishop about his relationship, or rather, non-relationship, with the woman.

"The woman and I were elementary and high school classmates. We were friends all those years and we went to prom our junior year. That summer, I had begun thinking that I might want to become a priest. I visited with several priests, even toured a seminary. I still wasn't sure that God was calling me, so I applied to NYU to study and figure out my vocation. She and I had many long talks about our future. I told her my plan was to attend NYU and ask God what He wanted of me. This upset her, but she still wanted us to date. I told her that we could still be friends and go on group dates like we had always done, but that we couldn't go steady until I figured out my life."

"What happened after that?" asked the archbishop.

"She was angry and avoided me our entire senior year. I felt bad because I hadn't wanted to hurt her. Then ..."

"Then what?"

Then a few years ago, she came to the rectory and we talked at length about our lives. To be honest, Excellency, I had thought about her, as I had thought about my other friends, but never in a romantic way. Toward what I thought was the end of our conversation, she stood up and began to undress. I asked her to stop, but she removed her blouse and bra. When she began to remove her skirt, I called on the intercom for my housekeeper. Upon hearing this, she immediately put her bra and blouse back on and was buttoning her skirt just as Mrs. Cleary walked into my office."

"That was convenient," said the monsignor, with a not-too-subtle sarcastic tone.

"Bill, that's enough. Please leave us alone for a few minutes."

The monsignor bowed and left the room.

"It's all here in my journal, Excellency. I was shaken by the incident, but I had the presence of mind to write it all down. Here."

He handed the journal to the archbishop.

"How do I know you didn't just fabricate this?"

Fr. Sullivan said in an even tone, devoid of the sarcasm that tempted him, "You'll see that I wrote and dated my recommendations for the music committee after the entry about the incident. They had met that evening. If you would like, Excellency, I can put you in touch with some of the committee members to verify my attendance."

"That won't be necessary," said the archbishop, "But I would like to visit with your brother and, of course, your mother."

"MY MOTHER?!"

"If you prefer, I can have the monsignor visit her at her home."

Fr. Sullivan could no longer restrain himself. He didn't appreciate the monsignor's condescending attitude and suspicion. "I'd prefer you resurrect the most fearsome torturer from the Spanish Inquisition to visit my mother."

"The monsignor will be gentle," said the archbishop, looking pleasantly at Fr. Sullivan. "He's on his way to your parents' house right now. Please sit, Terry. Would you like some tea?"

Chapter 18

Jack

Tuesday evening. I was exhausted from the stress of managing creative people, placating an unreasonable agency head, and appearing upbeat and engaged at countless meetings with clients' in-house ad people, whose goal was to make themselves look good in their bosses' eyes.

With Darby's wet, black nose rubbing against my hand I stood at the narrow table in my entrance hall and sorted through three days of mail. Respond. Throw. Shred. Thankfully, solicitations from numerous disease-related charities had slackened after I respectfully informed them that their constant bombardment served only to bring back a flood of bad memories. I assured them those memories did not convince me to support their research into diseases for which there were never going to be cures.

I heard the clatter of pots and pans being put away in the kitchen and yelled, "Helen, you left the door unlocked last week. Again."

She came out of the kitchen and stood facing me, wiping her hands on a dishtowel, her shoulders slumped.

"Sorry, Mister Sullivan," she said, so quietly that I could barely hear her. "My youngest kid called and I had to go to a school conference. I just forgot all about it."

"Forgot about locking the door?"

"No," she said, louder, but sadder. "The school conference. I do it alone."

"Did you call the lawyer, Helen?" I knew the answer but asked anyway.

"I forgot."

"Helen," I asked, "what happened to your notebook for lists of things to do?"

"Lost," she said, sheepishly. "I think I left it last week on the first bus I take."

"I've got plenty more, Helen. I'll help you make your lists. First, you need to go after your kids' father for support."

She ignored me, as usual when our conversations became uncomfortable.

"I ordered Thai for you, Mister Sullivan. Should be here soon. Can you just mail my check? I gotta pick up my kids so we can ride the bus together."

"I already wrote it," I said, handing her the check and two twenties. "Plus more for the bus pass."

"Thank you, thank you!" She took the check and money and, grabbing her purse and threadbare jacket walked to the door. As she opened it, I looked at her and only saw the side of her shoulder as she quickly closed the door.

"Call the lawyer, Helen. Have a good..."

I walked to the door and threw the deadbolt closed.

"... week."

A wet nose pressed incessantly against my left elbow. Darby's bladder had held out long enough and needed relief. When an Irish wolfhound tells you it's time for a walk, it's time for a walk.

"Just a little longer," I said hurrying into my bedroom, tearing off my clothes, pulling on a t-shirt, shorts, and slipping into my running shoes. Darby's head jerked so impatiently I had trouble hooking the leash and locking the door after we were on the stoop. No sooner had he pulled me down the steps, than he lifted his leg and peed on the first tree he saw. A lot. Poor guy. Must be more attentive, I thought.

"Good boy, Darby!"

The more we ran and the longer we walked that evening, the greater my stress relief. I marveled at the loyalty of this wonderful creature and the comfort he had brought me in the years after Missy died. Her dogs, Sigmund and Freud, had moped around and for several weeks had walked from room to room looking for her. I told them that she was gone, not just to the hospital for rounds, but to her new forever home.

Did they understand? I don't know if I believe they did, but eventually, they stopped wandering through the house and just laid at my feet. Whenever I allowed it, they climbed onto the couch and put their heads on my lap as I read or watched TV. I only allowed it when I was feeling especially lonely. I think they sensed that and knew they could get away with being on the couch. One evening, a few weeks after the funeral, I slumped on the couch with tears flowing down my cheeks, followed by sobs. Each dog jumped on up on a side of me and licked the tears off my cheeks. I hugged them so tightly they squirmed away. Extra treats for weeks. Two months later, I found them asleep in Missy's closet, only they weren't asleep. I rushed them to the vet. He said they had died of broken hearts. I cried for days.

After eating most of the Thai that Helen had ordered and a getting a good night's sleep, I awakened to a wet nose in my ear, which I briefly thought was some nebulous woman getting frisky early in the morning. But dog breath brought me back to reality. Time for my morning walk, it insisted – at 5:30!

Since I was up so early I decided to drive to the office. I quickly parked in my underground spot, which I could've found with my eyes closed, and scanned my day's schedule on my smartphone as I rode the elevator. No one met me when I reached the agency floor, so all was going well until I approached Lester's cubicle at 7:45. I could hear his sobs 10 feet away.

"Somebody die, Les?" I asked sympathetically.

"Nooooooo."

"Lose your apartment?" That's always a problem in the city, especially if you live in a rent-controlled building.

Lester sobbed even louder. I looked around. Heads had appeared above the cubicle walls, like the old "Kilroy was here" graffiti. This was getting embarrassing.

"Noooooo."

I walked into his cubicle and put my hand on his shoulder.

"Wanna tell me why you're crying like your doctor just called to tell you that you only have four days to live and he's sorry that he didn't call you three days ago?" Sometimes an old joke can lighten the mood, especially mine.

"Manuel," sob, sob, "dumped me for a Hungarian personal trainer."

"That shit," I said, somewhat less than sympathetically. "Les, you'll find mister right," I added. It was getting hard not to laugh at his histrionics.

"No I wooooonnnnn't."

"Who's Manuel?" I asked.

Before he could answer, a gaggle of female graphic designers crowded into Les's cubicle and elbowed me out.

"Jack, let us take over," demanded kindly Kristie, a 30-something Bohemian wannabe with curly black hair and too many turquoise beads around her neck and dangly feather earrings chiming against her cheeks.

"Sweetie, it's okay to cry," she said to Les, laying her hand gently on his shoulder. Mercifully, his sobs subsided. I was torn between wanting to let this play out or to strongly suggest that they all get back to work and deal with Les' love life on their own time. Being the caring sort, I decided to give this tragedy a few more minutes before reminding them that we were – in Langston's parting words to me Tuesday – on the clock and heading for the tape.

"Thanks, girls," Lester said, wiping tears with a tissue one of them had shoved into his hand. "You know what it's like."

"We sure do," said Kristie, kneeling eye-to-eye with Les.

"And I don't?" I asked.

"You've been out of circulation too long, Jack," Kristie said looking over the cubicle wall at me. "Les was Manuel's 'in-between' boyfriend, Jack. But he didn't know. The bastard didn't tell him."

"Lester, go home," I said with all the sympathy I could muster. "You're no good to me today."

Kristie and Les stood up and she gave Les a loving big-sister hug. Then the waterworks started again for both of them, so I slid into his cubicle, picked up his electric-blue messenger bag and handed it to him with a motion that said 'I mean it, go home!' He took the hint and hugged the bag to his chest as he shuffled toward the elevator. Kristie, fingers to her mouth, watched him until I said to her, "Please come into my office, Kristie."

We walked into my office. "Close the door, Kristie. I don't want anyone hearing our conversation." I sat in the leather chair nearest the windows. Kristie gave me a quizzical look before she closed the door. Then she sat down facing me.

"What's the whole story about Les, Kristie?"

She cleared the tears from her throat and dabbed her eyes to wipe away the mascara that streaked her cheeks. "Seems Les invested two months in a relationship that was doomed from the start."

"How so?" Now, this was getting interesting.

"Manuel had just gotten out of a long-term relationship with a cellist. He used Les to heal and get him back into the dating scene. When he found his soul mate at a soccer game and fell madly in love, he dumped Les."

"The bastard," I said, trying unsuccessfully to express my outrage.

"Don't be a jerk. It happens. People get hurt by being the in-between lover."

"You?"

"Jack, almost every single person either has been on the rebound or has dated someone on the rebound. It's the rebound relationship."

"Well, yeah, come to think of it...," I paused remembering my heartbreak. "During my last year of college, I fell madly in love with the national dairy princess. We got engaged. She cheated. Turns out, she broke up with her boyfriend of seven years just before we got together."

"So you were HER rebound guy!"

"Yep, she married the guy she was cheating on me with. I got over it by thinking that he was, uhm, having relations with my fiancé, but I was having the same kind of relations with his future wife. Poetic justice or irony, maybe both."

"But you've had a few dates since your wife died, right?"

"Usually disasters, or at the very least, uncomfortable," I said, looking out the window. "Client receptionists, after hemming and hawing and finally asking them out for lunch after several visits to the client's office, for fear of rejection," I laughed. "Mainly because they were not much older than my oldest daughter, or they had been single since JFK was elected."

"Really, Jack? Don't you think you're exaggerating?"

"Okay, maybe a little. But I always felt like I was cheating on Missy. Still."

"Jesus, Jack! How many years has it been?"

"Seven years, three months, two days."

"I doubt that she would mind if you met someone and fell in love. Let go, Jack. Let go."

"You may be right. But first, I need to spare some other schmuck the pain of dating a rebound girl. And second, we need to figure out how to deal with this Japanese car company. Now, please leave so I can work on the problem at hand on company time."

Chapter 19
Jack

Bobby and I were racing each other through Central Park. I was holding back so I could sprint at the end and demolish my brother. Darby was having no trouble keeping up with us, his Wolfhound legs being designed for chasing wolves, Irish poachers, and asshole younger brothers.

I looked over at Bobby. His cheeks were flushed, he was breathing hard, and sweat poured down his neck. Time to sprint. Darby and I pulled away. As we did, I heard a breathless "Prick" yelled at me.

Darby and I slowed to a trot and came to a complete halt at our pre-arranged bench finishing line. As I bent over so Bobby would think I was winded, Darby licked my face and neck. It was not refreshing, but I scratched behind his ears and he gave a satisfied growl.

I sat on the bench and Darby plopped himself beside it. Bobby, exhausted from trying to beat us, stumbled forward and slumped on the bench. He wiped his face and neck.

"Well?" I shrugged and maybe glared at him.

Bobby got the hint and struggled to his feet. He stumbled over to a bush and retrieved three water bottles we had stashed in a bush behind the bench. I cracked one open and Darby gamely rose to his feet and stood next to me, mouth open, tongue lolling so I could pour water in his mouth. When he drained it, I cracked mine open, but Darby wanted that, too.

"Forget it," I said. "This is mine. Go lay down." We went through this routine every time we ran in the park. Our little game. Bobby and I sat back and sipped our water. After a few minutes, when Bobby's breathing stopped sounding like he was climbing Mt. Everest without an oxygen tank, I laid out my plan to be a rebound guy.

"And you're wrong, Bob. Nobody will get hurt."

"Bullshit, Jack! You can't date a woman just to dump her. It's against one of the commandments."

"Only one?"

"I'm being serious, asshole...it's wrong to hurt people, especially women."

"But that's the beauty of my plan. It's a win-win for them. I've been hurt. That's why I want to prevent that for others, Bob. I'll find women who've just broken up with a guy, like the five women I've dated in the last year who dumped me for a bunch of different reasons and moved on, and I'll date them. Until they find their soul mate, that is, and dump me."

"And what happens if they get serious about you?"

"The minute I sense that, I'll know enough about them to start doing what irritates them. They'll dump me like I'm a convicted bigamist ...Guaranteed. I'll be their rebound guy so no other guy gets hurt. To use an overused management cliché, it's a win-win."

"And how, pray tell, are you going to find these unfortunate women?"

"To quote a Garth Brooks song, "I've got friends in low places!"

Chapter 20
Jack

"Let me get this straight, Jack. You want us to help you find women who've just broken up with a longtime boyfriend?" asked Denise, my assistant.

"Yep. Or a fiancé."

"Widows?" asked Kristie, with a great deal of incredulity.

"Only if they've already been on a few dates," I said. "I don't want to take advantage of their grief."

"Really, Jack. Widows?"

"I'm a widower, Denise, as you all know. Life goes on... After a while."

"I know a guy your age," Lester said, stifling a laugh.

"Les...I'm serious."

"Okie dokie, then. I'll ask my sister to be on the lookout. But you don't know what you're missing."

"I can only hope I never find out, Les. No insult intended."

"None taken, Mister Cranky Pants."

"Let's get back to work on next year's TV spots so we can actually make this a working lunch."

We were lunching at Metro Diner on Broadway on the agency's tab. Sometimes creatives' creativity flows more easily in settings outside a creative meeting room. Different sights and sounds can inspire new ideas, and folks feel freer away from the office to throw out a variety of ideas with less fear that someone, say a managing partner, will saunter into the room and call their ideas stupid. As Linus Pauling famously quipped, 'The best way to have a good idea is to have a lot of ideas.' Some of our best campaigns had developed from these sessions where we whittled down lots of ideas, combined some, and got excited. It made writing copy, doing storyboards, presenting those to the account executives, then to the clients, who could feel the enthusiasm from the creative team about the campaign, much easier. That is, if one of the partners hasn't intervened and displayed his or her seagull management style – swoop in, make a bunch of noise, shit all over the campaign, then fly off, leaving a mess for others, usually me, to clean up.

"And you're serious about this rebound guy dating?" Denise asked, obviously having trouble focusing on campaign ideas. She was my assistant in name only. In reality, she was one of the most talented creatives in the agency and I relied on her to channel my energies and to exercise her creativity when we had these sessions. She had breezed through her undergraduate years, then came out of Brandeis with a master's degree in English. Poor woman, she had actually wanted to work in an ad agency rather than teach freshman English to football players somewhere. Go figure!

"Okay, yes, Denise, I am serious. Now, can we get back to our campaign ideas?"

"Jack," she said, serious herself, "before I help you find your ... victims, I ..."

"They're not victims, Denise," I said, getting a little irritated at her suggestion that women on the rebound would be my victims like I was a vampire who could mesmerize them and then make them my personal blood banks.

"What would you call them?"

"I prefer to think of them as people hurting from a broken long-term relationship and me as the 'doctor' helping them heal."

"Oh, puh-leeze," Lester interjected.

"You're awake at last, Les."

"Awake and aware of this sounding a little creepy."

"It's no different than dating someone for a few weeks and then deciding that it's not working," I tried to explain. "The difference is that I will irritate them so much that they will want to break up with me. Get it? No harm, no foul. It's not creepy at all."

"But it's dishonest," said Kristie, ever the moral compass.

"It would only be dishonest if I pretended that I loved them, and I played them like a con man out to get their money, like Max Bialystock in 'The Producers'."

"And you're sure you can pull off these rebound relationships?" asked Kristie.

"Missy taught me a lot about self-confidence. And besides, my position in the agency demands a great deal of self-assuredness with Langston, his partners, and our clients, so, yeah, absolutely!"

"Well, if you're that sure, Jack, I'll be on the lookout for women who need your healing," Denise said, with a slight hint of sarcasm.

"No one will get hurt, I promise."

"You might," Kristie remarked.

Chapter 21

"Would you like some coffee or tea, Monsignor?"

Monsignor William Joseph McAllister and the archbishop had discussed at length how to question Fr. Sullivan's mother. They decided that he should be friendly at first in order to establish rapport and put her at ease. When he sensed the time was right, he was to be blunt, giving her no warning about the reason for his visit.

He had called the Sullivans the day before his visit and first thing that morning immediately after he said Mass and a Rosary in the small chapel in the archbishop's residence.

"My husband will be here," she told him that morning.

"Wonderful," he smiled into the phone, "I would love to meet him, too."

Like most New York residents do, he had taken a taxi to the Sullivan's house. When he got out of the taxi, he told the Sikh driver to pick him up in exactly 45 minutes.

"No problem, priest."

"Monsignor or father, please."

"Okay, father priest."

He gave the man 20 dollars and a smile through the plexiglass divider and exited on the curbside. He took two steps and turning back, said, "Forty-five minutes!"

He wanted to look his most clerical, so he wore the traditional red-striped cassock over highly polished black chukkas and a biretta with a red ball on top. In his black Floto Firenze Italian briefcase, which he had purchased during his first year in Rome, he carried a small electronic recorder, a matching folio, and a file on the allegation against Fr. Sullivan. It held nothing else because he didn't want to be searching for the file amidst other unrelated materials when he sprung the question on the Sullivans.

He removed his biretta as he sat down, smiled and politely requested tea. As Mrs. Sullivan walked into the kitchen, he asked Mr. Sullivan, "Mets or

Yankees?"

"Yankees! Great team, great history."

"Yes, of course."

"And you?"

"Boston Red Sox. Great team, great history."

Mr. Sullivan glared at his guest, then smiled broadly and they both laughed.

Mrs. Sullivan returned with a teapot and three mugs with a Celtic harp on one side and the Irish flag on the other. She set it down on the coffee table in front of her husband and poured. There also was a plate of currant scones, which she offered to both men. Both declined.

"What brings you here, Monsignor?" asked Mr. Sullivan.

So much for taking time to get to know them, the priest thought, putting his mug of tea on the tray. He reached into his briefcase, pulled out the recorder and set it on the coffee table.

"What's that for," Mr. Sullivan asked, point blank. He sat up straighter in his chair.

"Don't be rude, Patrick!"

"It's so I don't make any mistakes and so I can listen instead of taking notes," he replied, smiling ever so sweetly. Then he pulled out the file and opened it in his lap.

Looking directly at Mrs. Sullivan, he said, "When did Fr. Terrence tell you what a women in his parish confessed to him three Saturdays ago?"

Mr. Sullivan exploded, "What?"

"Patrick, really, I can speak for myself." She paused. "My son is a good priest, Monsignor. He would never tell me what anyone confessed. Where did you get such a ridiculous notion?"

"We have a reliable eyewitness who claims to have overheard Fr. Sullivan threatening to tell you about her confession or your son's, and, as you know, that's a very serious allegation."

Patrick Sullivan gripped the arm of the chair with his left hand and slammed his right fist down. "That's enough," he said through a clenched jaw. "This person probably overheard my sons joking around. That's all. And there's no proof that Terrence did what he's been accused of, right?"

"That's what I'm trying to find out, Mr. Sullivan."

"You can just find your way out of our house," Patrick Sullivan said, his neck growing a deep red.

"My son has never discussed anything about what anyone has confessed," Mrs. Sullivan said calmly, looking the monsignor in the eyes. "To me or to anyone else!"

"You're quite sure?"

"As sure as I know my own name, monsignor. And as sure as I know you're no longer welcome in our home," she said, rising from her chair and glaring at him.

The young monsignor calmly put the file back into his briefcase, reached out to turn off the recorder, and put it in his briefcase. He stood up, picked up his briefcase and his biretta.

"I've a taxi coming, so I'll just wait outside."

Mrs. Sullivan showed him to the door. To his surprise, she grabbed his elbow so hard it made him inhale sharply. She turned him toward her and pressed her fingers into the tender inside of his elbow, like guiding a bull with a ring through its nose.

She looked up into his eyes with fire in her otherwise pleasant blue eyes. "If anything happens to my boy, there'll be hell to pay. And the Irish in this town won't be donating to the archbishop's many churches. Do you understand me, boyo?"

With that, she let go of his arm, swung open the door, and shoved him down the steps. He tripped on the first step, caught himself by the third step and turned to face the door as it slammed shut. He squared his shoulders and took a deep breath, his elbow still smarting. "Understood," he said to the door. Turning around, he saw that the taxi was up the street. 'Thank you, God,' he mumbled as he walked toward the curb.

Back at the archbishop's office, he and the archbishop had listened to the recording three times, each time the archbishop took notes. After the third review, the archbishop looked up from his notes and reached into the middle drawer of his desk. He pulled out Fr. Sullivan's journal and handed it to the young monsignor.

"Don't look at it just yet," he said. "Tell me if you think she was lying?"

"Who?"

"Mrs. Sullivan."

"I'm good at reading people," bragged the monsignor, "and I didn't give her enough time to lie, so, no, I don't think she was lying."

"Now you can open Terry's journal. I've marked the pertinent pages, so take some time to read what he wrote about the woman's attempt to seduce him."

After a few minutes, the monsignor closed the leather-bound journal and looked at the archbishop. "It seems, excellency, that we have unnecessarily cast a shadow on Fr. Sullivan."

"I agree," said the archbishop, exhaling slowly. "But we had to be sure. The faithful can never, ever doubt the sanctity of the confessional." He paused.

"When was the last time you heard confessions in one of our smaller parishes, monsignor?"

The monsignor thought a few moments, his eyes looking past the archbishop's shoulder through the window. "I honestly can't remember."

"While you were away, I received a formal request from two adjacent parishes upstate to have their own pastor. They've been relying on Franciscans from a monastery approximately 30 miles from them. Tragically, the two Franciscans both died recently of heart failure. A terrible coincidence."

He looked at the monsignor and smiled gently. "You and I will attend the funerals at the monastery, and then travel to the two nearby parishes. Please pack all your clothes and vestments, monsignor. I'll be returning to New York and you will be the new pastor at St. Nicholas and St. Boniface."

"But, but, excellency," stammered the monsignor, "I'm a big city kid. I grew up in Brooklyn! I won't know how to act in a small town!"

"You'll learn about obedience and about hearing confessions in not one but two small parishes. You already know about parish finances after examining three months' worth of St. Patrick's books looking for irregularities and payments to the woman. The archdiocese's accounting firm has agreed to help you."

"You've already set this all up, haven't you?" the monsignor said in resignation. "Do you mind if I ask you when?"

"I've felt for several months that you were taking your station here too seriously and were losing sight of our real calling as priests. We serve God and his flock, not the archdiocese and its trappings. This is your opportunity to spend the next 12 years reminding yourself of that."

"Twelve years, Excellency?"

"Pack your things, Bill. We leave in an hour. And remember your chalice."

"I will, excellency," he said, softly as he bowed his head at the archbishop. "Thank you."

He turned and left the archbishop's office, quickly walking past the outer office and turned his head so the priest sitting at the desk couldn't see the angry, dejected look on his face. Once out in the hall, he quietly closed the ornate office door and not so quietly said at it, "Asshole!"

Chapter 22
Jack

My scouts had little trouble finding candidates for my Broken Hearts Rebound Relationship Club. Seems the city was awash with women who had recently broken up with or been dumped by a boyfriend.

To pick my first group, which some might call 'victims', I gathered as much information about each of seven women and then assigned points based on their circumstances. One point if they had been together with the guy but not engaged; two points if they had been engaged, but hadn't set the wedding date; three points if she had broken off the wedding; four if he left her at the altar; and five points for a recent widow. The lower the number, the higher they ranked on my list of future dates.

The points allotment had taken several days to work out in my mind, and I was only able to finalize the priority points once I had written down and thrown away the first three attempts at awarding points based on woman's circumstances. Each time I scribbled something, Darby raised his massive head and tilted it to one side as if to ask what I was up to. When I crumpled up the penultimate sheet, Darby got down from the couch and laid his head on my lap, nudging my arm with his nose.

"All right, boyo, I think I've finalized the points allocations."

And so, here I was with Louise Alexandro at Erminia, my favorite Italian restaurant, where I always took the person for our fateful breakup date. The actors were in place and the scene was about to begin.

"We need to talk, Jack," Louise spoke her line on cue, after gently dabbing the corners of her perfectly lipsticked mouth. Somehow, she had been able to eat her entire meal of a salad and one piece of French bread without touching her fork to her lips. I was impressed.

I wiped my mouth and nose with my napkin, which was covered in red sauce. I think some of it even came off on my nose because she gave me a look of pure disgust.

"I know," I replied, through the napkin, as I pinched my nose with it, "we need to talk about where this ... us. Where we're going."

"We're going nowhere, Jack," she said in perfect Vassar diction. "I've started seeing someone else, and I think he's my soul mate. I'm sorry, Jack. You're a very ... um ... nice guy, but he doesn't have your peculiar habits."

"Like what, Lou.?," I said, feigning hurt feelings.

"Like calling me 'Lou.' You know I don't like that. And ..."

I dabbed my right eye and then cleared my throat of nothing and pretended to spit quietly into my napkin. This couldn't be more perfect. It was as if I had scripted her lines myself. I guess in a way I did.

"That, Jack," she said, her eyes never leaving mine, as she threw her napkin on the table, slid back her chair, and got up. "It's disgusting and embarrassing. Goodbye, Jack."

I put on my best look of dejection and cast my eyes down at my bowl of half-eaten pasta, but I saw out of the corners of my eyes the embarrassed glances toward me from other diners. I raised my head trying to look embarrassed and saw Louise storm out the restaurant door. As it closed behind her, I smiled and, as unobtrusively as possible, pumped my fist at my side, and said in a stage whisper, "Yesssssssssssss!"

Bernie, and exceptional maître d' and my co-conspirator, sauntered over and handed me a plastic bag for my napkin.

"Another slam dunk, sir?" he said, with a sly grin.

"Close call, Bernie," I said as I slid the napkin into the bag. "It took me weeks to find out what irritated her. Weeks more for her to find her perfect match while I got more and more irritating. I was even starting to disgust myself."

We both laughed. Across the room, at a table with a guy, I saw a woman who seemed to be watching me.

"A very narrow escape, to be sure. Should I add your usual gratuity?"

"Double. Tell the crew they did a great job tonight."

"Certainly, sir. When can we expect you back?"

"I need a few weeks off. But I've got my eye on a nun looking to leave the convent."

Bernie coughed politely, a slightly surprised look on his face.

"You do love a challenge, don't you?"

"I'm kidding, Bernie."

"Certainly, sir."

"Goodnight, Bernie." I slid back my chair and headed for the door. On my way out, I spoke briefly to my waiter and thanked him for his good service. As

I continued my exit, I saw that the woman who had glanced at me earlier was an attractive blonde woman who I could swear I knew. As I passed her table, I gave her an innocent smile, the kind you give the people in the elevator as you get on. When I reached the door, I paused and turned to look at the back of her head. Where had I seen her before? Had I seen her before? I shook my head and walked out into the cool Manhattan night. Mission One done, I smiled to myself.

Chapter 23
Suzanne

I'd been watching a man, gentleman is a term that would give him too much credit, from across the room. He appeared to be the rudest, crudest boar in all of Manhattan. Or so it appeared. When the woman he was with stomped by my table, I looked quickly beyond my date and noticed the guy's reaction when his date walked out on him. Confusing, but interesting. I saw him talk to Bernie then get up and walk toward the exit, a path that took him right past our table. My God, it's him, I thought. I turned away and wiped my mouth, hoping to hide my face. But he must have stopped to talk to someone because I turned back to look where he was and our eyes met. Shit! But he simply smiled down at me as one polite stranger smiles at another. I smiled back and turned to continue talking to my date, a very mild-mannered actuary with a life expectancy, he had told me, of 82.75 years, based on his height of 73.15 inches, weight of 169.5 or 168.75, depending on the day, and his healthy lifestyle that includes semi-annual visits to the dentist. However, his recent divorce from his college sweetheart had, he figured, shaved 5.5 years off his longevity. She must have been patient to a fault, although any woman would admire his carved physique and dimpled chin.

"I just love the atmosphere here, don't you, Glen?" I said too loudly.

"It's very nice...and quiet. Suzanne, can we talk ... quietly for a minute."

"Only a minute?" I asked sarcastically. "Oh, just a minute? Is that all?"

I snorted and laughed at my own joke, then I executed the coup de grace mercifully ended both of our suffering. I picked food out of my teeth with the fingernail on my little finger.

Glen looked around at the other diners, none of whom were paying any attention to us. He looked mortified and spoke in a clipped cadence that must have taken him several minutes of rehearsal in front of a mirror, "I'm sorry, Suzanne, but this just isn't working for me." He paused, I thought, for effect and to gain courage. "And I've been seeing someone else."

"WHAT! You ... arrrgh."

"Please calm down, Suzanne, will you, for God's sake! She's my dentist and we just sort of hit it off after my root canal."

"Your fucking DENTIST!!!"

"I knew you'd do this. You always go way overboard lately. You know I hate that."

He slowly got out of his chair and looked around using only his eyes while he kept his head pointed in my direction. Gently laying his napkin on the table, he looked at me and shook his head slightly. "I'll pay on my way out. Enjoy the rest of your dessert ... and the rest of your life."

I didn't turn to watch him leave. I just smiled and took one more small bite of my tiramisu and placed the dessert fork upside down on the plate just as Bernard glided over to my table.

"Is madam all right?" he asked, politely, even though he was fully aware of what had transpired.

"Yes, Bernie. Just perfect."

"Another success, madam?"

"A tough one, Bernie. It took me an entire month to find out that loud women in quiet places irritate him. Lucky for me he needed a root canal."

We laughed.

"I'm sure they'll be very happy together," he said. "Would there be anything else?"

"No, except would you please apologize to the other diners for me."

"Certainly, Madam. When will we see you again?"

"Maybe in a few months. I'm working in Paris for two months. Then I'll try to find the next broken heart on the rebound."

"It's always a challenge, isn't it?"

"You know me; I love a challenge. And saving other women from the pain of being rebound girlfriends is definitely a challenge I'm enjoying."

"Good night, Miss Suzanne," he said sweetly as he pulled back my chair. "We all loved your last magazine ad. You were stunning."

"You're too kind. Good night, Bernie."

I walked out of the restaurant into the pungent night air of Manhattan. I looked skyward, and for a brief moment, I felt as if a weight had flown from my shoulders. It wasn't the weight of getting dumped, but the relief of finally being dumped. I took a breath and stepped off the curb. Raising my hand to my mouth, I whistled loudly to hail a taxi.

Chapter 24
Suzanne

There is so much to see at the Louvre that I go every time I'm in Paris. My current visit was more business than pleasure, though.

The flight from JFK to Charles de Gaulle Airport had been uneventful, so I caught up on sleep and even read the first few chapters of Janet Evanovich's, "Tricky Twenty-Two."

My agent had signed me on for a series of print ads for a pricey perfume, which were to appear in magazines across Europe, and, to my utter dismay, in the AARP Magazine in the States.

The crew and I had spent four days at several Paris locations, including a night shot at the Arch de Triumph that had required the ad agency to hire water trucks to wet down the streets. Water adds another dimension to dry concrete, which is quite ugly, and it also reflects light, I have learned. It also wreaks havoc with fancy negligée, which I had to wear in the middle of the street. The extra moisture caused the wardrobe people to swear in several languages, including Hungarian, I think, although they had been warned beforehand they'd have to deal with it.

To this day I still don't know how Jacques found me in Paris. I suspect he heard from an executive at the perfume company who had heard from the photographer the name of the model who had been hired to be the middle-aged face of parfum à vieillir. In my mind, the name roughly translated into, 'how to age gracefully by spending lots of money to smell good.'

He showed up the last day of the photo shoot. Between wardrobe and hair fixes, he strongly suggested in typical lothario style, that I should have lunch and tour the Louvre with him, or he would tell his friend at the perfume company that he could find some other exporter. I didn't like being extorted by anyone, especially not by an arrogant, pudgily handsome Frenchman, but business is business.

I admit our lunch of duck confit and Bordeaux the next day was delicious.

The conversation was even pleasant enough until Jacques started telling me how his latest love had broken his heart by leaving him for a painter. He knew from what she had told him shortly after they met that she had broken up with her fiancé three months before they had gotten together. I couldn't believe it. Half a world away from Manhattan, men and women were in rebound relationships.

As we stood admiring the Cheat by Georges de La Tour, Jacques put his arm around my waist. I gently removed it and turned to the side.

"And you come into my life just like THAT!? I am a man with needs, Cherie," he said loudly in his best Louis Jordan imitation.

"Sssshhhh. Besides, you are trying to get in my life! Now talk quieter, people are staring at us."

"They stare at your beauty. And mine, of course."

"I just adore your modesty, Jacques! It's so quaint!"

"More sarcasm from a ... an aging model?"

"Don't be cruel."

"You are the cruel one. My mistress treats me better."

"Your MISTRESS?!"

"Now who's making the scene?"

"You bastard!"

"Old drama queen!"

Jacques turned on his heels and walked away, bowing to people as he left in a huff. I found a bench, sat down and stared at Jacques' paisley silk scarf as he flung it over his shoulder.

I muttered to myself, "Can't let anyone get to me like that ever again!"

I spent the rest of the afternoon lazily walking through the Louvre, thinking about how I had been manipulated into a date, how it wasn't going to happen again and how I would keep up my guard as I carried out my plan. In the back of my mind, I wondered if it was dishonest to date men and then dump them, gently of course, so they could move on with their romantic lives. I knew it was dishonest, but no one will get hurt, I told myself. No one, and not me, that's for sure, because I would be in control of every situation, like a grand puppet master. Sometimes, though, I knew the strings got tangled and the show had to end before the final curtain.

Chapter 25
Jack

She was my second rebounded relationship and a true test of my celibacy pledge to myself and my brother the priest.

"As your spiritual advisor ..." Fr. Terrence started to say.

"Whoa there, bro! Since when did you become my spiritual advisor. I don't need you as my spiritual anything, other than confessor, of course," I shot back. We were sitting in his office, or rather, he was sitting and I was filing copies of parish financial statements as my penance for not donating to the pope's annual mission plea. I hadn't confessed that. Why would I? But there had been no envelope with check inside, and Fr. Terrence had decided that filing financials would encourage me to give the pope money. It wasn't working, but my brother was working on me.

"As I was saying, now that you've been single for a few years and you're now embarking on this, uhm, scheme to save women from the heartbreak of a real rebound relationship, you need to promise Jesus, Mary, and God that you will stay celibate until you get remarried."

"Well, that's probably not going to happen."

"Being celibate?"

"No! Yes! I mean getting remarried. And there ought to be a rite of celibacy for widowers. Something like, 'I've had great sex with one woman for twenty-some years and now I promise to be chaste, so help me God,' or something to that effect. I'm sure you and the boys at the archdiocese can come up with something."

"No, Jack, you just have to be true to yourself and Missy, until you meet another someone special, that is."

"Thanks for that, big brother. You've managed to lay Catholic Guilt on me for things I haven't even done yet!"

"Just doing my job."

Now, here I was with Hayley Hathaway, a most attractive and well-endowed woman in her early thirties, spending the afternoon at the Metropolitan

Museum of Art working our way through the Egyptian exhibition. On our first date, she told me that she had grown to the ripe old age of 16 in Skunk Hill Holler, a little more than a mile from the village of Skunk Hill, Tennessee, (so named, she said, because the village founders set their tent on top of a well-worn game trail, a favorite of the mountain's skunk families, and so were invaded by several families of polecats who refused to circumvent the tent). She was discovered by a documentary director who was in Skunk Hill to find people with teeth who would be willing to put a new spin on the Tennessee Valley Authority for a documentary he was hoping to sell to NPR. He had seen her and three friends lollygagging in front of the boarded-up Pamida. The store had closed several months before because the local coal mine had been played out, which sent the miners scurrying to towns out of the county and state to ply their black-lunged trade before the EPA forced all coal mines out of existence.

Hayley had beautiful white teeth because her Momma had nursed her until she was three and, in contrast to local parenting custom, had not allowed her to drink Mountain Dew out of a baby bottle or a sippy cup. Instead, she had boiled water from the stream north of the house for Hayley and then stuck in a buried cauldron to cool. The director had spoken to all four girls, told them a few jokes, and told them how pretty they all were. That prompted big smiles, but only Hayley had the requisite white teeth.

The director had given them all his business card and, with his female "assistant" as he called her, they had followed Hayley to the holler. Her parents' home was a well-kept four-room place built facing the valley, so stilts supported the front porch above either a stone basement or crawl space – the director couldn't tell. Hayley was so eager to talk to Momma about the director's offer to tell him.

"They want me to move to Memphis, Momma, and live in a big house and go to school there and everything," she had blurted out just before her mother had grabbed a shotgun. The gun was kept behind the recliner she had bought with settlement money she'd received from the mining company after her husband had been buried for two days under several tons of coal.

"You're one of them couples that turn young gals into hookers, now, ain't ya," she had said while racking a shell into the chamber.

"Calm down, Momma," Hayley said soothingly, as she approached the barrel of the shotgun and grabbed it.

"Momma's kinda protective since my Pa died in the mine three years ago," she explained to the strangers over her shoulder. Turning to her Momma, Hayley said, "They showed me pitchers of the house, and the school, Momma."

"Why are you doing this?" Momma asked the two foreigners, who she never did trust.

"Your daughter can have a better life," said the director, his voice quivering, even though the shotgun was now safely pointed at a picture of Jesus eating supper with 12 black-faced coal miners wearing hard hats and red, white, and blue coveralls. "I know the school in town is a good school, but in Memphis, your daughter can get a real fine education and I, we, think she has potential to become anything she wants."

"Like what? She can't have potential here in the mountains?"

"She can get her diploma and then maybe go to a trade school, learn how to be a dental hygienist or maybe a nurse, or whatever. We would just ask her to model clothing for some catalogs, to kinda pay her way, so to speak, but we'd give her a generous allowance, enough so she could send you money from time to time."

"Model?! She take off her clothes to be a model?"

"Momma, it ain't that kind of modeling," Hayley said, gasping loudly at her mother's assumption.

After three exhaustive hours of convincing, a flood of tears by both women and Hayley finally packing a grip her Pa had used when he went off and joined the Army, Momma Hathaway had served them sun tea from a gallon jar on the front porch. She had cried about not wanting to lose her only child to big-city life, but after promises that many photos and copies of the catalogs and newspaper inserts would be sent home regularly, she had walked with them down the well-worn game trail into Skunk Hill. Sitting on a bench between the former Pamida and the director's car, Momma had cried once more for several minutes. The turning point was when the director had said he would stay in town to finish scouting locations and writing an outline, while his assistant would drive Hayley to Memphis and stay there with her.

"I still don't like this one bit, mister," Momma said, watching the car carrying her daughter drive out of town. "If anything ain't right, if I don't get them pitchers and whatever, or if I EVER find out you make dirty movies with my little girl, I will bring my shotgun to Memphis. Carrying a shotgun in these parts ain't illegal, and sure as Jesus is the Risen Savior, I will find you and that woman, and there won't be enough left of you two to put in one grave, do you understand me?"

"I do," he had said, his voice quaking again. "I promise she'll be treated well."

In Memphis, some girls had made fun of her mountain accent, so she had joined the drama club and in four months sounded like a true Southern Belle.

One thing she just couldn't shake when she wasn't reciting her lines in a play, was her habit of storing up her thoughts and then blurting out full paragraphs in one breath.

Nor could Hayley believe her good fortune. Why me, she constantly asked herself as she drifted off to sleep each night after praising God and praying for Momma and her Pa. True to their word to Momma, she wore the latest casual wear fashions and athletic clothing while a photographer took her picture. Always a day later, she received several copies to send home, and usually about a month after that, she would get two copies of the newspaper insert or catalog. She kept one copy in a file box and mailed the other home to Momma.

Life had gone well, and Hayley had returned to Skunk Hill every Thanksgiving, Christmas, Easter (Momma's favorite) and during the one month each summer she had no modeling work. She had also saved enough money to pay for her dental hygienist school with some left over. Those savings allowed her to leave Tennessee behind and begin cleaning teeth in New York, where she also hoped to keep modeling.

One patient, a medical doctor, had become so enamored that he begged her to accompany him to a Yankees game. She had agreed reluctantly because she liked the excitement of being in a major-league ballpark. She had found him funny and charming, in a weird sort of way, and after more games, she agreed to more dates – most of which ended in bed. After he began to criticize her weight, which all the girls in the dental office thought was ideal, she had agreed one night to have her stomach stapled. He had assured her that her insurance would pay for it because he would write in her chart that her weight depressed her to the point of talking about suicide. It really hadn't, but she agreed to make him happy. The procedure and its after-effects made her ill so after asking another surgeon to remove her stomach staples, she had broken up with her boyfriend. She told another dental hygienist in her office she wished someone could relieve her loneliness after the breakup. That hygienist told another friend whose gay guy friend, Lester, said he knew just the guy – a fellow in his 50s whose wife had died and he was looking to start dating again.

So, we were on our fourth and, according to my plan, final date. I had hoped that a sidewalk vendor hot dog and a trip to the Met would be the perfect breakup date, but I was so wrong. She wolfed down two loaded dogs and a can of Mountain Dew (catching up on a deprived childhood, I suppose) and she loved the Met, twirling around like a ballerina in the large lobby, then racing to find the Egyptian exhibit.

"I just can't believe how large the pyramids are, can you, Jackie? I mean, they're huge! And the Egyptians grew grain and stored it over the winter so they could feed the slaves bread all year. That's why we have to struggle to lose weight, ya know. My last boyfriend tied off people's stomachs 'cause they ate too much bread and didn't have to build any pyramids. I know 'cause he tied my stomach, but the lawyer said I didn't really need it...that Selmer, my boyfriend, had this idea that I should be skinny, but how can you keep big breasts like I have and be skinny, I mean, really...", Hayley said rapid-fire in her uniquely Tennessee drawl while peering down at a miniature Egyptian village from 3,000 B.C. I backed away and quietly walked away.

"You like my big breasts, don't you...Jackie? Jack? Where are you??"

I had secreted myself behind a column to avoid being associated with her. As much as I liked Hayley and admired her spunk, it was time to end this.

"There you are, Jackie! Why are you hiding from me?"

Since we were out of sight from other visitors, I took her by both elbows, turned her so she faced me and gazed into her beautiful eyes.

"Look, Hayley, we couldn't be more wrong for each other," I said in all sincerity. I was playing this breakup thing by ear, having experienced it only twice in 30 years. "You're a wonderful person. I admire your drive and what you've done with your life." I was getting into the spirit of letting her down easy. I'll need to make notes later about the process, I thought.

"You need to find someone your own age, someone who's maybe a transplant from the South instead of a New York native."

I sure wasn't expecting her response, but given everything I had started doing on our second date, what surprised me was her response and the realization that my system, in its infancy, could, would, work.

"Well it's about damn time, Mister Bigshot advertising executive," Hayley yelled. "Y'all don't deserve me, old man. Y'all can hardly keep up when we walk to the subway, Y'all pick your teeth with your fingers, and Y'all won't have sex with me. And that hurts the most. I mean, look at my body. Look at my girls. Are you gay or something, 'cause a real man would have gotten into my Victoria's Secret panties on our second date?"

When she was fired up, she reverted to her Southern charm, I guessed.

People came out of nowhere and were staring at us, at me and snickering. A few even had the decency to cover their mouths, others just giggled. Some of the guys looked at Hayley in her tight red dress and shook their heads in disbelief and disgust at me for letting down the brotherhood of lechers.

With her final words about getting into her knickers, she pirouetted and stormed out of the exhibit toward the main entrance. A middle-aged couple slowly walked by me, and they both looked at me in pity.

"Not true," I said, looking them in the eyes. "I run ... a lot ... and ... oh, hell, never mind."

I strolled out of Egyptian history and to the present, the bright New York day. Outside the massive doors, I saw Hayley get into a taxi. For some reason, she turned toward the entrance and, seeing me looking at her, flipped me the bird. So much for Southern charm, I thought, but then realized that the plan I had devised in my head worked in practice.

I went for a long run through Central Park with Darby and thought about what had worked with Hayley and knew I had to formalize my plan. Otherwise, if I just winged it, I could get in trouble by not accounting for variables, like how widows felt differently than how divorcees felt and how differently they felt than a woman who had been dumped by a long-time lover.

Chapter 26
Jack

That evening, after another Thai takeout meal, I sat down with two fingers of Bushmills to refine the plan for helping women get over a breakup, divorce, or death of a spouse. Although I'd successfully survived two rebound skirmishes, I still hadn't thought the process through in detail:

Step One – Find woman somehow;

Step Two – Find out what iterates her about men;

Step Three – Act like a complete putz based on her pet peeves about men, which will cause –

Step Four – She dumps me and once again feels in control of her life.

I refined it, based on my experience with Hayley:

Step One – Find women through my circle of friends and staff;

Step Two – On first date, have her tell me her story. Guide her to tell why she dumped or got dumped or divorced. Be very gentle and circumspect with widows (Wow! Saint Me!), who may have dumped a guy before they got married, so I can use those offensive traits as my behavior guide in prompting them to end our relationship.

Step Three – On second date, subtly incorporate one such guy traits into my behavior; dates three and four, add in more idiosyncrasies, exaggerating them almost to the point of being comical – almost, and absolutely no sex, not even canoodling, because sex changes everything, unless it's a one-night stand, and I'll not be having any of those. The guilt would kill me.

Step Four – She gives me the heave-ho.

But what if she doesn't dump me? What do I do? Gotta have a contingency plan.

I took a sip of the Bushmills and asked Darby, "What do I do, Darbs, if the woman won't dump me?" He didn't even raise his head. Just looked at me with doleful eyes. Did he roll them? I took another sip. I was starting to give my dog human characteristics. What's that called? Oh, yeah, anthropomorphism ... I think. Not important.

If she won't break up with me by the fourth date, then on date five I'll set in motion my plan to gently break up with her. How? "That," I said to an absent Darby, who had by this time of night considered me to be loony and gone upstairs to hog the bed, "will depend on what I learn about her on dates one through three or four." Satisfied with the detailed plan, and having accounted for a major contingency, I took the last swallow of Bushmills, checked the locks on all the doors and windows, turned off lights, and headed upstairs to the bathroom.

The next day I was in my office reviewing some storyboards for one of our national clients, and Lester stuck his head in. He was dressed like a fashion model for Target or Old Navy, but I knew his clothes were ...

"Hey, Boss, how's the dental hygienist I lined you up with?"

"She broke up with me in a rather dramatic fashion on our fourth date, just as planned. The woman walked and talked like she'd was on speed, so I was relieved not to have to listen to her anymore."

"But isn't she the one with big, how do you straights say it, ta-tas, knockers, boobs? Aren't they what every straight guy craves?"

"I prefer breasts. It's more dignified. And, no, other body parts are more interesting. Besides, you're gay, Les. Why would you care?"

"Empathy. Besides, who do you think designs the clothes to fit over them? It ain't straight guys, Jack!"

"Go figure," I said. "And, yes, pun intended. Now let's talk about these storyboards."

Chapter 27
Jack

Another weekend and I ain't got nobody, to paraphrase a Sam Cooke song. But I'm far from lonely. The pizza just came out of the oven and I slid it onto the kitchen island right when the doorbell rang. Darby gave out a quick bark and lumbered to the front door, tail wagging in anticipation. When I opened the door, there stood a beautiful African-American couple and two adolescent kids, who were clutching sleeping bags and pillows. I looked from the astonishingly drop-dead gorgeous woman up to the hulk of a man smiling down at me.

"Can I help you folks?" I said to the woman. "The homeless shelter is four blocks away."

"Can I have the same room?" asked the young girl as she rushed past me, dropped her sleeping bag and pillow, and threw her arms around Darby's neck, which she could barely reach.

"Room? What room?"

The boy pushed past me, headed for the kitchen.

"Pizza. Cool."

"Whoa, kiddo. What makes you think that double pepperoni with extra cheese is for you?"

"Balloons, too? Can we live with Jack forever, Mom?" the girl looked up from Darby to the woman.

"Who are you people anyway?" I asked.

"You don't have to spoil them every time they stay with you, Jack," she said and then leaned in and kissed me on the cheek.

"Careful, Mrs. Tucker. Let's not make your tight end jealous."

"You wish," joked Tuck Tucker, the starting tight end for the Jets. "I keep telling you, she doesn't want an old white man."

"That's not what she says when you're at training camp," I said, trying to look serious.

Loretta Jean Tucker just rolled her eyes and shook her head like she always does at my witty banter with her husband. "We'll be back Sunday evening. No roughhousing and please, no horror movies. I'm still dealing with the nightmares from the Black Lagoon."

"I solemnly promise," I said, right hand over my heart, left hand in plain view with my fingers crossed. "Now leave us alone so I can turn your little rappers into Irish Riverdancers."

"Thanks a lot, Jack," Loretta said with her usual sarcasm. "One more thing...a few months ago my sister broke up with her fiancé. She needs to go out and have some fun...Would you do me a favor and take her out a few times... nothing serious, though."

"As long as I don't have to kiss her."

"Don't even try," Loretta said, far too seriously. "She's a little...um... prejudiced."

"Oh, that's just wonderful! Should I wear my Klan hood?"

"It's not what you think...I'll set it up."

"See ya Sunday, bro."

Loretta and Tuck walk down the front steps toward their BMW.

"Catch a pass this week so you don't embarrass your children again, Tucker," I yelled at him. "We'll be watching!" He didn't even turn around, and I got the one-finger wave from them both. He opened the door for Loretta and she smiled up at me and blew me a kiss. Tuck Tucker shook his head in mock disgust and slid his bulk into the driver's seat, which was my cue to wave and close the door. I walked down the hall and into the kitchen, where my charges had already begun devouring pizza and sodas.

"What'll it be tonight, you hoodlums...Alien Three or Shrek Three?"

After we ate, they helped me clean up the kitchen, I loaded the Blu-Ray player and we settled onto the couch to watch their choice – Alien 3. Of course. Darby crawled up and flopped down between the kids after turning a few circles, much to their delight. My attention didn't make it beyond the opening scenes before I reflected on my friends, Loretta and Tuck.

Loretta Jean Tucker is a neurologist who initially had been close friends with Missy. I first met her and Tuck one Friday when Missy invited them to join us on one of our regular "date nights." As a lifelong Jets fan, I asked Tuck how they had met.

"It was the usual story," Tuck started telling us. "She saw me across the room and was immediately smitten by my ebony handsomeness and athletic physique. Then she made her way through the crowd just so she could stand close to me."

Loretta, who had heard this fiction many times, put her hand on my forearm and asked in mocked sincerity if I thought my brother, Fr. Terrence, would think it a sin to murder her husband for such a line of bullshit.

"I believe he and God would forgive you," I said. We all laughed, Loretta then told the real story.

"We were both at a grand opening party for Casa Mono, one of Mario Batali's restaurants. I was with a doctor friend of mine, casual date. Tucker was with some South American model, who looked like every man's image of the 'Girl from Ipanema.'

"It was my turn to get drinks, so I went to the bar. Pretty soon this hulk cast a huge shadow after forcing his way next to me. Trying to be polite, I looked up at him and asked him if being big entitled him to be pushy.

"Don't you know who I am," he said to me.

"Well, no, I don't, but if I did, I'm sure I would be in awe."

"You're being sarcastic, aren't you?"

"At that, I picked up the wine glasses and walked back to my date. Next thing I knew, my date looked up over my shoulder and there was the hulk, looking down at both of us. He handed me a business card with his Jets helmet and phone number."

"Please call me so I can explain what I do for a living," he said pleadingly, and turned and walked back through the crowd. After he left, my date said, "Don't you know who that is?"

"No, should I?"

"He's only the best rookie tight end in pro football. Hell, even I know that!"

"I didn't call him, but that Friday he called my office. Apparently, the Jets orthopedic doctor knew my date, who gave him my office number. He begged me to be his guest at the next home game. It was so pathetic, but I thought it would be fun, so I went wearing the Jets jersey with his number on it he had sent to my office and sat with the other players' wives, kids, and girlfriends. I denied being involved with a rookie. Most of the girlfriends accepted that because Tuck's usual "Girl From Ipanema" hadn't been to a game in weeks.

"After the game, we attended a fairly tame party. Tame because the players were all nursing injuries and sore muscles and bruised egos because they lost. Tucker was self-deprecating, sweet, and witty, and attentive. He seemed genuinely interested in my medical practice and never left my side. Although he told me he planned to pursue his MBA during the offseason, I already knew he was smart. I had looked him up on the team Web site and learned that he had graduated with honors from Rice. It was apparent from our conversation that he knew a lot about the business side of major league sports. I agreed to see him again the Monday after the team's away game. Father, he was the smitten one. Like a little puppy. It took me a full six months to fall in love with the guy."

"Any rebuttal?" I asked Tucker.

"She's always truthful," he smiled, "except she fell madly in love when I sent her the jersey. That always gets 'em." He felt her stinging pinch over his left kidney, but because of where we were, he didn't make a sound.

While she didn't do the original diagnosis, Dr. Loretta Tucker sat in on three consults to lend her support to Missy and me. We had socialized with her and her jock husband, and during an offseason cruise on a tall ship through the Caribbean with them, something just clicked, and we became tight. Missy was with her when their first, Joshua, had come into the world screaming. Loretta had lined up home healthcare for us when Missy became bedridden and explained the progression of the disease to us and again to me after Missy lost consciousness. They were the first people, after my family, I called the day Missy died, and they came within the hour and stayed with me until the funeral home took Missy away. Solid.

Their long-term friendship prompted me to agree to seeing Letitia Washington.

Chapter 28
Jack

Despite her misgivings, Letitia Washington, Loretta's baby sister, agreed to meet me for a beer at Old Blarney Pub in Brooklyn. One beer, she had cautioned. We met, and kind of hit it off because she had heard from Loretta how much fun her two kids had at my place. She said she was a little jealous that her niece and nephew would enjoy their cross-cultural experience, which she explained meant spending a weekend with an Irish-American widower instead of their Gran and Gramps. I laughed when I told her they only came to my house when Granny and Grandpa Washington were with Loretta at an away game, something that only happened twice during the regular football season.

"They think you're funny, and they love your dog and how much you spoil them," she finally admitted, "I guess it's okay for them to interact with a white guy who's at their maturity level."

I let that one go, acknowledging that having her niece and nephew around brought out the kid in me, so she was right. Apparently, the only time a drug rep is polite is when she's trying to convince a doctor's receptionist to let her give the doctor a brochure about her company's newest miracle drug.

We talked through three beers and some pub food, which I don't remember. The next thing I knew, we were outside the pub looking for a taxi for her. When one pulled over, Letitia opened the door, told the driver to wait a minute, turned back to me, said, 'Oh, what the hell,' and, putting her arms around my neck, kissed me full and warmly on the lips. 'Call me next week and I'll let you spend money on me,' she had said from inside the taxi before closing the door.

Over dinner the following Friday, Letitia walked me through the twists and turns of her broken romance. Her fiancé, she claimed, wanted her to stay at home and have four babies instead of putting her advanced chemistry degree to good use as a drug company rep. The last straw – she told him in no uncertain terms that she was going to have a career of her own. He had quietly walked out of her apartment, but had slammed the door. She had sensed something was seriously wrong two days later when he failed to reply to her texts and phone calls.

"Sounds to me like he was ghosting you," I told her, using my best 'I feel your pain' tone. His tactic of cutting off all communications with her had, contrary to what the ghoster thinks, hurt her deeply, especially when they were about to set their wedding date. And what's more, they had been running buddies, having met on a water stop during a half marathon. One of their favorite activities on Saturdays was to run together, somewhere. They had never run through Central Park, so I suggested that we make that a standing Saturday date, then lunch at Shake Shack (yeah, I know, defeats the purpose and all that), then a movie later that day.

On our first run together, I let her run ahead of me because she was in top physical shape and, besides, after her painful breakup, I wanted her to feel in control. After that run, she made me promise that I would eat healthier and run more so I could keep up with her.

"It's bad enough for me to be seen running with a middle-aged guy," she said, "but worse when he's huffing and puffing trying to keep up with me."

Knowing how much pain she was in and knowing that sarcasm was her go-to way of expressing herself when she recalled the hurt she had felt when her fiancé had finally had the guts to break up with her, I let it go. What she didn't know was that I had just set her up to dump me.

Two Saturdays later, Letitia and I were running through Central Park. She wore a very expensive running outfit she had bought during a retail therapy trip to an upscale shop in SoHo. I was wearing my oldest sweatpants and a raggedy t-shirt. I appeared to be drenched in sweat, but it was actually water from a bottle of water I had secreted in a bush along the way that I poured on the front neck of my shirt after she ran around a curve way ahead of me. When I caught up to her, she was running in place in front of two park benches. I limped toward her and bent over at the waist breathing a little too heavily for effect; but hey, this is acting.

"C'mon, Jack," she said, breathing as if she had just walked 10 feet. "Run another three with me. It'll be good for your disposition," she said, mockingly, looking around to make sure no one she knew was coming.

"Throwing you in the East River would be better for my disposition," I said to the ground.

"I just don't think I can be with someone who doesn't take good care of his health, Jack," she said while bending over and grabbing the toes of her fluorescent green and pink running shoes. I turned my head in her direction just in time to admire her round, muscular glutes. Amazing, but not mine to …

She continued, sounding exasperated and disgusted. "We've talked about this...you promised you'd work out more so you could keep up."

Now I slowed the wheezing and heavy breathing as I stood up straight, hands on my hips, looking down at her chin, "I've let you down, I know."

"I am very, very disappointed, Jack. My sister thought you'd be good for me, show me a different way of thinking, help me get over my ex, and I love her for that. The more time we spent together made me think I could actually be with a middle-aged white guy and forget about finding the Perfect Black Man, but I just can't," she said, wiping away a tear of what I supposed was disappointment.

We walked to a sidewalk ice-cream vendor. She ordered a bottled water, I got two scoops of Rocky Road in a waffle cone.

"I know tonight will be our third date night, Jack, and I know guys expect to score on the third date, but I'm just not gonna get that deeply involved with a man of your ..."

"Color?"

"I was going to say 'age'."

"How old is your cut-off?"

"Do men still like sex after, like, 45?"

I just about choked on my ice cream. "I think a few rare old birds still have the desire."

"I could never go to bed with any man over 35."

"You're 39!"

"So I like younger men! I think that makes me a cougar. A black cougar. How old ARE you, Jack?"

"Thirty-four...20-something years ago."

"You're sweet, sugar. But old sugar just isn't my thing."

We walked in silence, but I figured it was time to let her end this, so I nonchalantly asked, "How about dinner and a club Saturday?"

At that, she stopped, faced me, and kissed me on the cheek. Then she turned and walked away.

"I'll call you for lunch sometime," she said over her shoulder. "Tell my sister I like 'em younger."

I tried to look dejected, just in case, she turned around to see if I looked dejected. She didn't, so I smiled.

"I'm running home. No need to run with me. Goodbye, Jack." She turned and sprinted away, giving me a last look at her gorgeous derriere, her ponytail flopping merrily side to side against her muscular shoulder blades.

"Bye, Letitia. I'll miss you. Good luck," I yelled as she ran out of hearing range. I watched her until she rounded a bend in the trail near the basketball courts where my friends and I usually played. As soon as she was completely out of sight, I started to run the opposite direction but stopped when Mrs. Steinmetz, who was sitting on her usual bench feeding bread to the pigeons, voiced her opinion of the scene she had just witnessed.

"Faker," she smirked.

"Morning, Mrs. Steinmetz," I looked at her wrinkled but still beautiful face and gnarled fingers from years spent in her late husband's tailor shop. They had been married 62 years she had told me several months earlier.

She was dressed in her usual black dress and had covered her grey hair with a black lace scarf that flowed down to her waist. Peeking out from under the dress was a pair of highly polished black lace-up shoes that reminded me of the kind nuns used to wear before they switched to any shoe that went well with their secularized habits.

I sat next to her and asked her my usual question, "What kind of bread are you poisoning the birds with today?"

"Jewish rye," she replied. "Just like every other day." She tilted the bag of bread slices my direction, I reached in and took a small pinch.

"You are such a bad actor," she said, not looking at me.

I threw the bread at a bunch of pigeons that had gathered at my side of the bench.

"You think so? I thought I was very convincing." I leaned over and kissed her on the cheek like always. She smiled, like always.

"Putz," she called me her favorite Yiddish term of endearment. I kissed her on the other cheek, turned, and sprinted off in the direction opposite the way Letitia had gone. Didn't want to take the chance that she might have figured out the ruse and was watching me. Was I getting paranoid? Nah!

"Tough luck, buddy," said a gravelly voice from behind a large elm.

I walked over to his tree and noticed a homeless Vietnam vet, according to his cap and vest full of ribbons, who had concealed as best he could, his shopping cart loaded with soda cans and other garbage, which I supposed he wanted to turn into cash.

"Not really," I said, admiring his industriousness.

"Gotta fin for a meal?"

"Nope, but you can finish this," I said, handing him my cone, which he accepted with a gray hand. I turned to walk away and had second thoughts, so I reached into my sweatpants pocket, peeled off a couple tens and handed them to him. "Enjoy a good meal."

I walked away wondering what had been the guy's turning point.

Chapter 29
Jack

This recruiting thing may be getting out of hand. Too many recruiters, too many recruits, and too much buzz about what I was doing. Maybe that's okay. I may need to end my rebound dating soon. I'm getting mentally and emotionally exhausted from playing with people's lives, although my cause is noble.

I was staring out the window at the Manhattan skyline when Lester stuck in his head, new haircut and all. He had paid good money to have the right side of his head shaved and the stylist had done a comb-over with what remained on his left side, which didn't move when he stuck his head into my office.

"What's with the new doo?" I asked, politely, not wanting to offend. "Lose a bet?"

He ignored the mild insult. "We found you another soul to rescue, Jack," he said with a definite lilt in his voice. "A lawyer." He was grinning with pride at his accomplishment.

"Sounds like a personal injury lawsuit just waiting for an injuring party... me," I said, looking back at the skyline. "But go ahead and tell me the story."

"Denise in the coffee kiosk says this lawyer just broke off her engagement to a stockbroker. They were high school classmates. How clichéd!"

"Not interested. Where's that campaign for Eastwood Publishing?"

"In the pipeline," he said much too quickly. "This woman needs you, Jack. Rather, the next guy she falls for needs you. Save his sorry straight ass. For the love of God!"

One last time, I thought. Maybe.

"Okay, get me her name "Where she hangs out. Anything I can use."

"She likes to go to the Met every Saturday. Loves the Egyptian wing. Always browses the store. Here's her photo from the New York Bar directory. She'll be expecting you."

"What?!"

"She's a lawyer, so we couldn't very well have her think you're just some random guy hitting on her in a museum. Denise described you to her and told her to expect you. Be gentle, Jack."

"Always."

I had worked late on Friday, much to the chagrin of Darby's bladder, which he barely managed to hold until we walked out the front door and he peed on the stoop. At least he waited. We walked our usual six blocks, getting waves from neighbors and stares from almost everyone else. We got home just before the rain started, but I let Darby out in the garden area anyway while I filled his food dish and refilled his water dish, which are nearly the size of a kiddie pool. He was only slightly wet when he came in, but smelled like a skunk that had been dipped in its own spray. I grabbed a kitchen towel and rubbed him down while he scarfed his food. Then it was my turn. Veggie omelet and iced tea. Simple, quick, and relatively healthy. Most importantly, easy to clean up, especially when using a paper plate.

After supper, I Googled ancient Egyptian society, royalty, and technology. Engrossing. Next thing I knew, it was midnight and Darby stood at the back door looking between it and me. I got the hint and let him out into the garden. He was well trained, so he lifted his leg on the back fence, thus watering the alley. Good dog.

Chapter 30

Jack

I don't quite understand why some women like the Egyptian exhibit so much. Maybe they imagine themselves as Nefertiti or Cleopatra. Or just maybe, like me, they appreciate the ancients for how they lived and their technology. I had discovered last evening that their advances could have put Europeans to shame, had the Egyptians not pissed off God and Rome.

So here I am, trying not to appear to be a stalker as I stroll a few paces behind a very tall dark-haired woman wearing a Yankees cap and a Harvard Law t-shirt over yoga pants and Nikes. Her black hair shone like wet pavement … no, no, bad simile. Like a lake at midnight in a full moon. Much better.

As she stopped to read the descriptions of a miniature farm display, I stopped just behind her left shoulder.

"Spoiled kid," I said.

"What?"

"Must have been a spoiled rich kid to have all these doll barns. What's that? A goat, or the kid's dog?"

"These were put in the tomb of the unknown rich guy to take care of him in the afterlife," she explained casually, without even a hint of condescension.

"Very interesting, but dumb," said the smooth talker within me.

"Laugh-In. Arte Johnson. And it's a terrible pickup line."

"You're older than you look," more smooth talking, which made her walk away. I couldn't tell from the back of her head if she was offended, but chances were pretty good she was.

"Thanks for the compliment," she said over her shoulder, which, even though it was mostly hidden by her gray t-shirt, was toned. "I have cable. And you must be Jack."

I followed her into the Met Gift Shop, where she stopped to look at the Egyptian jewelry.

"You put Cleopatra to shame," I said kiddingly, now knowing that she knew who I was.

"That's the world's absolutely worst pickup line," she laughed without looking up from the display case.

"So how about coffee, Cleo?"

This time she looked me in the eyes. She had light olive skin and a slightly hooked nose. He lips weren't full, but neither were they thin, and her chin was dimpled, which might have distracted me from her elegant neck had it not been so long and graceful.

"Only if it isn't Starbuck's. My name is Mallory, but you knew that."

We walked at a good pace to a bodega a few blocks away. I tried to order coffee for her, but she said to me and the middle-aged Pakistani guy behind the counter, "I can order my own coffee, thanks."

We sat at the counter across from the till that looked out at the sidewalk. We sat in silence for a few minutes, blowing and sipping boiling hot coffee. Then she blurted out, "I happen to like corporate law! I got my undergraduate in accounting. That's where I reconnected with Benjamin. He was such a geek in high school." I hadn't asked, but I knew her background, thanks to Denise.

"Geeks are cool," I said, using my biggest vocabulary words.

"He turned out to be. We stayed in touch when I went to law school and he went off to get his M-B-A and intern at a brokerage firm."

"Then?"

"Then, getting engaged just made sense. It was logical. Our families loved each other. We made sense."

"So what happened?"

We got off our stools and headed toward the door. I reached for the bar and pushed it open before she had a chance to open it for herself. She smiled at me and we headed back toward the Met.

She talked as we walked. "He lost some...no, he lost a lot of money. For himself and my dad. And some of my dad's golfing buddies. He was ashamed. I was embarrassed."

"Sorry."

"It never would have worked after that. Imagine Thanksgiving dinner!"

I laughed and took her left elbow. I was walking street side, like a gentleman.

"I'd really like to see you again," I said in all honesty. "I have tickets to the annual Subway Series next week. How about we go and eat expensive hot dogs and drink expensive beer. My treat."

"Only one game," she cautioned. "But only if you don't cheer for the Mets."

"Deal. Go Yanks!"

We arranged which subway station we would meet at and what time. We shook hands and walked off in different directions. I was going to need a NY Yankees shirt and cap. Oh, and tickets to the game!

Two days later, I called Lester into my office.

"Close the door, please, Les." He stood in front of my desk and I looked at him over my laptop screen. His combed-over hair had blue ends today, and he wore a skin-tight silk shirt and tight, shiny jeans that together must have cost more than the GNP of Bangladesh.

"Did you get me those damn tickets yet?"

"Calm down, Bambino. I called my friend at Vogue who called his friend at Sports Illustrated who called the Yankees P-R guy. Here are your tickets to the second game. At Yankee Stadium.

"You're my hero."

"You love me. You really love me."

"You know it, partner."

Chapter 31

Jack

I took Darby for an early walk so I could be on time at the subway station where I was to meet Mallory. Darby was always laid-back, but he also was eager to walk when I took his leash down from the peg by the front door. Smaller dogs would jump up and pant, Darby just licked his nose and pushed his massive head against my leg. We walked out of the front door just as my neighbor, Angela, came out of her brownstone next to mine.

Angela had married well three times, she had told me one evening after one too many gin and tonics in our adjoining garden areas, getting lucrative divorce settlements from her first two husbands, neither of whom could avoid screwing their secretaries, and hadn't managed to keep the affairs a secret. Angela's third husband, a retired floor trader who had little time or energy to cheat on her, had lived so long in a high-stress industry that he died within two months of an early retirement. He also had a boatload of life insurance, having heeded the insistent advice of his financial advisor, who warned him early and often in his life to buy more than enough term insurance to protect his assets and his family should he succeed and marry. He did, marrying Angela, his first and only wife, the day after he turned 50.

Angela had really loved the guy. He treated her well, and his death devastated her. Being the resilient sort, she grieved deeply for six months. During that period she vowed to anyone who would listen that she was never going to get involved with another man. The week after the funeral, her financial advisor urged her to put enough of her inheritance into a fund that would make her monthly mortgage payment and earn enough so she could pay the taxes on her other investments each April.

Consequently, Angela carried herself like the carefree woman she was because she never had to worry about running out of money or paying taxes. She spent her time volunteering at her church's homeless shelter and doing hot yoga. The former gave her a calming sense of purpose, the latter molded her tight, sculpted body and firm ... uh ... derriere that I couldn't help but noticing.

I admonished myself whenever I took notice, but how the hell could I ignore it when her regular ensemble featured tight yoga pants?

I looked over at her as we both locked our doors.

"'Morning, Angela."

"Jacko! Haven't seen you in a long time."

"I waved at you yesterday morning when you were running to your yoga class."

"That was you!? I just thought someone was hailing a cab."

This morning she was really into thinking every guy is a eunuch mentality because, in addition to tight yoga pants, she was wearing a running bra that left little to the imagination. I had difficulty keeping my eyes on her face. I admired her oval face and slightly curved nose, which sat over full lips. However, when she smiled, only her eyelids raised, not her eyebrows or her forehead, which was smooth as a baby's butt. Good for her for fighting the good fight, I thought.

"Nope, that was me waving at you," I said matter-of-factly, displaying my best I-promise-I'm-not-looking-below-your-chin expression.

We walked down our respective steps and met at the mountain ash surrounded by a two-foot green wrought-iron fence between our two houses. Darby pushed me aside and lifted his leg at the tree. Angela smiled and stepped aside to avoid the stream.

"Have you given any more thought to my invitation to worship on Wednesdays?"

I hated myself because she was talking religion, Darby was still peeing while I was focused hard on looking Angela in the eyes. I coughed slightly in the front of my throat to maintain eye contact. I also dug up the memory of her coming over four times to sit with Missy when I had to go to work early before the hospice nurse was scheduled to arrive or coming over after the nurse left because, like an idiot, I was working late. That calmed the beast.

"I'm Catholic, Angela, remember? We play bingo Wednesday nights to give us a reason to avoid services at Lutheran churches."

"You really are funny, you know," she said, matter-of-factly. "Our organist would just love you, Jack."

"I'm sure she would. I'm a big hit with church ladies."

Having finished his morning urination, Darby was insistently pushing his head against my leg. When I saw him head nose first into Angela's crotch, I jerked his leash just in time. She had reached down to pet Darby and didn't seem to notice his rude behavior. She scratched him behind one ear and looked solemnly at me.

"How are you doing, Jack? Really?"

"Fine...today. I haven't curled up in the fetal position in weeks now."

She reached up and gently patted my cheek and gave me a sympathetic look. "That's good, Sweetheart."

With that, she gave Darby one more scratch behind his ears, spun around and jogged up the street. I watched her go, admiring her until she turned the corner. Then Darby and I headed the opposite direction. At the first corner, I took his head in both hands and looked him in his big brown eyes.

"Just because you're big and she's a good friend doesn't allow you to act like a dog, Darbs," I said to myself as much as to him.

Of course, he had no idea what I was talking about, but at least I felt better for attempting to civilize one of us.

Mallory and I had a great time cheering for the Yankees, even though they lost. We even held hands as we left the stadium and on the subway back to the city. It felt right, but her hand was limp in mine. We both got off at her stop and I knew the inevitable dump was coming.

"Jack, it's been a great day, and you're more than an okay guy, but I'm just not comfortable being with a guy yet. Still reeling from the betrayal. I'm not giving up on love, just not with you."

"Mallory ...."

She pressed her hand to my lips.

"Good-bye, Jack. "You'll meet your Egyptian queen someday."

Chapter 32
Jack

I own three tuxedos. Goes with being an ad guy in New York. There's always an art gallery opening at which I would need to show my face. Missy and I had tried to attend an opera at the Metropolitan Opera House at least four times a year. It was our chance to get dressed up and hob-knob with the city's elites. Besides, we both loved the opera, loved the classics and always were game to attend any new one that sounded interesting.

We had reserved seats through the agency, and by maintaining our longstanding membership through the years, moved into the prime seating area. The Fletcher Group, whose motto is "On Target, On Time, On Budget." At least that's what we want our clients to think. We're always on target because we focus-group every campaign to death, and in our business, you've simply got to be on time. Two out of three ain't bad, considering how much we raked in buying media for our clients and retaining the commissions. "Somebody has to pay the media buyers," Langston Fletcher, founder and CEO, always joked, "and it sure as hell ain't gonna be me!"

Operatic enthusiasm was the common denominator in my next rebound romance. I had been referred to Phillipa Garcia by a talent agent who told me the details of Phillipa's messy public parting with an actor she had dated for 27 months who she had hoped would propose. He did – to his female co-star in the Mexican soap opera in which both played major characters. Heartbroken, Phillipa was very vulnerable and needed to gain confidence through a relationship that she herself would end. That was my cue.

We first met for drinks at a small upscale bistro in SoHo. She was amazing. Funny. Smart. Drop-dead gorgeous with a gutsy personality. We talked for hours. Well, she talked; I listened. She had become philosophical about the breakup, which had occurred on the sidewalk in front of the Metropolitan Opera House. During an intermission, he had confessed that he had proposed to his co-star and was leaving New York to go back to a house he and the actress had purchased together on the outskirts of Cabo San Lucas.

"You own a fucking house in Mexico!" she had screamed at him on the front steps after fuming during the third act. "A fucking house in a resort town!"

He had pleaded with her to be quiet and not so vulgar before he sheepishly turned away and slunk off to a taxi.

"You fucking coward," she had intoned basso profundo. Then she looked around to see the mostly stunned looks on faces, but women in the crowd had applauded and yelled "Bravo" and "You go, girl!" And what did Phillipa do? "I bowed and held up my hands in triumph," she said. Like I said, gutsy and gorgeous.

I liked Phillipa, a lot, but I had headed down a slippery slope greased by lying to protect the women I was rescuing, or so I tried convincing myself several mornings a week as I looked in the mirror to shave. I lied to a woman I liked and respected, which made me more guilt-ridden than I ever had been. It went like this:

"I just love La Bohème, Jack. What a romantic evening!"

I'm glad one of us enjoyed it, Phillipa, I really am."

"What's wrong? You didn't like it?"

She was wearing the most beautiful red dress I had ever seen at the opera. A gift from the asshole actor, she said. Wearing it reminded her to be on guard with men.

"Honestly?"

"Well, yes!"

"I thought it was boring and overdone."

"Then why did we go?"

"You love La Bohème. I just don't like the opera."

"You took me anyway? That's so sweet. I can't wait to tell my sister."

Uh, oh.

"Er, you think it's sweet? I thought you liked honesty. I wasn't being very honest."

"You were being sweet by sacrificing," she purred in her sexiest Latina accent. "That's just so wonderful."

At that, and to the envy of every man at the opera, Phillipa put her arm through mine and playfully leaned her head against my shoulder as we walked through the lobby toward the exit. She couldn't see the worry on my face. It was going to be more difficult than I thought to make her dislike me enough so she would break up with me. Crap!

Chapter 33
Jack

Another disturbing surprise awaited me the following Monday. My team and I were reviewing video storyboards for an upcoming international perfume campaign. In earlier discussions with the eventual photographer and client rep, we had decided that the face of the scent should be a mature model, one with enough beauty to spur men to buy the scent for the women in their lives. Simultaneously, we need to inspire mature women of means to buy the fragrance for themselves and their tennis partners. During our storyboard and magazine layout review, we came up with a list of detailed descriptors of the model and forwarded it to our modeling agency contacts.

"Great job, everyone," I smiled and sent them back to work. Lester was last to leave, but he hung back and closed my office door. He eased himself into one of the leather chairs in front of my desk, which were specifically designed for discomfort and selected by our architect to prevent people from sitting too long and wasting time with idle chatter. Lester liked sitting in them.

"How was La Boehme?"

"An absolutely stunning performance," I said truthfully. "One problem, though. Phillipa is growing too fond of me and enamored with our relationship."

"What did she do to make you think that?"

"For one thing," I began, "she acts like she's a woman in love. And when we said goodnight ... at her front door ... and I shook her hand and tried to kiss her cheek, but she pulled me in for a long, soft kiss and when we parted I was a little dazed and heard her say something that included the word 'love.'"

"She told you she's falling in love with you?"

"No, as I recreated the scene while I walked to the taxi, I know she said she could fall in love with me. There's a difference."

"You lied about the opera. You love the opera. You're like an opera groupie."

"A little white lie. I had to change tickets with Doctor Hammer. I didn't want the people around my season seats talking to me."

"It backfired?"

"If I have to, I'll tell her I set the whole thing up to avoid running into a woman I had just broken up with. And don't you have work to do?"

Lester slowly rose from the chair shaking his head. "This just keeps getting better every time you ..."

Just then, Robbie, our CEO's gopher, opened the door to my office and stuck his head in. He gave Lester a derisive glance, and then looked at me.

"He wants to see you, pronto, Jack."

To be polite, I knocked.

"Come on in, Jack."

Langston Fletcher knew it was me because apparently, I'm the only member of the management team that ever knocks. That and he had just sent his gopher to fetch me.

He sat at the conference table in his corner office that has a breathtaking view of New York. He slouched back in his chair, which had been designed for optimum comfort, as had the other chairs around the table. He had wanted clients and potential clients to be wrapped in soft leather comfort. He didn't worry about staff lingering because he knew that to end a meeting all he had to do was get up and go back to his desk to begin typing at his computer, which was the staff's cue to get the hell out.

Langston Fletcher was well-dressed every day, even on our casual Fridays, but today he wore a blue pin-striped suit that had to have cost more than the GNP of Myanmar. His light blue dress shirt and cufflinks screamed wealth, and his yellow and red tie set everything off. He looked like the king of Sweden going to a state dinner at the White House.

"Mornin', Langston," I said after I had taken in the details.

"Jaaaaack, so good of you to join us!"

"Like I had a choice," I said to myself. I smiled as I walked over to the table. I stood there waiting to be introduced.

"Jack's our crackerjack creative director. He's a writer by trade, like me," he said by way of introduction and giving me legitimacy, I supposed.

"Jack, meet Sukura Yukio and his brother Jiro," he said in his best 'I'm in charge here' voice. "They're the brains and drive behind Sukura Motors."

They stood up and I shook each of their hands as they bowed. I didn't bow in return, being the Ugly American I am and remembering my short military career. Americans don't bow.

"Pleasure, gentlemen," I said, honestly.

Langston frowned slightly when he looked at me, but then smiled. "I was just telling them it was your team that's been handling B-M-W. They like what they see, Jack."

"We think your agency would be a perfect fit for our introduction into the U. S. market, Mister Sullivan," said Sukura Yukio. "We'd like to tour your creative department, meet your team and see what other kind of work you can do for us."

"I'd love to. When?"

"Now, of course, Jack," Langston said as he slipped on his suit coat.

"But we're up to our eyeballs with the ..."

"Nonsense, Jack. Our creatives need a break."

"Can I ask ..."

"Gentlemen," Langston said to the two Japanese car makers, "Would you step out here so Louisa can show you the rest of my suite."

After they bowed their way out, Langston closed the door.

"You know I don't like contradictions in front of anyone, especially not new clients," his face was red and his lips were so pursed they were turning blue after he growled at me.

"And just how are we going to handle two major car makers? Lang. It's unethical."

"A minor detail," he said, waiving off my concern, which calmed him down. "We'll just create a spin-off agency so we can handle them both, see how it goes, and if BMW squawks, we'll resign their account."

"Lang, I'll lose people," I said. "They won't ..."

"Then you'll hire better people," he said, gripping my left arm just above the elbow and squeezing. Hard. I always flexed my triceps when he did this, just to let him know I wasn't intimidated. "Now let's go design our future, Jack!"

"Wait, Langston. We've handled B-M-W for seven years. We know them. We know their cars. Hell, they even ask our designers for ideas."

He squared off and looked me in the eyes. "Frankly, Jack, your attitude is getting tedious and your team's getting stale. Speed, style, safety, image...it's all bullshit. Car buyers want sexy, Jack, and sex sells sexy. Sexy women. Sexy androgynous males. That's the future, Jack. Get on board or get out of the way."

His neck still red with retreating anger, Langston jerked open the heavy door, but before he took a step out, he quickly composed himself. I followed him, but I was taken aback by his thinly veiled threat to end my employment. Of course, he would have to buy out my contract, plus give me a healthy severance package, so financially, I could survive quite well. However, losing a job I was good at according to my team, our clients, and even Adweek would be a disappointment and a shock to my ego. In the back of my mind, I started to plan my life after advertising. But that was only a future possibility. Now I was faced with the ethical dilemma of serving two masters.

Langston shrugged and straightened his shoulders under his impeccably tailored suitcoat, assuming the air of a man in charge of every aspect of his world.

"Gomen nasai, gentlemen," he said with what I could only imagine from behind, was a broad, phony grin. "Let's meet Jack's wonderful creative teams."

The four of us strode down the hall and into the creative bay. Upon seeing Langston leading a pair of Japanese business types into the room, all graphic artists instinctively switched their computer screens to screensavers to avoid revealing their work. Of course, there was no way they could know who these two men represented, it was just common practice to maintain creative integrity. I introduced the new clients to everyone without disclosing their business. After I introduced them to the final team member, Langston sneered at me with a look that said I was a traitor to his cause.

Chapter 34
Jack

I was glad when Sunday rolled around so I could relax with family and eat a great meal I didn't cook myself. I don't mind the cooking; I'm good at it. But as I'm eating alone, I'm thinking about kitchen cleanup. At my folks' house, though, many hands make light work, to coin another phrase.

As I drove through Manhattan to get to my folks' house, I thought about my date two days earlier with Phillipa. After she swung open her door and invited me in, she insisted we have a glass of wine before going to dinner at Erminia, where I have a standing reservation for every other Friday. Phillipa was stunning. Her red dress set off her olive brown skin, and the jade necklace and matching earrings were perfect accents. Her high heels made her perfectly firm derriere to even more prominent. I cleared my throat and mumbled, "This is going to be the hardest yet."

"What did you say, Jack?"

"Nothing...Just thinking out loud," I said truthfully.

"Are you sure you want to go out to eat? We could just drink wine and get silly."

"More sure than ever, Phillipa. I want to show you off." I gulped the rest of my wine and took her glass and set it on her island counter. "Let's go, or we'll be late and they may give away our table."

We were greeted with the usual formal warmness by the maître de, who took us directly to our table by the corner floor to ceiling window. I didn't blame him for looking over Phillipa as he sat her. She was most stunning, and, of course, she didn't know this was my usual table and the greeting was standard for these dates.

We ordered more wine, had antipasto served with a slight head-nod by my favorite soulful waiter, who I gave a stern look that Phillipa couldn't see.

As we drank our coffee, I quietly put down my cup and cleared my throat. "Phillipa, I need to come clean with you," I said as I leaned across the table. I forced my eyes to stay on her face, not her cleavage. I cleared my throat again.

"I lied about the opera. I love the opera and I thought if I acted like I hated it, you would break up with me."

"Stop, Jack. I know. When I went to the bathroom during intermission, I overheard two women talking as they washed their hands. They wondered why you weren't in your season ticket seats. I put two and two together when one of them said, 'He's probably hoping another one will dump him.'"

"But why did you tell me you could fall in love with me, and why on earth would you try to seduce me?"

"Acting, Jack. I'm quite good at it, so I wanted this to be uncomfortable for you. I pretended. I made up everything after I returned to my seat during La Boehme. I played you because you play with the hearts of women, and I detest you for it."

With those words, she pushed back her chair, picked up the water glass, brought back her arm and prepared to hurl water at me. At the last moment, she thought better of it. Instead, she replaced that glass on the table, picked up her glass of wine and threw it in my face. She stormed out of the restaurant to applause and hoots from many women in the room, some of whom I recognized as regulars.

"At least she broke up with you, Mr. Sullivan," said the maître de in his usual polite voice as he handed me a terrycloth towel kept handy for just such occasions.

"One way or another, Bernard, they always do," I said, dabbing the wine off my face and shirt as I gave him my 'satisfied with myself' smile. "Seems she's now ready for a new relationship."

I shook Friday's date with Philippa from my memory just as I narrowly missed clipping a taxi waiting for a fare as I drove past my parent's house looking for a parking place. I found one on the next block. The walk gave me the chance to further clear my head to prepare for the "Sunday Dinner Conversation of Doom."

After kitchen duty, I huddled with Terry in a corner of the living room.

"You can't be serious!" Terry exclaimed, a little too loudly.

"As a heart attack. They want me to go to Vegas with them ... and they hinted about finding a whorehouse, I whispered. "Please lower your voice Fr. Terrance...I don't want to tell everyone. I especially don't want my daughters to worry."

He leaned his head close to my ear, "What's your boss say?"

"He wants the account."

"So???"

"So, nothin'. He can take 'em. I won't."

"Dad would be proud. He'd tell you a man..."

"A man stands on principals, Jack, or he sinks in liberal quicksand," I said in my best impression of our old man.

"That's Pops," Terry laughed, "forever the righteous conservative."

We both laughed.

"What's so funny, you two?" Pops asked from his recliner across the living room.

Chapter 35
Jack

My presence on the Las Vegas junket had been more self-defense than supplication to Langston's command. In a matter of minutes, I had had to arrange with a neighbor to take care of Darby, no mean feat since all but one of my neighbors thought him a vicious face-licker. Langston insisted our guests not be allowed to pack since they were in a hurry to get to Vegas, so neither he nor I packed, but I had texted my entire family to fill them in.

"Our Gulfstream is supplied with complete toiletry kits," he had announced to the three of us, "so no need for anything. Besides, we'll buy clothes in Vegas at Suitsupply when we feel the need."

I had thought of refusing to go but decided that if I wanted to convince Langston to change course I would need to play along for a while. I knew we absolutely could not work for two major automobile manufacturers, and that his plan to start a new company to handle either BMW or Sukura Motors, was dishonest, unethical, and probably illegal. In addition, I wanted to keep my job – at least until I could design a parachute out of the agency.

The flight from Teterboro Airport in New Jersey was raucous. Evidently, Langston had planned our trip days before because the bar was stocked with Murai Family Daiginjo sake, Jack Daniels, Jameson and a wide assortment of fresh sushi, brought aboard minutes before departure.

Our guests were drunk by Ohio, but I had told them I was allergic to sake and raw fish, so they felt sorry for me and let me drink Jameson. Cagey Langston pretended to drink with them, and by the time we passed Iowa, they were ignoring both of us while they managed to finish off three bottles of the Murai Family's finest and demanding that the Geisha onboard open a fourth bottle. We had to rouse them when we arrived at our private gate in Vegas and poured them into the waiting white and gold-trimmed Hummer limo.

Halfway to The Strip, one of the brothers vomited in an ice bucket barely within his reach. When he finished, he wiped his mouth on his right sleeve and both brothers laughed so hard tears ran down their cheeks. Apparently, throwing up sushi and sake was hilarious in Japan. The rancid odor rising from the bucket was making me gag, so I covered it with a bar towel from the minibar and lowered my window to allow fresh air to sweep out the acrid smell. By the time we pulled into the casino's circular drive, my nausea had subsided.

Langston got out first and he and the driver helped the brothers out. Langston ushered them away from the limo as I got out, so I was left to tip the driver. I handed him a $20, all I had in my pocket.

"Well, thank YOU, sir," his displeasure evident. I ignored him, mostly because I was in a hurry, but also because he didn't have to unload any bags and didn't work hard.

As I approached the trio, Langston put his arms around the brothers' shoulders. "Welcome to Vegas, gentlemen!" he beamed. "We're going to rock this city!" With that, he ushered them through the massive brass and glass front doors, completely ignoring me. The Japanese brothers were all smiles as they turned full circle and took in the glitter and noise of the casino's gaming floor.

I don't know exactly how much money they turned into chips, but it was so much that a casino guard, who looked like an MMA fighter with brain damage, carried their trays of black chips and followed them around like a fierce puppy.

They started at the craps table, a tough game even if you're completely sober, but deadly if you're still reeling from too much sake. After five costly losses, the brothers moved on to a high-stakes roulette table. Of course, they bet the maximum on each spin. Instead of just betting red or black, they each insisted on betting a number, which meant they were losing big time.

Langston cheered them on, patting each on the back before every bet, and hugging them with an arm around their shoulders after each loss.

I hated to see anyone lose so much money. "They're losing their shirts," I said to Langston from behind.

"They've got plenty of shirts, buddy boy," he replied over his shoulder. "Don't be such an ass, Jack. They're having a fucking ball!"

Just then Sukura Yukio turned to Langston.

"We are bored," he yelled over the clacking, ringing, hollering, and cursing. "We want to see women dance with poles. Please take us. Now, please."

"You got it, my friend," Langston shouted. Yukio grabbed his brother, who was about to lose his final chips, and Langston ushered them away from the roulette table and through the crowd that had gathered to see two Japanese guys lose a bundle. I felt like a lackey as I followed them, without even a glance from Langston, who had his ear to his phone. Since no one was paying any attention to me, I scooped up the younger brother's suit coat and reached into a pocket, where he had hastily shoved some of his remaining chips. I pulled out two $100 black chips.

As we walked through the spinning doors into the brightly illuminated night, our limo pulled up, the driver came around and opened the back doors. Just before I got in, I handed him one of the chips to make up for the poor tip earlier. It wasn't my money, and he did have to clean up a bucket of barf, so I guess he earned it.

Langston told the driver to take us to Stripper King. When we got there, I handed the driver the other $100 chip. I wanted him to feel guilty for his earlier sarcasm. It worked. He kept his eyes lowered after I handed him the chip.

At the entrance, Langston told the doorman that we did, in fact, have reservations, which he confirmed and let us in. A raven-haired hostess dressed in a red dress that appeared to have been spray painted on took us to an open table at the stage. Just as we all got seated, a beautiful blonde waitress wearing stilettos, black net stockings and a black-and-red rubber corset with matching G-string, approached, like she had been waiting for us.

The Sukura brothers wasted no time stuffing money in the girls' G-strings. The girls were seasoned pros who allowed just the right amount of groping before gyrating their hips for tips. The boys obliged with all the lust and lasciviousness of a bunch of Soviet submariners on shore leave after six months under water.

Langston and I sat across the table from our guests. Langston nursed a whiskey and soda, and I was on my second Guinness. Now I was getting bored with this spectacle. Keeping his eyes on the stage, Langston leaned next to my ear.

"They're having fun, Jack," he said in a loud voice. "You should try it sometime."

"My daughters aren't much younger than these girls," I replied, just as loudly.

"These girls make more money in a year than your daughters ever will," he looked at me and laughed. "And besides, they don't have student loans."

I couldn't hide my disgust. Langston quickly looked at the girls. The Sukura brothers turned back to the table and motioned to us that they were tired. Langston waved to our waitress, who quickly brought our check, which Langston scribbled on, and the four of us got up and wove our way through the cheap seats to the front door.

Sukura Yukio looked up at Langston. "My brother and I want to go to world-famous bunny ranch," he begged.

"You mean a whorehouse?" Langston said, laughing.

"Yes, where we can do it like rabbits!"

"We'll see if we can make that happen, gentlemen."

Langston turned to me. "Make it happen, Jackie Boy."

I looked away and sighed, then I shook my head from side to side and took a deep breath before I spoke.

"I may be a word whore, Lang, but that's as far as my whoring goes. If you want to take them, go ahead. I'm going back to New York. I have real work to do," I said to his face. Then I turned and walked toward the curb to hail a cab.

"We're not through with this, Jackie Boy."

Enough is enough. I turned around, and hands clenched at my sides, walked over and stood facing Langston. The Sukura brothers stood anxiously by.

"I am not 'Jackie Boy', Langston," I said, low and slow. "As far as I'm concerned, we are through with this." For good measure, I stared into Langston's eyes. He blinked. Feeling a little victorious, I turned and walked back to the curb. I could feel Langston's eyes burning into the back of my head, so before I got into the cab, I saw Sukura Yukio approach Langston from behind. Since I was only two steps away, I heard their conversation.

"He very negative. We like positive people."

"Fuck him! Now, let's get you gentlemen some real action."

I got into the waiting taxi and stared out the window in thought, seeing only streaks of light.

At the airport, I booked a first-class seat on the next direct flight to LaGuardia. Luckily it was only a two-hour wait, just enough time to get through TSA's horrendous security and have a drink.

I quickly found my seat. When the flight attended asked, I ordered a beer. When she brought it, I leaned my head back and sighed, realizing that my job may be in jeopardy.

The two Japanese businessmen and Langston, all disheveled, walked down the sidewalk away from the front gate to the bunny ranch. Four ladies stood provocatively in the doorway to the building.

"Y'all come again real soon," they said in unison as they waved goodbye.

Sukura Yukio waved back. "I already come many times, Y'all."

Everyone laughed at his joke, then the three got into a waiting black stretch limo and it drove off, headed to the Las Vegas airport and the private jet.

Chapter 36

The first weekly meeting post-Las Vegas junket had been tense. Langston cut off any department head who tried to explain a lack of progress on a client's campaign, and he called on Jack Sullivan last but interrupted him in mid-sentence to thank and dismiss the others and told Jack to stay.

"We need to discuss how we'll handle our new client, Jack," he said, not without sarcasm.

Jack didn't say anything. He just got out of his chair, walked to the credenza that displayed an assortment of muffins, rolls, fruit, and cheeses, and poured himself a cup of strong gourmet coffee. Then he sat on a leather couch and waited. Langston had swiveled his chair so he could look out at the skyline.

Without turning away, he said to the windows, "We need this account!"

"No, you want this account," Jack said. "There's a big difference. Plus, the accountant just told you that we're on track for a banner year, so you and your partners will be happy."

Langston slapped his right hand on the table. "If I say I want it, we need it. You've never understood that."

Jack took a sip of the strong black coffee, got off the couch, put the cup back on the credenza. He slowly turned to Langston, who was still looking out the window.

"I have work to do that doesn't involve pole dancing and bunny ranches," he said, maybe a little too loudly and a little too sarcastically.

"We're all whores, Jack. We sell our talent to the highest bidder every day and these Japs are today's highest bidder."

Jack opened the door and left without saying anything more. Langston swiveled to face the door. He smirked and picked up the phone that was on the table by his elbow.

He punched in four numbers, paused, and then said into the mouthpiece, "Get that human resources lawyer up here. Now!"

Chapter 37
Jack

Our first three dates had been the usual progression—coffee and muffins at a bodega getting each other's life story; an afternoon showing of some chick flick, the title of which I thankfully can't recall, followed by burgers and malts at Shake Shack; then drinks in a loud Irish pub, after which we held hands in the taxi ride to her apartment and a glass of wine before I excused myself and said goodnight before any canoodling could start.

So Linda and I are now at a nightclub that features blues and rock. It's date four, the final one during which I hoped she would end our brief relationship. To ensure that she wouldn't want any more to do with me, I had not shaved for three days, which raised eyebrows at the agency, but I just mumbled to anyone who gave me a look that I was thinking of growing a beard; and what do you think of that, I'd ask. Also, I dressed like I had worn my clothes to bed, wrinkled, unstarched paisley shirt, jeans with a hole in the right knee, and scuffed loafers, all of which made me look like an overdressed Millennial IT guy.

So instead of paying attention to Linda, I focused on the blues singer, a thin Cajun woman who was belting out a throaty Zydeco version of Proud Mary. Linda looked painfully bored when I stole a glance at her, but she was determined to have a conversation despite the loud music, so she leaned close to talk into my ear.

"I'm really more into classical, Jack," she yelled, but I nodded my head in time with the music. Ignoring her was painful, but necessary.

"Great jazz group, isn't it, Lindie?" I said while still looking at the stage.

"I really do prefer 'Linda'. And classical."

"What?"

"Oh, never mind. Just never mind."

After the band played two more loud sets, through which Linda and I sat in silence nursing drinks. I could sense her steamy anger. A good sign. I grabbed her hand to get out of the booth and she quickly pulled out of my grip. I offered her my hand again, which she refused and pushed herself out of the booth stomping off through the crowd and out the door.

The mood in the taxi ride was as frigid as a mother-in-law's first kiss. Neither of us spoke during the 35-minute ride, but I occasionally hummed Proud Mary as I looked out the window.

After I paid the driver, I had to hustle to catch up to Linda just as Charles, the doorman, opened the familiar outer door to Linda's swanky building.

"Thanks, Charles," I said, quickly going to Linda's side as she unlocked the inner door.

"You're welcome, sir," I heard him say.

Linda turned to me after pushing open the door. "Let's say 'goodbye' here, Jack," she said, lips pursed in anger. He beautiful neck was as red as her lipstick.

"Don't you mean 'good night'?" I said in my best hurt puppy voice.

"You're a great guy, I think. But you never listen and we just don't have much in common."

"But we have so much in common. I thought..."

At that, she walked through the doorway, and without turning toward me, she said, "Oh, goodbye!"

I watched her with my head down in a hangdog expression of loss until she got on the elevator. Then I went out and stood next to the doorman.

"Well, whadja think, Chuck?"

"Four dates was pushing your luck, Jack."

"Her best friend told me she was hurting. The more they're hurting, the longer it takes to gain their trust so I can figure out how to convince them to break up with me."

"You'll be sainted shortly after death, sir."

"Now she's ready for a serious relationship. She knows what she wants and she won't settle. I was that guy."

"The rebound guy. Of course."

"Right. The one she dumps 'cause she doesn't want to settle for a guy who doesn't like Mozart and brunch at the Met."

"You should know that the brothers at the union hall were talking about you and your scheme. Someday some of these women are going to compare notes about the last guy they dated. And your world is going to spin out of control."

"This is New York. Remember, the big city."

"Your little charade can't last forever."

I handed him my usual $20 tip. "Nothing lasts forever, Charles."

"Thanks for that tip."

I walked to the taxi waiting at the curb. After Chuck opened the door, I turned to him, "Keep your eyes open for a decent guy for her," I said sincerely.

"I'll make it my life's quest."

"Sarcasm actually suits you, Charles."

The taxi driver had just honked the horn, so I quickly got in and gave him my address. 'Charles is right, I thought. It may be time to find a different hobby.'

Chapter 38
Jack

Jack and the heavyset man stood off to the side of a hot dog vendor's stand on the sidewalk just north of The Met. Jack had gone to The Met early on Saturday so he could beat the rush of tourists. He never got enough of seeing paintings by famous artists, so he often sat in front of them and wondered where they had got their talent when they first drew something, what was going on in their lives at the time they painted this particular painting. The thoughts always made him hungry for hot dogs. He got up from the padded bench in front of The Horse Fair by Rosa Bonheur and, in no hurry to leave, strolled through the gallery and out the entrance where tourists were queuing up to be tricked into paying more than the suggested $2.00 free-will offering.

Outside, he breathed in the aroma of New York and headed down the steps toward a vendor's stand. As he approached, he had seen the man get out of the black Navigator and walk up to the vendor. He ordered two dogs, and when Jack got close enough, he had handed one of them to Jack. Jack reluctantly accepted. Over the man's shoulder, Jack noticed two huge men with muscular biceps the size of thighs standing a few steps away. One of them watched the street, his head slowly swiveling to watch traffic both directions. The other, larger of the two, eyed Jack suspiciously.

"I don't know where you got my name or what you heard," he said to the man standing next to him, "but I am not a pimp."

"I never said you was," the man said with a mouth full of hot dog. He had red hair with a white stripe down the left side that skipped his freckled forehead and picked up again in the middle of his left eyebrow. It gave him an almost circus-clown look, especially considering his red bulbous nose. The man had on a well-tailored navy pinstriped suit draped over his large belly, wore a French blue shirt, and a red, blue, and silver tie. "I said I heard about your, you know, girls," he added after swallowing.

"My daughters? Stay away..."

"Naw, not them. Whadya take me for, huh? Tony Soprano or one of them gangsta rappers? No, I heard that you help sad girls get over their boyfriends after a breakup. Although you're kinda old. But what the hey. More power to ya."

"How on earth...?"

The man gave Jack a broad grin. "Word gets around, pal. Besides, I own a few cabs, ya know. Cabbies, they hear a lot. They listen. They talk."

Jack swallowed what was in his mouth and threw the rest of his hotdog away.

"You're wasting a good dog...Listen, Sullivan, my baby girl lost her fiancé three months ago... "

"Lost? What do you mean 'lost'? Did she forget where she put him? Did he run away?"

"You're a real comedian. Yeah, he just wasn't gonna fit inta the family, so we set him up with a little operation upstate. He's fine, if ya get my drift."

"I don't want to get your drift. You don't have other daughters, do you?"

"Six. All happily married to good family men. They work for me and I pay them well so my girls can raise their kids."

"I'm sure you do. I'm not convinced that I want to help your daughter."

He pulled out a pocket knife, opened it, and began cleaning his fingernails, concentrating on them instead of looking at me. "Let me put it this way to you," he said, "you know all those cab drivers I mentioned earlier? If you don't do me this little favor, then everyone in the city will know what you and that dame partner of yours have been up to."

"I don't have a partner," I said emphatically. "There's a woman doing what I do? Who is she?"

"Never mind her," he said, folding his knife and sliding it into his tailored slacks. Then he looked me in the eyes with a stern expression on his face that removed any reluctance I may have had. "You just help my little girl and your secret is as safe with me as it already is around town, cabs, union halls. I can put a stop to the chatter, or I can make sure you can never date another woman in our city."

"Okay, since you put it that way, I'll help you this once, but tell me about the woman you think is my partner."

He ignored me and turned toward the SUV. "Stanley, the briefcase."

Stanley reached into the SUV's back seat and pulled out a thin black leather briefcase, which he handed to me with a slight grin of victory.

My new friend pointed at the briefcase. "Twenty-five gees in twenties. To cover your expenses. Whatever's left is yours. Treat her well, and then get her to dump you. I'll give you a head start. She don't like slobs."

"Good to know. That will be useful. How do I get in touch with her?"

"Stanley!"

At that, Stanley, the larger of the two goons, reached into his coat pocket and handed me what was probably a burner phone.

"Her name is Jessica Brigit O'Toole O'Malley." He had finally told me her name.

"Jessica? Not very Irish."

"Yeah, the wife and I couldn't agree on a seventh Irish name, so we picked Jessica as she was being born. Anyway, Sullivan, her phone number is Speed Dial One. Use only this cell phone to talk to her and when she dumps you, call me on Speed Dial Nine with the good news, and then throw the phone in the river. Get it?"

"Got it!"

"Good," he said. "Now have fun! Not too much, though. I'll be watching."

When he said he'd be watching, he patted me on the cheek with his right hand and gave me an evil grin. Luckily, I didn't flinch. Then he turned and gave Stanley, who was holding open the door, a clap on the arm and got into the back seat of the SUV.

I stood, dumbfounded, holding the briefcase in my left hand. I wiped my cheek as the SUV roared off. I felt like a high school kid, corsage in trembling hands, who had just stared down the barrel of a shotgun aimed by his prom date's father. Regaining my composure, I remembered the man's remark about my so-called female partner and was even more dumbfounded.

I called Jessica two days later and we met for coffee. Because it was a work day for me, I was dressed appropriately in gray slacks, black tassel loafers, and a starched pink Polo button-down shirt. Jessica complimented me on my style, so I knew I would need to dress down if I was going to get her to dump me.

Over the next three weeks, we had seven dates, each one worse than the last. I started out being a good listener, dressing somewhat well, but by the time our final club date arrived, I had become an inattentive slob who dressed in clothes from the sale rack of a secondhand store.

We had arrived early enough to wait in line for only 20 minutes and eventually got near the front so Jessica could hear the music and dance as she peered around the massive shoulders of the door bouncer. She looked back at me a couple of times, and each time I tried to look more bored, which matched her look of disgust with me. I couldn't blame her. My lime-green faux-silk shirt was wrinkled and partially untucked front and back on the right side from my tight black pants and white belt. I completed the look with lime green Crocks. Perfect outfit to get dumped in.

A black SUV drove by slowly, the back window opened, and Jessica's father glared at me. He drew his hand across his neck in a slicing motion. I stared back at him and followed his car until it was out of sight. I wanted this Irish thug to know that he couldn't intimidate a fellow Mick. Besides, I had this under control.

I turned back to my date and put my hands on her well-toned hips. "Jessica, I can't wait to see this band," I said into her ear.

"Yeah, me neither."

The bouncer, wearing black Ninja pants, a black t-shirt under a skin-tight black leather jacket, looked us over as I gawked at the crowd and up at the tall buildings in my best dork imitation.

"Your daddy come to the big city from North Dakota, babe?" he asked Jessica.

"Him? He ain't my daddy, he's my old boyfriend."

"He's old, all right."

"We've only been together for a couple of months. I'm breaking up with him tonight after he buys me lots of high-class champagne."

I overheard this and smiled an open-mouthed, dorky smile.

"Make him buy you the good stuff," he loudly said to her.

"You mean like you?"

"For you, I'm free," he said to her. "I get off at midnight. I'll find you."

"Find us for what, Jessie?" I innocently asked her.

At that, Ninja Ned unhooked the rope and let us in. As Jessica passed him, he winked at her.

"Enjoy your evening, kids."

After two bottles of Dom Perignon, Jessica leaned across our table and broke the news to me.

"We can't continue this relationship, Jack," she slurred, loudly as she spit her words on my beautiful shirt. "You shore helped me stop thinking about my fiancé, but this just can't work. I'll tell my Da I broke up with you so we can all get on with our lives. Besides, I'd never marry someone your age, even if you are put together. I'm pretty sure you can find a good use for the rest of the money."

Chapter 39
Jack

I was writing some ideas for a two-years-in-the-future campaign for one of our biggest clients. Because of all the storyboards, client approval process, production, and media buys, we had to work in the future to design and implement viable campaigns. It's a little nerve-wracking, but not as nerve-wracking as when Langston or one of his account minions charges in demanding a hard-hitting campaign overnight. I was feeling good about this perfume campaign and I was writing in the zone, so when my intercom buzzed, I jumped a little but finished the sentence.

"Jack, Alicia VanDorn is here to see you."

I picked up the phone. "Nadine, I don't know a ... an Alicia Vanwhatever."

I looked out at Nadine's alcove and saw a well-dressed woman standing there, looking impatient and troubled.

"Jack, she says it's important and if you won't see her she'll scream that you're anti-Semitic."

At that, I hit CTRL S, walked to my office door, opened it, and said to the woman, "Please come in." As we entered my office, she regally removed her mink coat and handed it to me. 'Well, okay, I thought, I suppose I can hang it up,' which I did on the hook on the inside of my office door. Then I motioned for her to sit in one of the chairs in front of my desk and I sat in the chair to her left.

"I don't usually meet with prospective clients, Mizz VanDorn," I said, smiling as diplomatically as I could.

"It's Misses VanDorn. Misses Clark VanDorn. Please call me Alicia."

"Okay, Alicia. How's everything in the Hamptons?"

"My maiden name is Steinmetz. Sound familiar?" she asked me in a conspiratorial tone.

It did sound familiar, but I didn't want her to know it. "No...not really," I shook my head slowly as if I was trying to recall the person attached to the Steinmetz name.

She leaned forward, put her elbow on her knee and looked me in the eye, smiling. "It's a very small world, Mister Sullivan. Very small. Even New York, for all its anonymity and loneliness, is a very, very small town. You just never know who I know who knows you." I ran my index finger under my collar. I suppose it's my "tell."

"Take my dear, sweet mother, for example. She spends several hours most days on the same bench in Central Park."

"I'm almost certain I've never spoken to your mother," I clearly lied.

"When you jog by her you greet her and sometimes you even kiss her on the cheek. So let's cut the crap."

"I'm not sure...," I was caught, but I continued the charade.

"My sharp-eyed Jewish mother can describe in some detail your little scheme."

"Okay, you got me," I said resigning the game. "I wouldn't call it a scheme. More like acts of kindness."

"Depends on your point of view, Mr. Sullivan, I suppose," she said, still looking me in the eye. "I'll be frank. I need your services."

"I don't know..."

"You do know. And here's what you're going to do. My daughter and her lousy boyfriend just broke off a three-year relationship, thank God. You're going to help this beautiful, distraught, talented girl get back on her feet. And you will not get her on her back ... or you will incur my wrath, so help me!"

"I never sleep with my dates."

"It's not sleeping that worries me," she raised one eyebrow.

There was an uncomfortable silence. I cleared my throat. "I've never had a mother line me up. A few sisters, but never a mother."

She ignored that, leaned back in the chair, let out a breath. "Of course, her father and I don't expect you to wine and dine her on your own, so we're prepared to reimburse you for whatever you spend on her...within reason."

"It's a kind offer, but I can't take your money because I'm not going to date your daughter."

"Mister Sullivan...Jack...My husband owns the most respected legal publishing company on the East Coast. His friends are high-powered lawyers and magazine publishers... You can either date my daughter or, after we expose your little scheme, you can be a greeter at a Walmart in Westbury."

My mind ran through all the things in my comfortable life that could collide and cascade into the shitter. "What's your daughter's name, Mrs. VanDorn," I said, resignedly, "and how do I contact her?"

She reached into her Coach purse and handed me a very expensive note card, with Dalia VanDorn's name, address, and phone number written in elegant script. She rose from the chair and I retrieved her coat, holding it for her as she slid her arms in the sleeves. She reached down and, taking my right hand and wrist in both her hands, smiled at me. "Dalia's expecting your call. Her grandmother told her you'd be calling."

Chapter 40
Jack

Sunday dinner was Ma's world-famous corned beef and cabbage. The whole house smelled of cooked cabbage, but the meal was delicious and the conversation spirited. When the dishes were cleared and washed, Terry and I retreated to the living room with a bottle of Bushmills single malt Irish whiskey. After a few comfortable minutes of silence, Terry took a swallow and, looking at the contents of his glass, said, "The pastor over at St. Michael's asked about you. Wants to know if you're ready."

"Ready for what?"

"To go to a seminary for older guys like you," he said with a half-smile.

I snorted, then took a sip. The whiskey burned going down but gave me a warm feeling as it hit my stomach.

"You're such a tool, Jack," he continued. "One of Fr. Patrick's parishioners, a widow about your age, has been dating a lot but can't seem to find the right guy. And, surprise, you can't find the right woman."

"Not interested."

"We thought you'd say that. She said the same thing."

"You two have talked to her? What's wrong with you?"

"I just told her how broken up you are," he said. "She reluctantly agreed to have coffee with you Saturday morning at Pirelli's on 42nd Street."

"This is rich. Matchmaking clerics."

"At least have coffee. What can it hurt? Besides, Fr. Patrick says she is very attractive."

"So now I'm so shallow that I need to be told that she's good-looking to get me to go out with her? If she orders some light latte sludge, I'm outta there."

"Fair enough."

We sat in silence for a few minutes, me shaking my head in mild disbelief that my dating life was the stuff of clerical concern. I poured us another bit of Bushmills, then I reached down by the armchair and picked up the black briefcase I got from O'Malley to cover expenses for dating his daughter. I slid it onto the coffee table and opened it.

"Wow!" Terry stage-whispered.

"Twenty-five thousand. I got it from an Irish mob boss to date his daughter. It's for the parish. You can either buy new bingo equipment or better food for the homeless shelter…your choice."

"Jack, you can't buy your way into heaven."

"Since when?!"

"Since Martin Luther."

Chapter 41

Their phone conversation had been cordial and quick. Fr. Patrick had given Suzanne's cell number to Fr. Terrance, who had then given it to Jack and told him the best time to call her. As much as he hated set-ups, except for the ones with his rebound relationship dates, Jack had agreed to call Suzanne, if only to get the two meddling priests off his case. One coffee date. My brother's voice rang in my head, 'What could it hurt?' A slightly uncomfortable half hour and the matchmakers could get back to arranging bingo nights, he had thought.

So, exactly seven minutes past the appointed time, Jack had called her. They had laughed at the ridiculousness of their matchmakers, and after a few pleasantries, agreed to meet the following Saturday morning at 9 at a little Dunkin Donuts just off Fifth Avenue.

Jack told his brother Bobby that he would miss their weekly basketball game, and had lied convincingly about the reason – getting Darby's ears and teeth cleaned, something he'd put off too long.

Saturday. Jack arrived at 8:45, because, despite his recent experiences with blind dates, he was anxious and wanted to get this over. He sat at a table facing the sidewalk so he could watch passersby and everyone who veered into the store. He had on his Saturday best—gray Yankees T-shirt, comfortable jeans, Bass Weejuns without socks.

Suzanne walked in at 8:53 (Jack had looked at his watch every few minutes), scanned the crowd and spotted Jack, who was the only guy sitting alone. She arrived early to rehearse her conversation for a fast departure and have a quick cup. Her plan was to stay long enough to get her priest to quit meddling, report back to him after Mass the next day, and get on with her rebound relationships. Apparently, this guy was not a prospect for her rebound scheme. Fr. Patrick had told her that Jack Sullivan had been dating plenty of women, so he seemed, for all appearances, to have moved on after his wife's illness and death. She was surprised that he had arrived before her. A good sign? Was he too eager, or also in a hurry to get this over with? She approached him cautiously.

"Excuse me. Jack?"

"Suzanne?"

Jack stood up and they shook hands. Her grip was strong, but not crushing. Evidently, she's accustomed to shaking hands and not in a girly manner, he thought. And her hands were the softest he had felt in a long time. She was also dressed casually, but with style—red sneakers, tight blue jeans, red designer sweatshirt, and a Yankees cap, which immediately registered with Jack.

"Hi. listen," she said as they stood facing each other like foxes invading one another's territory. "I'm sorry about this. Pretty crazy being set up by celibate guys in white collars."

Jack laughed. "It could be the next big reality show."

"Last Chance Dating."

Jack laughed again. Good sense of humor and quick wit, he thought. Then he looked closely at her.

"You look very familiar. Have we met?" he asked her, quizzically.

"Save that line for a bar, desperado," she quipped, but not meanly. "I'm the spokesmodel for Lafonte Diamonds."

"Ah, yes," he realized. "Billboards and magazines. All by B-B-D-O, the competition."

"You're in advertising?" she asked.

"Right you are," he said still looking at her face and realizing that he had also seen her in person somewhere. It was difficult to not check out her figure, but he would do that on the sly because he was a guy. He stepped around and pulled out her chair. "Please sit and I'll get our coffee. What are you drinking?"

"No," she said, "You sit and I'll go up. I'm buying. What do you want?"

"Well, okay, if you insist. Large black bold, no cream or sugar."

"Isn't that what black means?"

"What?"

"No cream or sugar. That's how I like mine. Only I get two ice cubes so I can drink it faster."

"No I-V?"

Jack was beginning to like her. She certainly didn't behave like a spoiled model, and she was straightforward. He liked that. As she turned, he caught her figure. Every part of her seemed firm, probably from doing hot yoga, he guessed, and he sat and averted his eyes to the sidewalk, not wanting to be rude. He was deep in memory-wracking, trying to figure out where he'd seen her before, when she set down his coffee.

"I'm almost sure I've seen you out and about," he said.

"In church, maybe?"

"Let me see the back of your head."

She turned full around in her chair and removed her Yankees cap, counted to three, then turned back around but left her cap on the table.

"No, I don't remember your hair or the back of your head, so it wasn't church."

"You look strangely familiar, too," she said, a sly smile coming across her face. "Ever run through Central Park naked except for a Nixon mask?"

Jack laughed. "Not in the past three years. And what would you be doing in Central Park when men in Nixon masks are streaking through?"

"My little secret," she said. They both laughed and relaxed, shoulders no longer rigid. The conversation shifted to what it was like being on both ends of advertising campaigns, the perks and peculiarities of people in the industry. Anyone looking at them would think they were old college friends or former colleagues catching up.

"Want a refill? He asked her after she drained her cup. "My treat."

"That's a generous offer," she said, "since refills are free. But, no, I've gotta run. Meeting some friends for lunch and if I don't leave now, I'll be late, and I hate being late."

Too bad she was so much like him, Jack thought. I could get to like her.

They got up, and only then did they notice the four millennials glaring at them as if evil stares could get anyone to give up their table. As they passed the evil quartet, Jack smiled politely and opened the door for Suzanne. The evil ones rushed to their table, elbowing out an elderly couple that was approaching it. Nice work, thought Jack, shaking his head in disgust.

Jack and Suzanne stood close together, their arms touching, but looking uncomfortable.

"Well, Mr. Sullivan," she said looking up at him. He really is handsome, in a middle-aged metrosexual kind of way, she thought. And, this wasn't as painful as I thought it would be. Damn! "We did our dating duty for the church," she continued after the pregnant pause, "and no need for confession."

"Yet."

"In your dreams, Mad Man!"

"I need more to tell my brother so we can put this to rest," he looked at her, "Not in the confessional, though. How about dinner next Tuesday? I know this great wine bar in Brooklyn that serves a mean sea bass."

"Oooh, a reason to live," she muttered to the street.

"What? I didn't catch that smart-ass remark."

"I said that's a good reason to give," she lied. "You seem innocent enough. But I can tell you my weakness is Chablis and baked Brie.

"Very European," he said, his voice dripping with the sarcasm.

"You have my number," she said, smiling sweetly. "Call me with the place and time and I'll be there, but there better be a bottle of Chablis and a plate of baked Brie on the table."

"I'll see to it, your Highness."

At that, they shook hands and hugged like a monk and a nun leaving a conference at the Vatican. Then they turned and walked in opposite directions. After a few steps, Jack turned to look back at her, still wondering where he'd seen her. He shook his head in unrequited memories, turned back, still perplexed and resumed walking.

When Suzanne reached the corner, she turned up the side street, then stuck her head back around to watch him walk away, trying her damnedest to remember when and where she had seen Jack Sullivan before.

Chapter 42

Suzanne's plush apartment was a loft in SoHo, where she had lived since the second anniversary of Richard's death. After grieving for 18 months she put the brownstone on the market and barely had time to sell most of their furniture on eBay before the place sold for more than her asking price. Bidding war, the listing agent had said. And because it was a cash sale (who has that much money, she wondered?), she had had 25 days to get out. Fortunately, she had often shopped in SoHo, and her agent knew an agent who specialized in lofts. After an exhaustive three days viewing seven lofts, she had settled on one move-in ready, with a great view on two sides, modern plumbing, and new appliances. It had an island in the kitchen, which she hadn't even known she wanted until she saw how it divided the open floor plan.

SoHo had a much different vibe than the old brownstones of her previous neighborhood. It was upscale without being pretentious. On her way to a photo shoot in Manhattan, Suzanne could dress like a middle-aged dock worker without drawing a second look. Or, she could don sweats, a slouch hat and Uggs and wait with three suitcases at the curb for her taxi ride to the airport. She loved that no matter what her outfit or whether she wore makeup, she blended into the eclectic neighborhood.

She and Jack Sullivan had enjoyed their dinner date, or at least she thought they both did because he had asked her out again and she had said yes. He said he'd come up with a different activity, so she was curious enough to look forward to it.

But now, sitting on her couch in the Lotus position and relaxing in her favorite PINK sweats, she was listening distractedly to Zack, her latest rebounder, whine on the phone. Thank the Lord, he had finally taken the many hints she had dropped and called to break up. She focused on a stubborn hangnail on her left ring finger.

"Yes, I understand, Zack," she said sympathetically, grabbing the pesky hangnail with tweezers. "I told you not everyone appreciates my sense of humor." Then she listened and gritted her teeth. "Ouch," she yelped away from the phone when the hangnail pulled away as she listened a little more intently.

"You said if I ever touched you like that again, you'd have the Irish mob feed me to pigs at their feedlot in Queens. Were you serious?"

"NOOO, of course I wasn't serious!"

"Sounded damn serious!"

"Really, Zack? Do you really think the Irish mob has a hog feedlot in Queens and that I know them?"

"You didn't smile ... You scare me."

After a few moments of silence on her part, she rolled her eyes. "If that's how you feel...Goodbye, Zack," she said into the phone. "Zack?" "Zack?"

She sucked on her finger tasting blood and walked over to her large windows that overlooked the city. After a minute, she looked to see if her hangnail had stopped bleeding, then pumped her fist and did a victory dance.

Chapter 43

The following Thursday, Suzanne, and Michael, who still wore his dark gray suit, French blue shirt, and black tie, sat 10th row, mid-court in Madison Square Garden watching the Knicks. In sharp contrast, Suzanne was decked out in full Knicks gear and held a hat shaped like a basketball, which she playfully handed to Michael.

"Come on, Michael. Put it on," she yelled over the crowd noise.

"It's beneath me," he sneered, looking at the hat and then at her. His brown eyes expressed his embarrassment and disgust. "I hate basketball."

"Then why'd you come?" she leaned closer and yelled. She already knew he hated team sports, preferring squash and handball where he could dominate and humiliate his opponents by outscoring them by large margins. A real narcissistic sadist, she had determined after consulting a psychiatrist friend. "Be careful with that one," Dr. Odell had warned her. Tonight, she hoped to goad Michael into storming out, then she would watch the rest of the game and leave with her game buddies.

Michael yelled back, his neck as red as a baboon's butt, "I thought I could ... Expand... Grow. I can't. I HATE basketball! And I hate ..."

"You hate what, Michael?" she egged him on, dangerously, possibly.

"I hate where we're going, Suzanne," he yelled, becoming even more exasperated trying to yell his feelings in a loud crowd, as he looked around. The two Knicks fans behind them averted their eyes back to the action on the floor when they caught him turning around. Turning back to face her, he said into her ear, "I need someone who wants to do what I want, someone like ..."

"Like Amy, Michael?" She was getting close to pushing him over the edge, but that was the whole idea with this guy.

"Like Amy," he admitted, not wanting to.

"Michael, she dumped you for her super-hot hot Pilates instructor, remember?" she reminded him. The two guys behind them laughed, which, of course, embarrassed Michael, whose whole face up to his hair-plugged scalp turned redder than a baboon's butt.

Fully embarrassed now, he glared at her, "And, bitch, I'm dumping you. Now!"

Slapping the basketball hat out of her hand, he struggled from his seat and squeezed out of the row, but as he turned to go his feet got tangled and he stumbled, up the steps, barely catching himself in time to save his head. Suzanne watched him until he reached the mezzanine exit, then turned back to the game. Joakim Noah was shooting a free throw. As the center bounced the ball, one of the guys behind her leaned down to her left side.

"Her yoga instructor! That's so rich," he said in a normal voice.

"Poor guy. Well, not really, but at least now he's had his rebound girlfriend."

"That had to be your best yet!"

"It was!"

"Where do you find these losers?"

Suzanne just shrugged. "Can you walk me to the taxi stand after the game?"

"Sure thing, Suzanne!"

They high fived and as she turned back to watch the game, she felt a shudder of doubt cross her mind.

Suzanne was running out of energy for her rebound-girl scheme. It was getting scary, or at the very least, nerve-racking to get inside some guy's head to discover what will make him dump her. Some were easy, like the self-absorbed money broker who hated basketball; others more difficult. There were those who defied all attempts to figure them out until they made some comment that finally gave her a clue. Like this guy.

Adler Sebastian Throckmorton, stage name "Black Adder", was a 67-year-old British rock musician with snake tattoos on his arms, neck and, Suzanne imagined, his torso. His numerous piercings always set off airport security alarms and during the ensuing pat-down always caused him to ask with the utmost indignation, "Don't you fuckin' know who the fuck I am, you fucks?"

So, after several painful dates to several New York clubs over the course of four weeks, he had finally revealed during a Narcotics Anonymous meeting that anything other than loud music and sweaty dancing bored him to death. He told the other recovering addicts that it was only through the grace of his higher power that his ex-wife and his now current squeeze enjoyed his sobriety crutch.

Upon hearing that at the meeting, Suzanne had decided on a potentially dangerous course of action. She had lied to Adler and told him she had to scout out a location for a jewelry photo shoot at the Metropolitan Museum of Art.

She couldn't believe he had accepted that without question because no one sends the model to scout a shoot location. Thank God for ignorant old rock stars, she had thought.

"It will be a growth experience for us both," she had told him. "I'll look at exhibits through the lens of the camera," she said enthusiastically, "and you'll learn something."

They now stood looking at the recreation of an Egyptian village. Fingers of both hands fidgeted with the seams of his skin-tight silver and mauve leather pants. His black silk pirate shirt covered his arm tattoos, and its high collar hid his neck tattoos, which Suzanne had told him would scare any school kids touring the museum. He had insisted on wearing his silver sparkled platform boots because, she knew, made him tall enough to tower over her.

"This is so, like, sucky, Babe," he whined.

"Just try, Adler," she mock pleaded. "Think about the people who made these tools and weapons. Picture yourself in their time."

"I picture us naked," he whispered lasciviously down her neck.

"Sssshhhh. Think of something else."

"Don't shush me! I can't because you won't. My old lady liked being naked with me."

"And with the gardener, and the pool kid, and the caterer, and ..."

"But she dumped me, that ungrateful, cheating bitch!"

"She did after she'd saved up all that money she told you she was spending on drugs while you were touring," Suzanne reminded him. "Very clever of her, though," she continued. "She moved it to an account in the Caymans and then took off after a few years. All that time the Feds wanted to know why you didn't turn her in for an expensive drug habit. Or at least make her go to rehab."

All his pent-up anger welled to the surface, and without thinking, Adler turned on Suzanne, grabbed her arm and twisted her to face him. She would later see the bruises left by his fingers. Unfazed, but slightly shaken, she gave him her fiercest look of defiance.

"You have a smart mouth, bitch, that's gonna get you in trouble someday," he sneered.

"But not today, Ad. Look around."

Adler slowly looked up from Suzanne's face and turned his head to see people were staring at them. He reluctantly released his grip.

"You knew I can't stand fucking museums and art galleries, but you made me come anyway, and I sure as fuck can't stand to be with you!"

He spun on his clear plastic platform heels, nearly twisting his ankle and pushed his way into the crowd. Just as he got to the first people, Suzanne, now visibly shaken, said loud enough for him to hear, "She dumped you because you're an asshole..."

Then she became painfully aware that women and a few men were covering their children's ears. They and many others looked angry and embarrassed.

"I am so sorry," she said to the crowd at the entrance to the exhibit. "You know how those Brits are, ever since they lost the wars against us."

A museum guard wended his way through the crowd and approached her. "Everything all right, ma'am?"

"Just fine... Boy, would you look at those jewels!"

Chapter 44

Jack had played the hypochondriac routine to the hilt. So easy. How else would you get a doctor to dump you? It had begun honestly. Somewhere, from someone, he had caught a massive bout of the flu or a cold, but nonetheless, the misery was real. It's just that he got over it in three days, a Friday to Monday, without missing a day of work. But he continued to fake symptoms for weeks, hoping that Dalia would tire of his whining and finally cut him loose. In a last-ditch effort to force her, he had come to the Emergency Room during her 3 – 11 shift, wearing a goose down parka, grubby sweats, a stocking cap, and a blanket wrapped around his shoulders. With his left hand, he held the blanket together and clutched a bouquet of wilted flowers in the other. And he sniffled louder than an anteater with a sinus infection.

Just as he looked up from his watch for the fourteenth time, Dr. Dalia VanDorn, dressed in navy blue scrubs, came out of the swinging doors of the ER and stood like an MMA fighter in front of Jack.

"Jack, what are you doing here again?"

"I brought you flowers this time," he sniffled as he showed her the wilted bouquet.

"For the hundredth time, Jack, you're not sick. You may have a little virus or an allergy, but you're not sick enough to be here. See these people? They're sick and injured. they really need a doctor."

"Well," he whined, even more pitifully, "viruses and allergies make people sick."

"They can, but you have hypochondria."

"Now that sounds serious."

"It does….," she said, sympathetically. "Look, Jack, you're an okay guy, but you shouldn't date a doctor. Besides, I spend so much time here that right now I don't have time for a serious relationship. I think we'd better say goodbye. I'll tell my mother and grandmother you did your job."

"Your mother and grandmother?" he coughed.

"Don't be coy, Jack. They confessed."

She leaned down and kissed his cheek. He handed her the flowers and wiped his nose. He slowly stood up and wrapped the blanket tighter around his shoulders.

"Take care, Dalia," he croaked. "I'll miss you."

"Get some help, Jack. I can refer you to someone. Think about it."

Hunched over, he turned, waved to her with one hand over his head, and shuffled out of the ER waiting room. Outside, smiling, he wrapped the blanket around an elderly woman being wheeled to a cab.

Dalia watched Jack walk out the door and then handed the bouquet of flowers to a woman and new baby being wheeled out by her husband. She re-entered the ER through the swinging doors and walked to the nurses' station. An attractive female nurse approached and, looking around to make sure there were no prying eyes, put her arm around Dalia's shoulders.

"What did you tell him?"

"That I'm too busy for a relationship right now."

"Including with me?"

"No, I just have to figure out how to tell my mother and grandmother about us."

Chapter 45
Suzanne

It's a rare Tuesday that Melissa and I are both in the city and between jobs at the same time. We have a standing arrangement that whenever that happens, we have brunch at the Clinton Street Café, then spend the rest of the day shopping or going to art galleries. That's followed by wine and apps at Aldo Sohm Wine Bar, which we discovered years ago by accident before it became wildly popular, so we always make reservations as soon as our schedules sync.

Melissa is one of National Geographic's most in-demand photographers, and I always drag her to one of her exhibits because she takes beautiful jungle landscapes, wildlife shots and enchanting photos of children the world over. Of course, she's modest, but not too modest to take the exorbitant paychecks and royalties. She buys most of the time. I insist.

We both enjoy dressing up for our girls' days out. I know Melissa enjoys wearing clothes other than ranger boots, field khakis, a jungle shirt, and baseball cap. She's a real clothes horse and looks stunning today in fashionable boots, black yoga pants, an over-sized dark gray sweater, Burberry check scarf, and her blonde shoulder-length hair falling loose. People stare.

"Tell me more about this latest guy," she politely ordered as she searched through a rack of slinky black dresses, apparently looking for the perfect one to wear to an evening of opera in Melbourne. "Is he a broker, divorced, widowed, gay?"

"He's in advertising. Widowed. Two years."

"Well?" she persisted, as only a good friend would be allowed to. I knew she was serious when she took down a slinky dress and held it against herself like a flour sack.

"I just can't get over the eerie feeling that I've seen him somewhere before we first met for coffee, though. I'll remember. Anyway, we laugh. He makes me laugh ... a lot," I said, remembering all the goofy, fun times we had together. I stopped looking at tops and stared out the window.

"You like him! You really like him, don't you?"

"Yes...No! I'm not going to let myself. Oh, I don't know!"

"Suzanne! You're falling in love!"

"Am not. He's just different. And he's already been dating. A lot."

"Anything serious?"

"He claims not."

"So you can still be his first serious rebound girlfriend?"

"That's my plan."

Melissa looked over the store. Her eyes locked on a mannequin.

"Suze," she said pointing her head at the mannequin. "Didn't you wear this to last week's runway extravaganza?"

"I looked better. More alive."

"You wish."

We laughed and walked toward the door. The three 20-something women working in the store stared as we walked past the cash register empty-handed and scrutinized us until we waltzed through the anti-theft detector at the door. Then they just scowled. Outside the store, we turned, and in our best immature gesture, stuck our thumbs in our ears, wiggled our fingers, and stuck out our tongues at them. "Let's drink some wine," we said in unison, laughing hysterically to stares from staid New Yorkers.

Chapter 46
Jack

When Bobby, Lew, and I got to our usual court on Saturday morning, three guys who looked as if they had just missed the NBA draft by a half-inch, were playing a rough game of three-man 21, blocking and hip checking allowed. After a short huddle, we decided to ask them to join us for three-on-three, winners buy losers lunch. They laughed, which we took to mean they would expect us to buy them lunch after they scored 60 or more points to our 20 or less.

What started as a civil pick-up game quickly turned into all-out war, with the short guys on the receiving end of a massive shellacking. I had a fat lip from an elbow to the face as I drove to the basket for a lay-up. Lew, for all his upper-body strength and intimidating Navy SEAL tattoos, didn't worry these guys one iota. In fact, it seemed as if they took it as a challenge to skin a SEAL. Lew upped his game but suffered as a result.

"Time," he yelled, holding the ball at midcourt, after a hard-fought rebound. "Hold up. I got a cramp."

I walked over to him. I was drenched in sweat and breathing harder than the last horse in the final race at Aqueduct. "You okay?"

Lew turned his back to the court and looked at me sideways. "Tell me about this new chick," he said, still breathing hard.

"What? Now?"

"I never see you anymore. I have to hear shit about you from friends and family, who I do see. Terry told me."

"Where?"

"In the confessional."

"Bullshit. You never go to confession. You're a Lutheran."

"I go into the confessional. He knows it's me because I start out 'Yo, Terry,' Lew here,' and then we discuss your love life. It's the only way I can keep up with your dating life. Now tell me."

"I can't believe he allows you to desecrate the confessional," I said, in my best appalled staunch Catholic voice. "Anyway," I said, breathing a little easier, "You see her everywhere, but you don't know it's her."

The other guys were hollering to get the game going again, so Lew threw the ball back over his head. Then he grabbed his side again and bent over. As he turned his head up, he said, "Where?"

On billboards, New Yorker, The Post."

"The Times?"

"Nah, you know nobody reads The Times anymore."

"She a mob gal, like that Irish girl?" he asked, finally straightening up.

"Could be, I suppose, but I doubt it. She's a model. Has been for years. Even after her kids were born. Was married to a heart surgeon."

We trotted back onto the court. To Bobby's obvious relief, we threw in the towel and offered to buy the NBA wannabes a dog at the nearest stand. They declined, so we just grabbed our towels and hobbled off the court as they returned to their previous game. We, however, needed a dog, so we headed to a stand. Lew and I walked ahead of Bobby, who seemed to be a lot worse off than we were. Good thing he was straggling because he couldn't hear us.

"Any kids???" Lew half whispered.

"Three. Boys. One Marine lieutenant and two in college."

"A jarhead? Yikes! You met them yet?"

"No, don't want to. That would make it harder to get her to break up with me."

"Pretty cocky, mi amigo."

"Not cocky. I've just perfected how to make them hate, despise, and otherwise want me out of their lives ... for the rest of their lives."

I drank half a Coke while the vendor prepared my dog, mustard, onions, sauerkraut. "No refill," he barked when I handed him the cup. I knew that, but a guy can always hope.

We grabbed a bench and slowly ate our dogs.

"What were you guys talking about so secretly," Bobby asked, mouth full of hot dog drenched in ketchup and bun, some of which he spit out as he talked. He was the only New Yorker I knew who put ketchup on a hot dog. Blecch. Who raised this guy?

"How embarrassed we are that those three guys beat our asses without breaking a sweat," I said, after chewing and swallowing my last bite.

"Yeah," Bobby said, "that was a beat down."

Chapter 47
Jack

Once a month, both of my daughters drive home on a Friday after classes to get a couple good night's sleep in their old bedrooms, spend quality time with their Dad and Darby – mainly Darby, who they take for long runs on Saturday. Then they go to lunch or dinner with Dad. No, that's in Lifetime movies. In real life, they meet friends for sushi and go shopping with Dad's credit card, handed over reluctantly and with a great deal of guilt over them being half-orphans. They come home just in time to help fix supper before going out again, wearing the scandalous outfits they bought that afternoon. Of course, they always come home in time to get a good night's sleep so they can go to Mass at 10:30, then to Grandma and Grandpa's for Sunday dinner before fleeing amidst long goodbyes to drive back to school.

The three of us are at the kitchen island chopping celery, bell peppers, jicama, radishes (the only allowable underground vegetable in this salad), and some unidentifiable mushroom they picked up in Chinatown.

The boneless, tasteless, free-range chicken breasts were on their first side under the broiler, and we had just scraped the veggies onto the romaine and kale, thrown in some balsamic and EVOO, and admired our handiwork.

Washing her hands and looking out the kitchen window, Abby said, "Daddy, I'm glad you can go out with all these women and have fun. But my Mom died, and I miss her, and I don't want you to replace her so soon."

"Dad misses her, too," Kelley tried to assure her. "You do, don't you, Dad?"

"Of course I do, and I'm not going to replace her anytime...soon," I just had to add. Sometimes my mouth engages before my brain says 'STOP, DON'T SAY THAT!'

Quick as a hummingbird, Abby picked up on that. "So you WOULD get married again?!"

"Honey, if I ever feel the same way about another woman as I did about your mother, I might. I ... I just don't know."

"Abby and I want you to be happy again, Pops," Kelly said sincerely, I hoped.

"Speak for yourself, Kel," Abby said, tears welling up in her eyes. "I want my Mom back so I can be happy again."

That was my cue. I walked to Abby and put my arms around her. She resisted at first, then relaxed her shoulders and melted into my arms. I put my cheek against the top of her head.

"I miss her every day," I said, fighting back tears because when I cry I sob, which I may have foolishly decided, is not good for daughters to see this long after the death of their mother. "She was my best friend, Abby, and sometimes I selfishly forget that you lost your mother."

"I miss her so much, Daddy," Abby said, through her tears.

"So do I, Peanut. So do I."

I felt warm arms around my waist. Kelly said into Abby's back, "Group hug!"

We did, then the smoke alarm went off and we barely had time to turn over the chicken breasts before they got nearly as black as the olive oil that coated them. The salad was edible, though.

Chapter 48
Jack

I had promised Suzanne a different dating experience, so instead of the usual drinks and dinner, or dinner and a movie, we met in Central Park. Having spent the entire past week studying its history, I told her that I would be her tour guide, relaying as much trivia as I could about various aspects of our nation's most famous inner-city park. At that, she seemed genuinely interested but rolled her eyes just to tease me. Of course, as a New Yorker, she knew the park's history! How could I be so stupid?

Entering the park, Suzanne put her hand on my forearm, then slid it into my hand. My God, she smelled wonderful and dressed casually like the model she is. I gently entwined our fingers and held on feeling a warmth generate up my arm into my soul, a feeling I hadn't felt since my first date with …

But then the spell was broken by a woman sitting on a bench feeding pigeons. Oh, crap! Mrs. Steinmetz!

"Putz," she mumbled, still looking at the pecking pigeons.

"Pardon me?" Suzanne said, as I quickly steered her away from Mrs. Steinmetz. "Wait, Jack! What did she mean by that? Who was she calling a name? You?" Suzanne protested.

"Just some crazy old woman, Suze. You know what's happened since they let them out of institutions. Sad, really," I said with all the sincerity I could muster, knowing that this particular crazy old woman was quite wealthy and had a nice home.

"But, Jack, she called one of us a putz."

"I'm sure she forgot her medication this morning," I explained, as we hurried away, but we didn't get far enough before we heard, "Don't trust him, Honey!"

"Please wait here," I said lovingly to Suzanne. "I'll be right back. I'm just going to see if she needs me to call her caretaker." Reluctantly, Suzanne leaned on a nearby tree, put one foot up, and stayed vigilant.

I loped back to Mrs. Steinmetz and sat next to her. I gently picked up her hand that had just thrown Jewish Rye on the ground and looked at her. "I'm sorry if I hurt your granddaughter. It was never my intention. And remember, she broke up with me."

"Why didn't you tell me she was one of those gay girls?" she asked, a tear welling up in each eye.

"Well, in the first place, that's news to me," I said, hiding my shock. "And in the second place," I explained, "even if I had known, Bubbe, it would not have been my business to tell you. Capiche?"

"She said you didn't know," she admitted. "Now go back to your lady friend. She looks like a keeper. Please run by again, Jack Sullivan. I like seeing your cute old tush."

I laughed. "I will," I said. I jogged back to Suzanne. As I neared her tree, she pushed off and grabbed my hand again. There's that electric feeling again.

"Did you call anyone to come get her?" she asked. "What did she say?"

"Not necessary. And nothing, nothing."

I hurried away. Suzanne looked back quizzically at Mrs. Steinmetz, then shrugged her shoulders. 'Something's going on,' she thought.

We walked through the park and talked about our lives. I hadn't opened up to another human being, let alone a woman, this much since getting to know Missy – when I didn't have much of a life history to share. This relationship with Suzanne was getting dangerously close to love, and I needed to get her to dump me soon, or I would tumble into the abyss and ...

She was saying something about waking up an appetite and if we didn't find some sushi damn soon, she was going to be "hangry," and model or no model, when she needed sushi, things could get ugly. We headed to a five-star sushi restaurant on West 58th, sat at the sushi bar, and proceeded to stuff our faces. I don't like sake, but even that was good. We helped each other wipe kernels of rice off the corners of our mouths and split the bill. Gotta love a woman who automatically pays half! Then, whether due to stiff muscles or too much sake, we left. Once outside, Suzanne grabbed my lapels, pulled my face down to hers, and gave me a warm kiss. I kissed her back, long and slow, as I put my hands on her cheeks. The moment passed when some jerk yelled: "Get a room!" We broke apart, slowly, tenderly. The old Neil Sedaka song, "Breaking Up Is Hard To Do," suddenly came to mind, as I thought that making her break up with me will be hard to do since I don't want her to.

I hailed a taxi, we climbed in, and Suzanne sat so close to me she was almost on my lap. I couldn't help myself. I put my left arm around her shoulders and hugged her tightly and held her hands in my right hand. She nuzzled her head into my shoulder. My God, she smelled good! Breaking up is for our own good, I thought. I will have to make her think beyond a doubt that dumping me is her idea, no regrets, no take backs, and absolutely no "we can still be friends," which never works. A clean break. That's the only way. Her doing, my maneuvering.

On the way to her apartment, the long afternoon walk, full stomach, and good sake made her doze off. I was watching the meter tick off our fare until I heard her snort. I looked down and gently wiped the drool off the corner of her lips and chin with my finger. She woke up and groggily asked, "Are we home yet?"

"Almost," I answered, softly, into her hair, as I wiped my right index finger on my pant leg.

I know I should have said good night at her apartment front door, but being weak and having enjoyed one of the best days I'd had in years, I accepted her invitation to come up for a glass of wine and more "talk."

We sat on her couch, looking out at the fabulous New York skyline, drinking a delicious Chardonnay, and actively holding hands, our fingers exploring each other's palms. That electricity just wouldn't go away.

Suzanne

We sat in a warm silence for a long, yet, comfortable, time, which was worrisome, because I was becoming too comfortable around this man. And too attracted to him. I had yet to find anything about him that would want me to break up with him. Will need to dig deeper. Worse yet, ever the gentleman, he wouldn't talk about why he broke up with all these women he had been dating since his wife passed away. I was having a hard time cracking that good-guy shell, and if I couldn't, I'd need to take him to Erminia and lay on the line that, even though I had been playing the field, getting back in the dating pool, nothing serious, mind you, with you, Jack Sullivan, especially because of all the fun we have, it feels like I'm cheating on my late husband, so this can never work because I'm still a grieving widow and I could never ... At which point, I hoped, he would slowly wipe the marinara off the corners of his mouth, and, with red anger rising up his neck and tears running down his cheeks, call for the check, grab it from the maître de, throw down his napkin, walk by me, lean over, and say, 'You've broken my heart, and I hope I never see you again.' At least that's my plan.

I carried our second glass of wine over to the couch and handed him his, almost filled to the brim because he got the last of the bottle.

Jack

After the silence of our first glass, she poured us another one, sat facing me, and for the next 15 minutes, told me the wonderful and infuriating things about her late husband. She capped it off with the crap his lecherous friends had said to her before his body was cold in the grave.

I couldn't help myself. I laughed. She had meant the last part to be funny, and it was. "Now it's your turn," Jack."

"I didn't come up to talk about my wife. You sure?"

"I told you about my husband," she said, matter-of-factly. "It's your turn to share."

"Missy was a remarkable woman. I was working on an ad campaign for the hospital where she was a resident. As you can imagine, we had a hard time getting together, so I finally had to wrangle a lunch date with her in the hospital cafeteria. Over salads and chili, we hit it off. Later, she told our friends it was love at first sight. I told everyone that love hit me when I walked through the hospital's rotating doors that day.

"Over the course of the next six months of casual, infrequent dating, I learned she had been an active little girl, always getting into mild trouble, winning science fairs and then being a knock-out cheerleader, science nerd in high school. That got her an invitation to every prom and every jock's back seat, which she politely but vehemently declined. She had scholarship offers from several schools but chose Columbia because it had the best pre-med program and Harvard Medical. Then there was an internship and residency at the hospital where we met. She'd never had no time for any kind of relationship, rarely saw her family, but since she had chosen a specialty, could work something akin to regular hours. We fell in love, had a big Catholic wedding at which my brother Fr. Terrance presided, honeymooned in the Catskills because they were close in case of an emergency and settled in to love each other and make two beautiful girl babies.

"She cared about people, especially about her staff, her patients, and our girls..."

"You? Where did you fit in?"

"Yes, but I think I was last on the list because I was always there for her. Everyone loved her. So did I, more at the end. We had been rediscovering each other...as lovers and friends. Then she got sick."

Suzanne touched my face. Just what the hell is she trying to do? Make me fall in love?

"The doctors all said there was nothing they could do. Nothing."

I had to look away because I was choking up. Damn her and damn her wanting me to share! I took a deep breath and regained my composure. "Sorry."

"Don't be, Jack. I still cry late at night after a day at Martha's Vineyard that Richard would have enjoyed."

"On that note, I should leave."

"Don't."

Suzanne put her wine glass and mine on the sofa table behind us, got up on her knees, puts her arms around my shoulders started kissing my neck and working up to my cheek. I turned and kissed her on the lips, then I pulled away.

"I really should go, Suze. I just can't do this."

Suzanne gave me one last long kiss, running her tongue lightly past my lips, into my mouth, past my teeth, and onto the tip of my tongue. I met her tongue with mine and enjoyed the feeling it generated from the tip of my tongue to my toes. Then she slowly pulled her arms away.

"Go," she whispered. "Next time you won't be so lucky."

I grabbed a pillow and got up slowly, covering my erection. I turned so she couldn't see it or my red face, and walked to the door. Suzanne followed me, laughing. No more erection! Red-faced, I opened the door, faced her, and pushed the pillow at her.

"Nite, Suze. I'll call you."

"I may not answer."

"If I call, you'll answer."

I kissed her goodbye, long and lovingly, turned and quickly walked down the hall. I heard her close the door. At the elevator, I leaned my head against the wall and pounded it. 'You are such an idiot. You're falling in love. How are you going to get this woman to break up with you without breaking two hearts?' I knew just the place, just the plan. It would work ... I hoped.

Suzanne

I closed the door and smiled, clutching the pillow to quiet the butterflies in my stomach. In spite of myself, my body told me I had enjoyed our day a little too much, especially our last few minutes on the couch. But a plan was forming to get Mr. Jack Sullivan to break up with me and I needed to implement it. Soon!

Chapter 49
Jack

I called Suzanne Monday for a dinner date Thursday. I knew she would be in the city because I had one of our talent scouts call her agency and request her for a few Japanese automobile still shots – maybe two days' work, big pay. The talent booker was told Suzanne was leaving for Paris on Friday afternoon and would be gone for two weeks. Moreover, he was informed she doesn't stand next to, sit on or drive cars for a living, so don't call again, which is exactly what we knew would be the answer. Like lawyers, our model agency coordinators had learned in the past that she wouldn't appear in automobile campaigns.

Suzanne and I agreed to meet at Erminia at 7:30 to beat the late dining crowd. Our taxis arrived simultaneously, so we exchanged kisses on the cheek as we walked to the entrance. Each of us had made reservations under our own names, so when we walked up to the hostess and gave her our names in unison, she was a little confused and more than a little perturbed that she had reserved two tables for two in the back. However, Bernie, the unshakable maître de approached with two dinner menus and two wine menus, then whispered something in her ear that made her neck turn red. She mumbled a half-hearted apology and turned to help the next couple.

Bernie walked us past tables that were all set for two, toward our table near the back of the restaurant. It gave me the feeling the restaurant was designed so a Mafia boss and his girlfriend could enjoy dinner away from his family while his wise guys stood behind them and watched for any danger. It wasn't, but I have a vivid imagination.

Bernard held chairs for Suzanne then me and once we were seated, he walked over to his station by the kitchen and signaled to a waiter I knew.

"Not a word to either of them," he said softly in the waiter's ear. "Act like you've never seen them." As the waiter started to walk away, Bernard grabbed his arm just above the elbow.

"Wait. Be cordial, Smile. Don't say their names. Capiche?"

The waiter nodded ever so slightly.

"Tell the others. No, I'll tell them. Do not say anything to anyone!"

Suzanne was talking to me in this high-pitched nasal baby talk, the kind some grandmothers think their grandkids and dogs want to hear. It's most irritating. I don't know where she ever got the idea ... oh, shit, I may have mentioned it weeks ago when I was telling her about my neighbor. What the hell is she up to? No, it couldn't be her! The Rebound Woman. Well, I'll be damned.

"And I just so adore my sister's little Pomeranian" she squealed. "She's such a poopsie whoopsie."

"Your sister, or her dog?"

"Her little dog, silly boy," again with the baby talk voice.

Two can play that game. Time to put MY plan in motion. I took a big swig of wine, signaled the sommelier to pour me the rest of the bottle, and as he did, I rolled up the corner of my ruby red napkin and dug deeply into my left ear it. After looking at the corner of the napkin, I wiped it on the tablecloth, and reached into my pants pocket, pulled out a nail clipper, and cut off a hangnail. Then I put the nail clippers back in my pocket and withdrew a small mirror, held it up to my face and began to check my teeth for bits of arugula.

I looked up through my eyebrows to see Suzanne staring at me in pure disgust. Score points for me!

Bernard silently approached our table. "How are the salads?" he asked. Before either of us could answer, a voice came from the middle of the restaurant. Leon, a long-time waiter at Erminia, had taken off his coat, flung it on the coat-check counter, and strode down the middle of restaurant. He spotted me and gave me an overhead wave as he approached our table. Suzanne didn't see him coming.

"Yo, Jack," Leon said. "How's advertising treatin' ya?"

Bernard rushed up to the Leon, trying to shush him. Suzanne turned toward Leon's voice. Leon recognized her and looked shocked and surprised.

"Miss Suzanne?!" Leon exclaimed. He didn't know her, but I had shown him a couple magazine ads so he would recognize her, or so I thought. Other diners, their romantic interludes rudely interrupted, were staring at the four of us. Bernard grabbed Leon and pulled him away. Suzanne glared at me. "You said you'd never been here, Jack!"

"And you said the same thing. What gives, Miss Suzanne?"

"He must have recognized me from my work."

"How did he know your name? They don't put it on billboards or on print ads, Miss Suzanne!"

"People or Us, maybe," she lied, again. "How did he know your name?"

"Uh...he worked at a little Italian place near my office. Got to know him there. Best salads."

"Bullshit, Jack!" she leaned across the table and hissed through clenched teeth. "You brought me here to break up with me...no, wait, you're hoping I'd break up with you...you...putz!" Suzanne pushed back her chair, no mean feat on the rich carpet, the chair fell over backward. Ignoring it, Suzanne turned and headed for the door.

"No, I didn't...honest!" I yelled a white lie after her. "But..." Then it finally dawned on me. "You...you...you brought me here so I'd break up with you!"

She turned around at the hostess stand, feet apart in a linebacker's stance, and said loud enough to hear over traffic outside, "No, I didn't, Jack Sullivan! But I am through with you now...I brought you here to tell you I think... thought...I was falling in love with you," the truth, but still a lie for all the wrong reasons. Then she pushed open the door, nearly knocking over a young couple trying to open it.

"Uh, well, sister," I yelled, right back, "that's why I brought you here," I lied. I looked around. The other diners watched silently, mouths agape.

"Hey, folks, we're in a reality show... you've all been punked. Dinner's on me." What the hell was I thinking there? Just then Suzanne stormed back in. The crowd began to applaud. She glared around the room until they stopped clapping. She clomped through the restaurant and grabbed her purse from the bejeweled purse hanger on the table and stormed back out of the restaurant. In a second she was back at the coat check to get her coat, which she madly struggled into and then paused, hands on hips, to think at the door. Composure regained, she stormed back to me. I watched her as I bravely sipped my wine.

She put her purse over her left shoulder, drained her wine glass, and leaned on the table with her hands clenched in tight fists. "Very clever of you, Sullivan," she said, with clear understanding. "You set this whole thing up just so I'd break up with you. That old woman in the park was right. You can't be trusted," her voice almost cracking. "Well, mister, it worked. You win...I never want to see you again," she said, with all the finality of a broken heart.

I looked in her eyes and hoped she couldn't see the remnants of the tears I had wiped away as she had headed toward the door the last time. "You can't break up with me, moopsie poopsie because I'm breaking up with you!"

As Suzanne swung around, the bottom of her coat knocked over her empty wine glass, bouncing it on the carpet. She squared her shoulders and stormed out, for what we all hoped would be the last time. After an uncomfortable interlude, Bernard came to our ... my ... table.

"I'm sorry, Jack," Bernard said most diplomatically. "I tried to stop Leon."

I felt his presence when Leon came up behind me, so I reached into my pocket, pulled out a folded, crisp hundred-dollar bill, and handed it to him.

"Sweet! Thanks, Jack," he smiled. "But I can't take this," he tried to hand it back.

"Don't you have a First Communion or Confirmation coming up in your family soon?"

"Yeah, but ..."

"Use it for that, Uncle Leon. You'll be a big hero."

"Thanks, Jack! I'll tell this story until the day I die."

"Which will be soon if it comes back to bite me in the ass, Leon." The three of us laughed. Leon waited politely.

"Why, you sly dog," Bernard looked down at me and grinned.

"We were getting too attached. I had to pull out the big guns. Sorry I didn't tell you."

"Leon, I need red meat. I'd like a medium-rare ribeye with a side of gorgonzola polenta and garlic bread, please? I'm dying here!"

"Right away, Jack."

Bernard shook his head. "I am in awe, Jack. You truly are the master of this game you've been playing."

I looked pensively at the door and sighed like a dying lion taking his last breath. Then I slowly shook my head and took a last sip of wine. "I sure am, aren't I," I said to no one.

"Bernie, another bottle of your best Cabernet, please?"

Suzanne

I stopped crying as I hailed a taxi. I was hurt because, in spite of myself and my damn rebound dating plan, I had fallen in love with Jack Sullivan – who was nothing like the vein, crude asshole in the restaurant who had set me up, tricked me, played me like a fiddle. Only he had gone too damn far, and we had had too damn much fun, laughed too much and were a date away from intimacy, or so I knew we hoped. All of which made me madder than a wet hen in a rainstorm, so my initial tears were from anger more than hurt.

Finally, a taxi stopped and pulled over too far from the curb so the only way I could get in was to step in a puddle in the gutter. I was not going to ruin my Manolo Blahniks, even though they were a gift, so I took them off and stepped in cold water to open the back door, which brought more tears of anger and frustration.

The driver, a handsome Sikh wearing a black silk turban, turned his head and asked the front passenger window, "Where to?"

"SoHo," I said, sobbing.

"Um...guy troubles?" he asked as he pulled into traffic to the sounds of several honking horns.

I wasn't in the mood to discuss my troubles, so I said a little too loudly, "Just drive, dammit."

"Yes, ma'am!" he said firmly, looking at me in the rear-view mirror.

"I'm sorry," I apologized. "Yes, a guy."

"He breakup with you? In a restaurant? Man, that's rude!"

"Yes ... no. I broke up with him, only I didn't really want to. He made me."

"Oh, that guy!"

"What? You know him?"

"Heard about him. Everyone calls him The Rebound Guy," he said, narrowly missing a parked police car with lights flashing. I cringed and reached down trying to warm my toes. "Yeah, they say he dates women just getting over a serious relationship, finds out what bugs them about guys, then does that so they'll break up with him."

"You seem to know a lot about this guy," I had quit crying, now I was more inquisitive. "And why do they say he does that? Please pay attention to your driving. You're giving me a panic attack."

"It's supposed to help these women and keep their next guy from being the rebound guy. That way he doesn't ever commit, either. No one gets hurt and everyone's happy. Or so they say."

"Not everyone."

"Weird thing, though, miss," he said, looking at me in the rear-view mirror and missing a traffic barrier by a fraction of an inch. "I hear some old chick's doing the same thing with guys."

"I don't think she's so old," I leaned forward to hear him better. "You seem to know a lot about these people."

"I listen, I learn."

I looked out at the rain streaming down the window the rest of the ride home and started to plot my revenge. It was the only way to make things right in the world. True to the way the night had gone, after I paid the fare, I again had to step into a puddle in the gutter. "Really, you fucking asshole," I yelled at the driver as he pulled away, his rear left tire splashing me, again to the sound of horns announcing a near collision.

"Suzanne!" A stern voice near the entrance yelled at me, I turned to see my lower-floor neighbor, Mary Abbye Haworth-Jones, who claimed to be a distant relative of the original Pilgrims on the Mayflower, but never produced a lineage chart. With her Airedale's leash in one hand and five-year-old son's hand in the other, she admonished me, "My son shouldn't have to hear that kind of language!" As she said it, her little darling in a Land's End rain slicker stuck out his tongue at me.

I was still angry and hurt and mad at the stupid taxi driver, so Mary Abbye felt my wrath. "It's 10:30, Mary Abbye! Your son is five, for Chrissake. He should be in bed where he wouldn't hear this kind of language from anyone but you yelling at your husband." She flipped me her pedigreed bird and stormed off down the street, dragging her precious son and dog.

My toes were too cold to throw anymore swear words at her, so I slid in my stocking feet through the main doors, buzzed myself in, half-slid into the elevator and to my loft, leaving wet footprints along the way. I threw my coat on the hook, my purse on the hall table, and plopped down on the couch so I could stare at the rainy night. Perfect night for a disintegrating romance. I stared out for at least an hour and went to bed, then stared at the ceiling, my mind racing with revenge. It would take some time to pull off because I knew 'Revenge is a dish best served cold.'

Chapter 50
Suzanne

Bar Americain is always crowded at lunch, which is why we had reservations for 11:45. Not that we wanted to eat that early, but it gave us more time to enjoy Bobby Flay's excellent wine selections. Melissa, Monique, Doreen, and I are enjoying our first glass of Anthill Farms 2014 Pinot Noir, the first of many to come. It's Saturday, and we're all dressed like we're doing a runway show mid-afternoon. We aren't, but the other girls like to tease guys. I just dress up to feel good.

Over the pleasant clatter, Doreen leaned across the table and said too loudly, "Let me get this straight. He wanted you to dump him?"

"Suzie, did he know what you've been doing?" Melissa asked, incredulously.

"He's been doing the same thing for months!" I replied. "Maybe even a year!"

Doreen hooted, "You two just happened to end up together? How does that work?"

"Not very well, thank you."

Then Doreen asked the Million Dollar Question, "Are you going to keep dating guys and making them break up with you?"

"No, I'm done," I answered, firmly. "It was fun, most of the time, but I didn't think anyone would get hurt, especially not me."

"Sweetie, you've got to lay low," Melissa chimed in. "Then we need to teach your Mister Sullivan a lesson."

"One he'll never forget," said Monique, with an evil laugh, as she signaled to our waiter for another bottle. We were getting tuned up.

"Are we all going to screw him together?" asked Doreen, lewdly.

"Doreen! Get your mind off your film career," we all said in unison.

Melissa looked at each of us as the sommelier poured our wine, "We're going to screw with him, though, aren't we?"

"I don't want to hurt him," I said. "Just teach him a lesson he'll remember for the rest of his miserable life." I looked over the rim of my wine glass, stared out the window, and my times with Jack flashed before my eyes.

"There will be pain, and he will gain," clever Monique snapped me back to the table, igniting laughter.

"We need to order before they kick us out," I joked, not feeling funny at all.

Chapter 51

Monique had made good use of her MBA from Harvard. Unable to get the high-paying position she thought she deserved, she started working as a teller at the Bank of America, where she met some of Wall Street's highest placed money managers. Of all things, they came in to help their kids open checking and savings accounts. She always gave them her BOA business card and her personal business card with her full name, Monique Delaquarte, B.S., M.B.A., Harvard, and her cell number.

One day, a customer with whom she had spent an extra amount of time explaining the penalties for bouncing checks to his twin 10-year-old daughters, told his girls to wait by the lobby coffee table and came back looking intently at her business card.

He nudged aside her next customer. "Sorry, I think I forgot my wallet," he said, smiling at the mildly disgruntled woman, then he leaned down to the narrow space beneath the bullet-proof glass teller's window. "Do you really have an M-B-A from Harvard?" he asked her, disbelief in his voice.

"Yes, is that so hard to believe?" she looked straight into his eyes, "Class of 2010."

"What the hell are you doing working as a bank teller, then?"

"I wanted to learn about banking from the ground floor," she answered, almost honestly.

He handed her his business card. "Call me tomorrow for an appointment," he said. "I want to talk to you about something before you forget everything you learned at Harvard," he almost smiled, but a guard approached.

"Everything all right, Monique?"

"A-Okay, Larry. Just fine!" she had assured him quickly. Larry Masefield was an ex-Army Ranger with many skills and personality traits that suited him to his job, but patience and tact were not among them. He looked at her customer with a jaundiced eye and then at her. She winked at him and he slowly backed away, hand on his stun gun.

"Thank you, Mr. Harmsworth," she bent down and said under the window as he walked toward his daughters. "Thank you!"

Three years after the phone call and four interviews later, Monique had an office with a view of Wall Street. Not a corner office, but she had a window and a handful of clients who trusted her.

Monique looked out at the office building across the street as she talked on her cell.

"Darling, I just need you to get him to go for a drink tonight so I can introduce him to my grief-stricken friend," she said, her voice dripping in sarcasm, which she knew Lester appreciated.

"I don't know, Monie," Lester said, looking out Jack's office window overlooking the Manhattan skyline. "He's been working late then going straight home ever since he fell for some model who dumped him, er, who he conned into dumping him," he looked at Jack, who was listening, feet up on his desk, smiling and giving him the thumbs up.

"He really fell for her?"

"Yes, Monie, he really fell for her. Hard. Like, in love hard."

"Don't say," she said to the guy with his head buried in his computer screen in the office across the street and smiled wickedly. "Just get him to Bar Americain at eight, Lester. My friend and her fiancé broke up a few months ago, and we're trying to get her over him. Please?"

"You owe me," Lester said, looking right at Jack, who swung his legs off his desk and started typing, then he paused and looked up at Lester. "Good job," he mouthed.

"Certainly, Luv," Monique said, triumphantly.

She ended the call with Lester and called Doreen.

"Okay, Doreen. We don't know if he'll be there for sure but meet me at Bobby Flay's midtown at seven-thirty tonight so we can rehearse again. And look your porn-star best."

Chapter 52

As usual on a Friday night, Bar Americain was crowded with trust-tube babies, short-sell geniuses, money managers, along with a smattering of lawyers, ad women and men. Of course, there were a few escorts, who, if the bouncers knew who they were, would be directed to some other high-end lounge up the street.

Suzanne wore a wig, floppy red hat, and huge beach sunglasses, which were not conspicuous at all, and Melissa had on a tastefully low-cut red dress taped to her cleavage. Their table was a short way from another where Monique, fresh from work, and Doreen, looking like the porn star she had been before she quit three years ago, sat sipping their Cosmos like sophisticated ladies, watching the front doors. Doreen had "retired" after a particularly violent scene in which she was forced to do things no human being should ever do, ever. After a period of healing mind, spirit, and body, she had launched her phenomenal career in commercial real estate.

When Jack, Lester, and Lew walked in, Lester made eye contact with Monique who scowled. Lester gave her a look of helpless resignation and guided Jack and Lew over to the table where she sat with Monique and Doreen.

"Hell-O, girls!"

"Les, what a nice surprise," said Monique, ever the amateur actress. "This is my good friend Doreen."

That was her cue. Doreen leaned toward Jack showing her deep cleavage, and just the rim of her right areola. She reached forward revealing, even more, to shake hands with Jack and Lew. Lew stared at her chest, giving Monique the desired result.

"Nice to finally meet you in person. I've...," Lew choked out the words, and gulped. Jack looked at him, then noticed he was shuffling his feet like an altar boy caught with a Playboy in the sacristy. 'Geez,' Jack thought, 'the guy did God-knows-how-many village sweeps in Afghanistan and this woman has him acting like he's never seen a porn star before.'

"You know my work?" Doreen asked, demurely batting her eyes.

"Only heard about it ... er, uh ... from friends," Lew stumbled.

Jack elbowed him in his ribs, which felt like elbowing a brick wall.

Lester finally broke the uncomfortable, embarrassing silence. "Aren't you going to invite us to sit?"

"Of course, sweetie," Monique, said. While smiling at Jack and Lew, she leaned over and pulled Lester's lapel before he could sit, and whispered in his ear, "What the hell are you doing, you little shit? You were supposed to bring him alone!"

"Jack's given up on dating," he whispered back. "He thought Lew could help your friend get over her breakup."

"What are you two plotting?" Jack leaned in and asked, jokingly.

As if on cue, Lester looked around and asked, "What's everyone drinking? I'll run to the bar."

Across the room, Suzanne watched Jack over her sunglasses using her best spy in a trench coat acting technique learned from a long-ago magazine perfume shoot. She saw Jack look right at her and too quickly pushed the glasses up to the bridge of her nose. He looked right by her, surveyed the room and turned away, smiling a mostly innocent Machiavellian smile.

His evil was cut short when Lester and a waiter brought their drinks. Lester took the drinks from the waiter's tray and handed them out. He had to squeeze between Doreen and Lew, who were obviously falling in lust, even without vodka tonics.

Monique threw back her Cosmo in one gulp and slammed down the glass nearly breaking it. She grabbed Doreen's elbow at the soft spot just above the joint and said, "Excuse us, Doreen and I absolutely must to visit the ladies' room."

"We do? That hurts!"

Monique pulled her off the stool and headed through the crowd to the ladies' room. Monique walked by each stall and pushed open the doors to make sure they were alone, just like she had seen done in cop movies. Then she locked the door, which caused a near panic outside. "Hey, I'm gonna pee, and I'm not wearing panties! You hear?"

"That really, really hurt, Doreen!"

"You're supposed to hustle Jack, not this Lew!"

Ignoring the whiny bitches pounding on the door, Monique grabbed Doreen by both shoulders and faced her.

"Well?"

"But Lew's younger!"

"I don't care, Doreen. The whole idea is to get Jack to fall for you, just like we planned. Then, in a couple of weeks, I'll seduce him away from you. Then Melissa will take him. Then we'll confront him and make a big scene. Get it?"

"Seems mean."

"He deserves it after tricking Suzanne."

The pounding had become louder and more demanding. "If I ruin these shoes, bitch...!"

"But wasn't she tricking him too?" Doreen pointed out.

"You'll never understand, Doreen," Monique said, exasperated. "Just go out there and shove your tits in Jack's face. Got it?"

"Oh, well, okay."

"Put a paper towel over your mouth when you go out."

The pounding had stopped and there was the sound of a key unlocking the door. A bouncer scowled at Doreen as she squeezed by him and seven women stampeded by him to get to the stalls.

"Sorry, sorry, ladies. My friend just returned from Mexico. She got Montezuma's Revenge and had it coming out of both ends. You didn't need to see it. It was so fucking gross!"

"Lying bitch!" they yelled in unison.

Back at their table, Doreen obediently sidled up to Jack provocatively.

"Sorry about your breakup," Jack said, sympathetically and almost honestly, but he had to put his fist to his mouth to keep from laughing.

"Breakup?" Doreen asked, innocently.

"Yeah, you know, Doreen, is it? With your fiancé."

"Oh, yeah, him," she remembered her role in the play. "I'm just getting over it," she said, remembering what Monique had told her. "We were engaged for two years. And three months. And ..."

"Honey," Monique said, cutting Doreen off before she could expose the entire ruse, "why don't you have Jack take you home?"

"Can't, Monique," Jack apologized. "Have to get home to my dog, who's been cooped up all day. But Lew would love to see you home, wouldn't you, Lew?"

"With pleasure, I hope," Lew said, finally regaining his SEAL courage.

"Down, boy!" Jack laughed. "Just take her home without embarrassing either one of us."

"Aye, aye, Cap'n!"

Monique scowled at Doreen, who leaned over and whispered in her ear,

"I'm gonna get laid tonight and you're not!"

Lew took Doreen by the hand and led her through the crowd.

"I'm meeting people here in a bit, Jack," Lester said.

"Okay, see ya mañana, Les."

Jack finished his drink and wended his way out of the restaurant. As he did, he walked past Suzanne and smiled at her without any sign of recognition. He turned and bumped into a table full of people.

"Sorry, folks, sorry."

He turned around to look again, but Suzanne and Melissa had mysteriously disappeared.

"Shit, oh, shit!" Suzanne said from under the table.

"Do you think he recognized you?" Melissa asked.

They both turned their heads to see a man's legs at their table, toes pointing in.

"Shit, shit, SHIT!" Suzanne said, sounding totally unsure now.

Then Lester's head appeared.

"Hello again, girls! Lose something? Like your...minds?!"

"Oh, shut the F up, Les! Is he gone?" Melissa had the presence of mind to ask.

Lester lifted his head from under the table and pretended to look around, except the only direction he looked was toward the front door. He watched Jack go out and hail a taxi. Then he stuck his head back under the table.

"All clear, girls. He just got in a taxi. You can try to regain what's left of your dignity."

Suzanne and Melissa scrambled from under the table, smoothed wrinkles from their dresses and brushed themselves off. Suzanne had retrieved her floppy red hat while nearly stepping on her cheap sunglasses, which she held up to show people who were staring at them. "Found them," she said, smiling as if relieved to have recovered the most expensive Oakleys. They gave her thumbs up and turned back to their drinks.

The taxi Jack was in slowly turned the corner and drove by the window outside Suzanne and Melissa's table. "Slow down a little more, please," he commanded the driver. Jack peered into the bar just as Melissa and Suzanne crawled from beneath their table. Jack watched the women gather themselves and he gave the thumbs up sign to Lester after they sat down. Lester watched the taxi creep by, held his hand behind Suzanne, whose back was to the window, and returned the gesture.

"Okay, Miguel," Jack said, "Vamoose!"

Chapter 53
Jack

Mondays are crappy days to hold creative meetings. Everyone's still scrambling to finish campaigns they worked on at home Sunday afternoon, against my orders, and prepare them for presentations to clients later in the week. Account executives occupy entire Mondays regaling one another with tales of sandbagging their golf games so prospective clients could win by just a few strokes, and then submitting four rounds of McCallan 25 as meals. Accounting had strict orders from Langston to pay their weekend expenses by end of business on Monday, no matter how shady. Conversely, the end of every month my team had to beg for each sheet of foam core.

Mondays are my days to prepare for the rest of the week, which includes gearing up for any confrontations with Langston about how unethical it would be to represent two major automobile manufacturers, even if starting a subsidiary agency was created. I spent part of this Monday thinking about last Thursday and how well a devious plan comes together when the actors are committed to the con. I smiled a lot, maybe too much, throughout the day.

My team had assembled around my conference table bright and early Tuesday. To my left stood Lanny, our most talented and most weirdly transformed graphic artist. During her interviews, Lanny looked like the sweet blonde kid she appeared to be – a graduate of the Rochester Institute of Technology with two years of experience designing websites and billboards for a small agency in Rochester. Six months after joining us, one day after completing her probation, she waltzed off the elevator sporting purple and pink hair on the left side of her head; the other side shaved to reveal a Chinese dragon tattoo and an earlobe pierced to the helix (hey, I was married to a doctor). She was wearing black high-top, platform patent leather boots, skin-tight yoga pants, and a black cardigan, which proved to be one-tenth of her new ongoing daily wardrobe.

Jet, as Jeremy Windsor liked to be called, is our lead video liaison. He was an excellent director, so we counted on him to convey our clients' needs and our storyboards to outside directors and film crews we always hired. It's cheaper to hire freelance professionals than to have employees sitting around cleaning lenses and oiling dollies between shots. Jet came to us from Hollywood after a dispute with the Director's Guild protesting their admitting a certain actor who Jet believed could barely direct himself to the nearest portable toilet on set. So, he packed up his two Oscars, three Director's Guild awards and headed east. Langston hired him on the spot when he walked into our reception area while Langston happened to be there. That was seven years ago, and I must admit, Jet is everything you'd never associate with a Hollywood type – genuine, honest, and not a flashy dresser. He prefers Levis over Gucci, Bass Weejuns, and okay real Polos.

Tall and muscular, Amanda Lewis is an anomaly in advertising. She's an honest-to-God writer with unbridled curiosity and exceptional skills backed by a rich imagination. She always sat across from Jet, hoping she could get him to tell her about his life. Not even Lester knows Jet's sexual orientation, not that it was anyone's business, but you can't blame a former WNBA player for trying.

Amanda had grown up in West Des Moines, Iowa, the daughter of a press operator at Meredith Publishing and an English professor at Drake. During her interview, I learned she had played college ball at the University of Iowa, had refused to drop her final year there to play in the pros. Instead, she completed her degree in English Lit then, much to her mother's pride, earned a Master's degree in secondary education. At the ripe old age of 23, Amanda had been drafted by the Minnesota Lynx, where she played for three years. Amanda was the starting center her final year until a hip check by an opposing player caused her to land awkwardly, tearing her ACL. When she returned to the court the balance of the year she was hobbled by a futuristic-looking knee brace after surgery and recovery, which prompted her retirement. The only good thing to come out of the whole experience, she said during her job interview, was meeting her future husband, an EMT-RN in Minneapolis. He was an inch taller than her and held her hand during her MRI because he was at the end of his shift and told her he liked the way she looked in basketball shorts. That earned him an excruciating, he later admitted, slug in his solar plexus. Once he could breathe again, he informed her she owed him dinner at an expensive restaurant. She had laughingly agreed because he was almost handsome for a tall white guy and he made her laugh. She didn't know how he had arranged it, but he had also been in the recovery room after her ACL repair, warming her icy hands with his. The damn nurses even called him by his first name, she vaguely remembered. He kissed her forehead, a complete shock, when they loaded her gurney into the team van, then disappeared. She hadn't seen him for a few weeks after that, but she was busy with therapy, doctor visits, and team meetings, so she only missed him a little every day. One day, he was waiting for her outside the team practice facility in a camouflage uniform. She recalled their conversation as only a writer would:

"Hey, Michele Jordan," he said, as I hobbled out, looking like the Bionic Woman.

"I thought you gave up on me, you jerk."

"Never. Guard camp. I'm a medic. Had to treat blisters, heat stroke, the usual. What, no crutches?" he asked.

"Went to a tent revival and threw them down. I've been healed!"

"We laughed. Then the damn guy hugged me like he meant it and gave me a kiss like he had missed me, and I kissed him back like I had never kissed anyone. We got married eight months later in Des Moines, and after our honeymoon in Tahiti, he applied for a job with the NYFD, which he got after two months on the waiting list, and you've seen my samples and I know I can be a good copywriter."

"What did your parents think?"

"About what?"

"Your husband is white, right?"

"You didn't really just ask me that, did you?"

"Let's pretend I didn't, but you mentioned it a few minutes ago."

"Okay ... so I did, but if you hire me, I'm going to hold it over your head for a very long time. Yes, he's a Minnesota Norwegian, so he's so damn white he's almost translucent. But my parents love him because he loves me, and they know we can both beat the shit out of anyone who looks at us weirdly. The great thing about living in New York is that no one ever does."

And then there's Gregory, junior account executive, who we all know is the office snitch. He must be about 29, but no one knows for sure, and we don't know anything about his background or education. He always dresses well, has perfectly styled black hair, smells like a perfume counter, and makes a beeline for his supervisor's office after every meeting he sits in on.

"So our challenge, then," I reminded them, "is to create a dynamic campaign that's going to make Americans want this hybrid in their garages. And that, my friends, will create and keep jobs for the automaker's workers, which is what marketing is all about."

Ever the smart ass, Gregory was quick to say in a stage whisper, "And create billable hours and media commissions."

Some nervous laughter, but it ended quickly.

"Thanks for that insight, Greg," my voice dripped with sarcasm, as it usually did when I responded to Gregory's remarks.

"That's the reality, Jack," he said, always needing to have the last word, like the spoiled shit he is.

"Okay, let's start listing what turns people on about this particular model."

"Instant death in a crash?" quipped Lester.

Even I laughed.

"Ninety miles to the gallon?" Lanny asked.

"Close, Lanny. Forty-two."

"Saving the environment?" asked Jet.

"Tax benefits?" asked Amanda.

"All good points," I said. "But, I've driven one, and this car is fun to drive! One option is a ruby red convertible."

"Models in tight wet tank tops front and back. That's sexy. Langston will love that," Gregory, Langston's sycophant eagerly chimed in.

"Langston thinks sex sells everything, Greg," I said, knowing full well that would go directly back to our CEO. "We can be sexy without being tawdry."

"Subtlety lost Barnabas, Shadows, and Collins this account, Jack," he said, smug as ever.

"No, Greg, following the crowd and padding their bills lost them the account," I informed him, rather firmly, which embarrassed him. "Besides, we're doing this on speculation. They can tell us they hate it and then use it in six months, which is why we're going to mail ourselves a certified copy of everything we produce. Now..."

Before I could continue, Gregory stormed toward the door, turned around, and, voice quaking, said, "Langston wants sexy back, mister creative director. Last I checked, he signs the checks around here."

He swung open the door, but unfortunately, his left foot caught the bottom and it nearly knocked him over as it swung back. He stormed out, trying to recover what was left of his dignity.

"Okay, the Greg Show is over for today," I told the rest of the team. "Let's get back to work. Forget the car's features; we need more benefits to families?"

"You're always welcome, Gregory," Langston said as he slowly looked up from his computer screen, "but you do need to knock. It looks suspicious when you just barge in."

"Sorry, boss, but you need to hear this right away." Gregory related what

had gone on in the creative meeting he had just been asked to leave, he lied.

"They kicked you out? How do you know they won't do sex in the campaign?"

"I don't, but Jack's a good two weeks from even doing storyboards," Gregory accurately explained. "And, and ... they're talking about consumers as if they're smart enough to care about anything except getting laid!"

"We're meeting with the client in three days. I'll tell Jack he needs a dog and pony show then. And if he can't, I'll find someone who can meet my deadlines, whether they know them or not."

They both laughed.

Chapter 54
Suzanne

I haven't felt this miserable-happy since I hoped my husband would ask me to marry him. I was sure he wouldn't, so if he didn't on our fourteenth date, I was going to ask him, but to his credit, he beat me to the punch, or I would have socked him in the gut and then when he was doubled over, I would have helped him straighten up, looked him in his beautiful brown eyes, and popped the question. At least, that's how I had imagined it would have gone.

Now, try as I might, I just couldn't get this damn Jack Sullivan out of my head ... and my heart, for good reason.

Melissa and I sat on my couch, everyone's favorite spot, looking out at the entrancing NYC skyline. We were drinking a delicious bottle of Bordeaux, a gift from Jack, but I didn't tell Melissa.

"Hon," she said, "you haven't been on a date in two months." As if it were a crime against womanhood.

"Fifty-seven days."

"Still too long."

"I'm far too busy."

"Bullshit! Your last shoot was three months ago."

"Eighty-three days."

"Oh, whatever...You need to get out."

"I'm just not in the mood to deal with men."

"You mean with one man?"

"No, men. They're all so much work."

"You love him, don't you? Don't you? That's why you walk past his office building every day."

"I am not that desperate! My agent happens to be in the next building. How did you know?"

"I didn't. You just told me, sweetie."

"I dumped him, he dumped me. We dumped each other the same night. I won't go through it again," I said, smiling out the window.

"Call him!"

I turned to her and smiled in a 'schoolgirl going to prom' way, "I don't have to," I said, "He called, I answered, and he invited me to dinner to meet his daughters."

"You horrible, sneaky bitch! I love you!" Melissa said. "More of Jack's wine, please?"

"How did you ...?"

"Never mind."

Chapter 55
Suzanne

I had made a few calls, called in a few favors and spent the day before running around the city picking up chef's aprons from Mario Batali, Wolfgang Puck, Bobbie Flay, and Martha Stewart. Between stops, I phoned to my two sons about how to talk to college girls.

"How the hell should I know, Mom?" Jimmie asked. "I still get tongue-tied unless I've had four shots of tequila and a couple beers!"

"You better not be drinking that much," I hollered into the phone. "Or I'll have Mark rip off your lips."

"Jeeze, relax Mom! Strong talk for such a petite woman. Anyway, I'm just kidding. I only drink that much on the weekends, which start on Thursday and end on Wednesday."

"James!"

"Gotcha again! Anyway, don't try to be too chummy. No hugging. No Hollywood kisses. And absolutely no fawning bullshit. Just be your normal, pampered-model self, and they'll kinda like you."

"Thanks for that wonderful advice, James," I said sarcastically.

Mark had been slightly more helpful, but not much. "You probably don't want to wear your usual tailored clothes, expensive perfume or a lot of makeup. Just something simple and understated – and don't try to be their best friend right away. Maybe even for a few months, if you and Jack – that's his name, right – are together that long. Oh, and Mom, don't talk down to them. They're adults, so don't try to talk how you think college girls talk, so don't start every sentence with 'like'."

"Got it. Thanks, Mark."

"After all the losers, I hope this guy's the one, Mom. I really do."

"I'm pretty sure he is, Mark. And I think he feels the same way. I hope."

"Bye, Mom. Good luck. Remember, you're not their pal ... yet."

The next evening my nerves were on edge as I walked up the brownstone's steps with the bag full of chef's aprons worried about being accepted by Jack and his daughters.

Jack swung the door open after the bell barely had time to ring. He wore an apron covered in red sauce, so we shook hands, he took the bag from me and motioned me into the hall. I slid past him and then he grabbed my arm and spun me around. He had taken off the apron and he slid his arms around my waist. Jack kissed me like a sailor who'd been too long at sea. I responded like the girl who'd been missing him far too long. Then a hairy head came between our hips and there was a duet of 'Ahems' from the end of the hall. Jack ignored them and whispered in my ear, "God, how I've missed you! I was a complete jerk. It was all my fault for not being honest about my true feelings. I'm so, so sorry about everything."

Breathless and embarrassed, I looked deeply into his eyes and mouthed, "Me, too, Jack, me, too." I squeezed his biceps to punctuate the point, we parted and he picked up the stained apron and the bag. Turning to the end of the hall, he pushed the massive dog aside, saying, "Girls, I'd like you to meet Suzanne."

They smiled politely as we shook hands. Their handshakes were firm and they looked me in the eyes like a mongoose looks at a cobra. Nobody ever said getting on the good side of young women would be easy.

When we got to the dining room, I offered them the autographed aprons. The girls picked their favorites, I took Bobby Flay's (Sorry, Bobby!), then Abby and I followed Jack into the kitchen, where he was checking on chicken enchiladas and putting fresh guacamole on the table with a pitcher of sangria.

Jack excused himself for a moment and Abby and I were alone; she showed me where her dad kept the silverware while she pulled red plates from a glass-fronted buffet. Apparently, Kate was rummaging around in a closet somewhere looking for Mexican-themed napkins and a matching tablecloth. I supposed that's where Jack had disappeared to.

"Your dad seems to be a great cook, Abby," I said, carefully using her shortened name.

"He didn't used to be."

"Did he take cooking lessons?"

"Not really," she said, placing the silverware on the plates. "He and my mom cooked together a lot," she explained, "but then she'd get called to the hospital to deal with a psychotic patient and my dad would have to finish the meal. He always kept a plate in the oven for her when she had to leave. Or, when she had to work late. He just started cooking all the time so she could do her dictation. When she got sick and had to stay home, he just kept cooking, one meal for her and another for us three..."

"He's quite a guy, your Dad."

"You're never going to take her place, you know that, don't you?"

"I'd never try, Abby," I said sincerely, putting my hands on the island and turning to look directly into her sky-blue eyes. "But maybe you and I can be friends, like maybe a favorite aunt and her favorite niece."

"Whatever," she said, picking up the plates.

"Wait, Abby, that word is very dismissive, and if we're to be friends, please don't use it when we talk and I'll promise to get you a free lifetime supply of Cover Girl cosmetics." That got her attention.

"Really?!"

"Really," I said, still looking into her beautiful eyes, which now had turned up in smiles at the corners. "Just one of the many perks of being their aging, former model."

"I can't be bought."

"Of course not!" I said with a small laugh. "Just think of it as a huge tax-free bribe."

"It's a start...You're kinda funny. My mom was funny, too."

'It's a start,' I said to myself. "Let's set the table, shall we?"

The meal was beyond delicious, the sangria flowed freely as did the conversation and the laughter as I told stories about the hilarity that has happened on commercial and ad campaign photo shoots throughout my career so Abby and Kate didn't think it had been all flowing gowns and champagne. Then, when they were in tears of laughter, I launched into stories about my rebound girl dates, leaving out the ones that had become nearly abusive and dangerous. Jack then told some of his rebound guy stories, and the girls suddenly stopped laughing and their jaws dropped.

"What the fuck, dad!" Kate said, loud enough for Darby to scramble out from under the table and head upstairs.

"Language, Katherine!" Jack said.

"Really?" Both girls exclaimed in unison.

"You never told us you were doing that, too," Abby said.

"You are at school and it just never came up," he said, calmly.

"Well, shit," Kate said.

"Did you sleep with all those women?" Abby asked.

"Not a one," Jack promised. "That was one of my basic rules because sex changes the game."

"Mom would be so proud," Kate said, her sarcasm filling the room like smoke from a blocked chimney.

This was followed by an uncomfortable silence until Darby snuck back into the room and began to lick food from my plate. It broke the tension, and I stood up and took everyone's plates into the kitchen. Jack excused himself to go to the bathroom. Too much sangria, I supposed. I heard low tones of argument, then Abby finally said to Kate so I could hear, "Dad deserves to move on, Kate. You have, so have I. And Suzanne is nice. I like her. So does Dad. I think she'll be good for him."

Through the kitchen door, I saw Jack enter the dining room and start putting away the salt and pepper shakers and then rolling up the tablecloth. The girls came into the kitchen carrying silverware and baking dishes. Kate put the silverware in the dishwasher and filled the pan to soak. After rinsing her hands, she turned to me, stepped in close and hugged me warmly, "I'm sorry for what I said. I know Dad likes you, and I hope you like him because if you don't, I'll make Abby give me all the free makeup."

"Deal," I said, through tears, hugging her back as hard as I dared. Then we heard the crash. We rushed into the dining room. Jack lay crumpled on the floor, a chair overturned on top of him, the tablecloth unfurled on the floor.

"Call 9-1-1," I said as calmly as I could. Jack was pale and unresponsive, but one of the girls, I don't remember which, slipped a couple aspirin between his lips. He spit them out.

"Bitter," he mumbled.

"Chew these," I commanded as I slid them in again. He did. I can't lose him, God. Not after all we've done to get together.

"Are you having pain down your neck and left arm?" I asked.

"No, I think I just fainted. Too much sangria. Dropped tablecloth. Stood up too fast."

Just then the doorbell rang. Abby let in the EMTs, who administered more aspirin and hooked up Jack to EKG wires. After a few minutes, one of the EMTs announced, "The EKG doesn't indicate a heart attack, but we need to take you to the ER for observation, Mr. Sullivan. Standard procedure."

They allowed the girls and me to ride in the ambulance to the hospital. We were greeted by a lovely doctor who immediately recognized Jack. She leaned close to his head as she lifted each eyelid.

"Now what have you done, Jack," asked Dr. VanDorn. She directed the EMTs to transfer Jack to an empty bed. "A real health scare?"

"He's fine, Doc. Just fainted."

"You gave us a scare, Jack," I said. "Don't ever do that again."

"Okay."

Dr. VanDorn asked us to wait and in a few minutes pulled back the curtain.

"You can sit with him. All systems seem in good working order. I'll discharge him as soon as I do some paperwork, but we all need to talk about why Jack fainted."

The girls and I stood at the foot of the bed, one on either side of me, our arms interlocked, too nervous and relieved to sit.

"You gave us a scare, Jack," I said. "Don't ever do that again."

"Okay."

Dr. VanDorn returned and closed the curtain surrounding the bed. She looked solemnly at Jack.

"You've been running this dating game of yours for quite some time, haven't you?"

"I..."

"That was rhetorical, Jack. And, I suspect your work is highly stressful, from what I recall."

"I guess ..."

"Listen! And to top it off, you work out like you're thirty years younger, right?"

"I ..."

"Rhetorical! So, here's the plan. You're staying home for one week. No work. No running or basketball. Thirty-minute walks every day. Plenty of bed rest. Someone will need to stay with you night and day to make sure you get the rest and exercise you need. Otherwise, this exhaustion you're experiencing can lead to serious health issues. Got it?"

She looked at Jack, then at the girls and me, then back at Jack. "I suspect you have someone here who will volunteer to be your caretaker for the next week or more. Go home, Jack. Get some rest. I don't want to see you back here. Ever."

Wedged between the girls and me in the taxi, Jack was silent. It was hard for him to be otherwise.

"We have to go back to school, Suzanne," Kate said. Abby agreed. "We have tests, and papers, and stuff."

We all agreed that I would move in and take care of their dad, walk Darby and with him, cook, deal with the housekeeper, call his office, and, just to reassure them, and Jack, stay in the guest bedroom.

We were exhausted from worry and the late night, so the girls went straight to bed and Jack and I spent a half hour scheduling the week.

"You don't have to do this, Suzanne," he said every five minutes.

"Just shut up and tell me about Wednesday's."

The next morning, I grabbed a taxi to my loft, asked the driver to wait, packed a suitcase with a few days of clothes knowing I could always do laundry and was back before Kate and Abby left for school.

"Please take good care of him," Abby said as she hugged me before getting into the driver's seat. Kate stood off to the side and waved goodbye. But then she took three steps and hugged me. "You're good for him," she whispered in my ear.

I pressed my hand to my mouth to keep from crying as I waved with my left hand. It was hard to believe we had become so close in such a short time.

Jack shuffled through papers on his coffee table as I walked into the living room, Darby at his side.

"What are you doing?" I almost yelled.

"Just getting ready for Monday."

"Are you nuts?"

"No, my team counts on me being there."

"They're going to get along without you Monday and all week. Doctor's orders. And my orders. I'm not losing you, Jack."

He put down the papers and looked at me. "You're serious."

"As a heart attack!"

"Bad analogy."

"You get the point. You're staying home and I'm staying with you. Now, we're going to bed."

I grabbed his shoulders and pointed him up the stairs. "Get undressed while I take Darby out. I'll be up to check on you soon, so don't make any business calls, got it?"

"Got it, Sarge."

Darby was almost too much to handle, but he was well behaved and did his business without delay.

I got upstairs in time to see Jack's naked derriere trying to slip into bed.

"What have you been doing all this time?"

"Took a shower, brushed my teeth. The usual."

"Well, get in bed. It's 11:00!"

He slid under the covers and I went to the other side and laid on top next to him. I put my arm over his chest and snuggled with him until I heard his regular breathing. Then I gently squeezed his chest and made my way to the guest room where the sheets had been turned down and a mint placed on the pillow.

At 7 Monday morning, Jack called his personal assistant and told her he was taking personal leave all week and not to call, text, or email, and briefly explained it was for health reasons.

"She's clearing my schedule but says she can't promise Langston will understand."

"He doesn't have to understand."

"You don't know Langston."

"And I don't want to, either. You can tell me all about him if you want, though."

"Maybe later."

"Jack, tell me about your brothers."

"Let's have breakfast first."

After oatmeal and fruit, doctor's orders, we sat on the couch drinking French Press coffee.

"I suppose we were pretty typical Irish Catholics. Terry, Father Terrance, was the nice guy of us three. We were all altar boys, but he went beyond. He joined Bible studies in high school, although he went on group dates; he never really dated any one girl, although there was one who fawned over him. Anyway, Terry wasn't holier-than-thou. He pulled pranks, was on the wrestling team, and stood up to bullies for younger kids. In college, he just decided to go to the seminary to see if that was for him, and it was. Mom and Dad think they're going straight to heaven because they raised a priest."

"Are they?"

"Probably, but that's not why."

"Why?"

"Because they put up with Bobby."

"Tell me more!"

"Terry and I swore Bobby was adopted because he was too smart and too stupid at the same time. He never studied, still got good grades, and spent more time in the principal's office than any other four kids because he was always challenging the teachers. One time he called Sr. Anne Marie stupid during Algebra because she solved some problem wrong and still got the correct answer. Well, after she smashed his nose with the textbook, she sent him and his bloody handkerchief to the principal. When he got home that afternoon and Ma saw his swollen nose, she marched right to school. She told Sr. Anne Marie that if anyone was going to break her Bobby's nose it would be her. Sr. Anne Marie transferred to another high school and Bobby was elevated to school hero. Ma made him do all our laundry for a month. It was great!"

"And you, Jack Sullivan?"

"Me? Just the average high school jock who wrote and had a good imagination, joined the Marines, went to college on the G.I. Bill, started as a copywriter, worked my way up, met Missy, took care of her, then came up with a cockamamie scheme that led me to you."

"That's quite the synopsis."

"We have time for details. Now, how about you?"

"Let me think about it for a day or so. I don't want to leave out the good stuff."

We read that afternoon. Since it was Monday, Jack had a hard time relaxing. He kept looking at his watch. Finally, I reached over, grabbed his hand. "I should have done this sooner," I said, unclasping it and sliding from his wrist. I stuffed it between the couch arm and cushion. "There. No more checking the time. Now, let's cuddle, then we can take naps after I start some laundry."

Cuddling led to a little more than that, but still platonic. "Off you go to bed. I'll be up in a while. We need to establish a pattern for the week so you're well rested when you return to work."

Tuesday was the same, except no laundry. We relaxed. Jack and I walked Darby. Three times. I cooked. He had settled down and minded me. Afternoon naps were restful. I was enjoying the time off and being together. We learned we could just be together.

After breakfast on Wednesday, we faced each other on the couch drinking coffee.

"Tell me about becoming a glamorous model."

I had laid in bed the night before and ran through a timeline because I knew Jack would ask me about my life.

"My modeling career probably began typically," I said as I bent my leg up onto the couch. "My mother enrolled me in ballet at three, and one day, after a lesson when I was five, one of the other girls' fathers watched as we walked out. He stopped my mother and said something to her, I couldn't hear what, and I saw her smile politely when he handed her a business card. On the ride home, she told me he owned a clothing company and wanted me to model their children's clothes in catalogs. That was the start of my career. I wasn't an ugly duckling who grew into a swan. I always had blonde hair and blue eyes. I worked. Had tutors all through school. Paid for college. Modeled during breaks and summers. Had a reputation for showing up on time and not being difficult. That's it."

"And how did you meet your husband?"

"Not an exciting story at all. I was modeling a line of raincoats in front of the hospital ... don't ask ... and he sat on a bench across the street and ate his lunch during the entire shoot. Staring. It apparently was the end of his shift, otherwise, he couldn't have sat there the entire time. As we were packing up to leave, he came up and asked me for my number so he could call me for a date. I looked up into those gorgeous eyes of his and said, 'Go away!' He got my number from hospital administration who got it from the agency and he called. I hadn't had a date in a long time, so I agreed to go out, but with our schedules, it took a while for us to get together. We had a great first date and every date after that, and a great marriage."

"I'm sorry he died. How did it happen?"

I told him about being on the shoot in the Caribbean and the traumatic flight home. As I talked, Jack held me tight and gently wiped tears that I couldn't stop. Despite the early hour, we fell asleep in each other's arms. Darby, ever-demanding Darby, woke us up for his mid-day potty break.

The rest of the week went per doctor's orders, and we celebrated with a date night on Saturday and Sunday brunch, followed by dinner at the Sullivan's. It was during that week that I fell deeply in love with Jack Sullivan.

Chapter 56
Jack

After my week off, I felt like I had been gone a year, but as soon as I got off the elevator, four of my team launched a combination of welcome backs and here's our big challenge, so get ready. I walked to my office, saw that my computer had been booted up, had a gazillion Sticky Notes all over it, so I promptly shut it down and walked to the conference room where my team had already assembled.

Brooklyn Brewery had decided to go nationwide, starting from its base on the Eastern Seaboard to the Mississippi next year and two years later to the West Coast. They had picked our agency because of my creative team and our knowledge of national rollouts, so we are comfortably brainstorming the initial campaign after they had arranged distribution (with an assist from an Irishman I knew who still felt he owed me) and finessed all the complexities of state licensing.

We had pulled in Jane Garfield, one of our ace researchers, to detail her department's findings over the past six months.

"The last two focus groups preferred the taste of our beer four to one over all competitors," she explained, as she wrote some beer names and figures on a whiteboard.

"We could show a taste test," Lester piped up.

"Let's piggyback on that idea. Anyone?" I said looking around the table. Then Gregory stuck his head in my office, like a snake looking for its next meal.

"'Scuse, please," it hissed.

"What is it, Greg?" I asked him.

"It's 'Gregory'... And management wants your team in the thirty-first-floor conference room. Pronto!"

Everyone, including me, got up to leave.

"Just your team, Jack," Gregory said with a smirk. "They don't need you ... just yet."

The others looked at me quizzically, but I motioned for them to go and indicated that I would be there later. I went to my desk and tried to check my email. Strange, I thought, something's wrong. System must be down. I tried the scheduling program. Access blocked.

I pushed a button and called my assistant. "Nadine, please call I-T and have them send a tech up here. I can't access the server."

As I punched a few more keys, my office door swung open and in walked Langston, wearing a Ralph Lauren ensemble, another guy in a fancy suit, and two of our security guards from the ground floor, each carrying two banker's boxes.

"That won't be necessary, Jack," Langston said. "Nothing's broken."

Nadine peered around the door jam and looked past the guards at me, tears in her eyes. I smiled weakly at her. Then the fancy suit gently pushed her out, but she said loudly, "Get your hands off me or I'll file a harassment claim with HR, you goon!"

"I am the HR attorney, Doreen!" he said, as he quietly closed my office door.

While all eyes were on that little dustup, I had time to reformat the hard drive on my desktop. Childish, I know, and quite possibly illegal, but it wouldn't take an I-T genius more than an afternoon to reinstall the necessary programs. Small price to pay, in addition to the large severance package they made me sign as the guards packed up my photos and trophies.

"Sign it now and get your year's salary and banked leave and swear you won't sue for unlawful termination or age discrimination. "Or," he said as he looked down at me as he slid the single page across my desk, which he obviously had had days to prepare, "you leave with nothing, and we'll see you in court."

My mind raced through the benefits of signing. I read the document three times as Langston tapped his fingers on my desk. Just to make sure there was nothing in it about creating a hostile work environment due to my objections to working for two major automobile manufacturers at the same time, or Langston's sometimes crude jokes about Catholic guilt and Las Vegas Bunny Ranches. Nope. The genius had failed to include that, probably because he was too embarrassed and knew his HR lawyer would hyperventilate at the mention of including it.

"I'd like my signature notarized on the original and on my copy," I politely demanded, not wanting to make this easy, although they HR lawyer had anticipated my request by including a notary space at the bottom of the document. He punched a number on his cell and slimy Gregory, wearing a "gotcha" grin, waltzed in carrying his notary stamp.

The ride down the elevator was silent. I couldn't think of any appropriate smart-ass remarks, and the two guards weren't offering up any words of warning or wisdom. They had taken my key cards and given the main floor front desk guard what looked like a wanted poster with my picture on it and the headline DO NOT ADMIT in block letters below it.

As I finished loading the last of the four boxes into the trunk of a taxi, James, one of the guards, who I'd known for years, closed the trunk lid for me.

I stepped up on the curb and grabbed James' elbow. "Thanks, James."

"No problem," he said. "See ya, Jack."

"Ya, see you sometime, James."

"You're the real talent, Jack. Everyone knows his arrogance is completely unjustified. You got a raw deal. And you can call me Jimmy."

"Thanks ... er, Jimmy."

Despite feeling relieved to be rid of the office games and Langston's unethical bullshit, I was still in shock as the taxi carried me away from the building where I had spent so much time and talent for nearly 20 years.

I should have recognized the signs a lot earlier. Langston, or one of his partners, had been shutting down my creative ideas during executive meetings the past few months. And Langston never let an occasion go by without some snide anti-Catholic remark, especially Ash Wednesday when several people in our building, me included, showed up with what he called 'dirt' on their foreheads. I always noted them.

"For the third time, buddy, where to?" the exasperated taxi driver asked. I gave him my home address, he cursed and made a U-turn as horns honked and tires squealed.

I laughed until the tears rolled down my cheeks.

That night I called my daughters to tell them what had happened. They asked if I was okay. I was still in shock, but I told them I would be okay once my mental dust settled. I knew the girls were worried about their college expenses, and I didn't blame them. I told them I would look over all my finances the next day after I had a good run with Darby and a gut-busting brunch at the Clinton Street Café with Suzanne. Then I called Suzanne and told her. "That bastard!" she yelled into the phone. "I'll tell you all about it at brunch tomorrow if you're available," I said, rather calmly.

"Of course!"

Chapter 57
Jack

The next morning, I ran hard, so hard almost had to drag Darby the last two blocks. Both our tongues were dragging as I wiped his slathering jaws and filled his water bowl. I stripped off my sweat-soaked clothes, shaved, showered, called Uber and rode to the Clinton Street Café where Suzanne was third in line on the sidewalk in front of the entrance. We both smiled, kissed warmly, then she pushed me back and looked at me with a worried mother's look. "Are you going to be okay?"

"You bet," I said, honestly, "after bacon and fluffy pancakes!"

We held hands in line, so I guess we had reached that PDA stage. We ordered one stack, bacon, two plates, two coffees, and grabbed a table at the window as soon as a young couple got up.

"Do you want to tell me about it," Suzanne asked, very concerned. So I told her everything, a lot of which she punctuated with, "That bastard!" I explained that during my run I had gone over everything, my finances, my 401K conversion to an IRA with my investment broker, my savings, and what the idiots had omitted from my severance agreement. Everything. She took it all in stride, especially when I explained how I had Abby's and Kate's college expenses and student loans covered so they would graduate debt-free. I also knew I could pay the real estate taxes on my brownstone until I was 104 years old, and follow her to Paris or wherever she went to be the face of some perfume.

After brunch, we went back to my place and she helped me write everything down on a legal pad and then enter it into a spreadsheet I could show Abby and Kate when they came home Sunday. When we finished that, we played strip poker but chickened out when we got to our underwear. Then we switched to backgammon, which she won, and Scrabble, which she also won!

She teased, "Aren't words your life, Mr. Writer?"

"Gloating is beneath you," I said. "Besides, you've been cheating by using big words I don't know."

"L-O-S-E-R"

"Okay, enough, enough. How about we see just how smart you really are, and you come to family dinner at the Sullivan house tomorrow?

"I'll wear something slinky and low cut."

"You do, and my mother will find you a black head-to-toe shawl and my brother will perform an exorcism to cast out my demons, you among them!"

"I'll wear my best Catholic schoolgirl uniform."

"Deal. And exciting!"

We spent the rest of the evening holding hands on the couch trading rebound date stories, laughing at ourselves and how two people could come up with similar schemes. As she told me about talking to her husband's gravestone about the horrible things his friends had suggested she and they do together, it hit me. I looked at her as if I had been struck by lightning.

She was startled when I grabbed both her shoulders.

"Do you, by chance, have a Burberry raincoat, and is your husband buried at St. John Cemetery?"

"Yes, and yes, but how did you ...Oh, my God, Jack, you're the guy I tripped over at the cemetery!"

Neither of us could believe it. It was if some unknown force had brought us together. We shuddered at the thought but accepted the whole last two years as mere coincidence. Sometimes, great minds, or even grieving minds, think alike.

We were too stunned to talk much, so we sat and held hands; our conversation was clipped --

"Do you think...?"

"No, do you ..."

"Well, no ..."

"But ..."

"Maybe ..."

"Couldn't ..."

Later Suzanne fell asleep in my arms, so I carried her up to my bedroom and covered her with a comforter. After I took Darby out for his nightly bladder duty, I made my bed on the couch and crashed.

Next morning, Suzanne was licking my face at six to tell me she was going home to shower and change. Well, no, Darby was licking my face; but Suzanne was smiling down on me, coffee cups and her shoes in hand.

With a sultry lilt in her voice, she asked, "Why didn't you come up to bed, Jack?"

"I didn't want to spoil our evening," I said after a sip of great coffee. "Besides, I want our first time to be special, and I have really bad breath."

She sat on the coffee table and brushed the hair out of my eyes. Putting her hand on my wrinkled cheek, she smiled sweetly and said, "Score one for Jack Sullivan." She walked to the kitchen, put her cup on the counter, and walked down the hall. "See ya later, alligator," she said over her shoulder as she opened the front door.

"After a while, crocodile!" I hollered.

Just like that, she was gone. I was up, putting on my shoes, and trying like hell to get Darby's leash on his weaving neck so he could pee; but me first, old dog.

On my way to Mass Saturday evening, I texted Suzanne my parents' address. At church, I prayed Bobby would have a near-death experience that would keep him in the ER until Sunday evening. Nothing serious, just enough to keep him from grilling Suzanne throughout Sunday dinner.

Family dinner. Pot roast. Biscuits. Bobby. Shit! Suzanne looking fabulous in a tasteful Kelly-green dress, white blouse, and off-white scarf with shamrocks. What a suck-up! Both my daughters were there, having a great time talking and joking with Suzanne. That relieved me beyond belief and didn't give Bobby an opening to ask her many questions. She also was a hit with my mom during dessert, which she ate down to the last bite. She told me afterward she would need to do an extra two hours of hot yoga to burn off. What a trooper!

Mom, Pa, Bobby and his wife retired to the living room. Abby, Kate, Suzanne, who insisted on helping with the dishes, and I cleared the table and laughed about blocking Bobby's inquisition. The girls were getting more relaxed around Suzanne. A trip to the ER with good old Jack can do that.

Once we finished the dishes, we went into the living room where they thanked their grandparents for the meal, kissed them, and Suzanne and I walked them out to their car. They hugged me warmly and hugged and kissed Suzanne. As they drove away and waved through the windows, I looked at her.

"How much did you pay them?"

"Free make-up for life."

"I gave them life and all I got was a hug," I said, feigning hurt feelings.

"You gotta know how to satisfy their needs, Jack!"

"What I need now is you, Suzie-Q!" I said, pulling her in and kissing her like I should have last night. Then, she pulled away and, breathless, said, "Look at the living room window."

The curtains were parted, and four heads peered out like a totem pole. Mom and Dad and Bobby's wife were smiling, Bobby had his tongue out and was flipping me the bird. Ever the class act. Where is a near-death experience when you need one?

Chapter 58
Jack

The next few months were a whirlwind of activity. I spent my days writing, working out, reconnecting with friends and poring over my finances with my financial adviser. One day over our third lunch in five weeks he said, "Jack, you're my friend, but I don't want to see you until our annual review in 13 months. You're giving me a nervous tick – you have plenty of money, the girls will be well taken care of whether you live or die, and you and Suzanne should just get married and quit dating."

Whenever Suzanne took a job, she stipulated that she be back in the city by Thursday. That way we could be together all weekend. Many times, she was passed over by new clients due to scheduling, but her regular clients always accommodated her request, so it worked out. When she worked overseas, she was always well rested by Friday evening and all smiles when I picked her up.

We acted like two kids in our 20s, but two kids who could afford season tickets to the opera and dress accordingly. The first night, I happily introduced her to the regulars who sat around me, which hadn't happened with any of my other dates. They were standoffish at first, but after the third performance with Suzanne on my arm, they all caught on. After that, everyone had a great time together during intermissions, drinking champagne and sharing stories about past performances.

Suzanne had Knicks season tickets – we each had jerseys and caps – you couldn't ask for a better fit. The guy sitting behind us kept leaning in and asking Suzanne if she needed any help with the old guy. She just laughed and put her arm through mine and hit me on the head with her foam Number One hand. Two games later, he asked again, and she pulled me close and kissed me. He gave her a thumbs up and bought us beers. He became a good game friend.

We also did typical touristy things New Yorkers seldom do unless they have out-of-town relatives in town. We strolled through the Metropolitan Museum of Art, enjoying the paintings, other exhibits, and each other. We paid our fee and rode the elevator to the observatory of the Empire State Building, looked through the scopes, looked around to make sure no one was watching and kissed like lovers from the Midwest until we heard giggles from a gaggle of Japanese schoolgirls taking pictures of us with cell phones. Then we smiled and waved.

The following week, when Suzanne returned from what turned out to be her final photo shoot in Paris, we boarded an early ferry to the Statue of Liberty, trying unsuccessfully to avoid the crowds. Neither of us had seen it since we were kids. While we waited our turn to ascend to the torch, we shot a hundred pictures of each of us clowning around. We even managed to get Suzanne posed so it looked like she was holding the torch.

On the ferry ride back, we finalized plans for the afternoon. First stop, the nearest bodega, then a taxi stand, finally the cemetery. We asked the driver to wait while we each bought the biggest bouquet of flowers that looked fresh, then had him head to the cemetery, where we asked the cabbie to wait again.

"This better be worth my time," he yelled, over the soundtrack to some Bollywood movie he was playing at full blast.

"Only if you turn off that damn music," I yelled back from five feet away. "Have some respect. This is a cemetery!"

To his credit, he turned off the music and lit a cigarette. Small victories.

I walked with Suzanne to Rick's grave, then walked back to Missy's.

Suzanne

I gently put the bodega flowers at the base of Rick's headstone as the petals fell like confetti at a tickertape parade.

"I'll always love you, Rick," I said, surprisingly choking back only a few tears. "I love someone new, a great guy who loves me more than you did, if that's possible, and we're happy together, happier than I ever thought I could be during my darkest days. I know you approve. Goodbye, Rick."

I kissed the fingers of my right hand, bent down, and touched them to the top of the headstone. I stood up straight and walked to the new love of my life. I smiled at him as I wiped a lone tear from my cheek. He reached out and gently took my hand. I noticed that his bouquet had begun to disintegrate, too. As we walked arm in arm toward the taxi, I took a chance and asked, "What did you say to Missy, Jack?"

"Nothing out loud," he said. "I just listened. She knows we're deliriously happy and she approves. She just hopes you won't trip in the wet grass this time."

I hit him. Hard. In the stomach. He anticipated it. It hurt my hand.

Chapter 59
Jack

I snuck around quite a bit before our date that was just supposed to be a romantic evening to relive and laugh about the rebound breakups we had had at Erminia. First, her second-eldest son had picked out one of her favorite rings that fit her left ring finger and had given it to me to take to Tiffany's so I could get the right size engagement ring. Now, I know, the woman is supposed to be along to pick out the engagement ring, but I knew from her comments about rings other women wore, the size and shape of the ring she liked, so I felt safe picking out a half-carat princess-cut diamond flanked by diamonds running down the band and set in platinum. After I picked it out while she was in Rome and was given a pick-up date, I gave her son back the ring, which he returned to Suzanne's jewelry box without her knowing it was gone.

Before she returned, I made our reservations at Erminia, and asked our friend, the maître d, if he would be kind enough to call a few of the other regulars and invite them so they could witness the proposal instead of a breakup. I also swore a nearby florist to secrecy, even if any woman attempted to bribe him to discover any recent large orders and deliveries to Erminia. That doubled the cost of the flowers.

I picked her up in a taxi, thinking a limo would be too much of a giveaway. She recognized the driver and cursed when she did. Apparently, there was bad blood between them, but he ignored her dagger stares and I put my arm around her and held her hand, which made him look at me and smile. My palm was sweating, and I kept wiping it on my pants, which she must have thought was odd, since after each wipe I felt my coat pocket for the telltale bulge of the Tiffany's ring box.

We made small talk during the ride.

"How was Rome?"

"Old and crumbling. Good food and wine, though."

"I missed you. Terribly."

"That sounds horrible. Couldn't you have missed me wonderfully?"

"That would mean I was happy you were gone. I had a hollow spot in my heart."

"Me, too. The photographer had to coax smiles out of me for every frame. He got pissed until he told his assistant to get me a bottle of wine and then he made me drink three glasses. I smiled during the rest of the shoot."

"I'll remember that trick."

We kissed just as the taxi pulled up in front of the restaurant. Suzanne insisted on paying and I didn't argue. I checked my blazer pocket one more time, then I helped her out of the taxi and barely had time to close the door before the driver roared away into traffic. Suzanne just shook her head as we walked into Erminia.

Even I was taken aback by all the flowers in the dining room. Money well spent. Suzanne merely smiled though, as the maître d escorted us to our breakup table, past tables of diners with their heads down or turned away. Strange, I thought.

The wine and caviar arrived, and the sommelier poured me a taste, which I approved, then each of us a half glass.

"Suzanne, these past few months have been, well, magical and wonderful," I said, a little too loudly so I didn't choke up. "I know I've already told you, but I love you with all my heart."

I cleared my throat and slid back my chair. I slowly got up as diners put down their salad forks and soup spoons to watch and listen. I went to her side of the table. Out of the corner of my eye, I saw the restaurant staff gathered around the kitchen door.

"Are you going somewhere?" Suzanne asked, looking up.

"Not this time. I'm staying right here," I answered, tears in my eyes. I got down on one knee and pulled the Tiffany ring box out of my pocket.

"Suzanne, I never thought I could feel this deeply in love again," I said, looking into her eyes. "Now, I simply can't imagine the rest of my life without you. I know, because I've tried." I opened the box to reveal the diamond ring that I hoped she would love. "Suzanne, will you make me the happiest struggling novelist in the Western Hemisphere and marry me?"

"Oh, Jack, no," she said, putting her hand to her mouth. "Don't you dare do this!" She looked down at me for what seemed like an eternity with tears in her eyes.

"Get up, please, Jack," she said quietly so only I could hear her. I was confused. Does she hate the ring? Is she breaking up with me? I stood up. She looked at the ring in the box.

"Please sit down, Jack."

Magically, if on cue, my chair was behind me. Then Suzanne stood in front of me and got down on one knee. She took my sweaty hands in one hand and held the Tiffany box in the other.

"I am so in love with you, Jack. I fought it, denied it, but love won. Being with you, loving you, laughing together, has made me truly happy, happier than I thought I would ever be again. I don't want to spend another day thinking about my future unless you're my husband. So, Jack, I'll let you put this beautiful ring on my finger, but only if you'll marry me soon."

I stood and helped her off her knee, then slid the ring on her finger. "Why, Jack, it's a perfect fit," she said, winking. We kissed long and passionately. The crowd exploded with applause. Then Fr. Terrance tapped us on the shoulder to break off our kiss, and Ma and Pa and Bobby and his wife, and my daughters and Suzanne's two younger sons, and Lew got up from their tables and all gathered around us. We cried. They cried. I would cry more later when I saw the bill.

Suzanne had booked a room for us at the London NYC, which she told me about after the last guest had drained the last bottle of champagne.

"How the hell did you know?" I asked her after we got in the taxi.

"The ring, Jack, remember the ring," she grinned.

It was after 1:00 when we got to the room, and the hotel didn't mind that we had no luggage. We were like a couple of high school kids on prom night, tired high school kids, but at Suzanne's urging, I had stopped drinking alcohol around 10.

"Why?" I had asked, puzzled.

"I want you in tip-top shape," she whispered in my ear.

"For what?"

"Don't be stupid," she whispered as she kissed my ear.

We walked into the room, with its fabulous view, and immediately, Suzanne turned down the lights and opened the curtains. Music came on somehow. She kicked off her shoes, and I was way ahead of her.

"Is this special enough for you?" she asked throatily.

No way could I get any words out as I unzipped her dress and, as it slipped to the floor, I thought I would unsnap her bra one-handedly, which wasn't there, nor was she wearing a thong.

"Your turn."

She stood on her tiptoes and put her lips gently on mine as her fingers adeptly undid my belt and peeled off my shirt. She even got down on her knees, pausing midway, "Oh, God," I said, to take off my socks.

Then we moved to the couch and, well, that was the first time. Wrapped in each other's arms, we moved to the bed, and lay there talking about what a great evening we had had and how we had fooled each other into thinking we had fooled each other, which turned into how much we had come to love each other during the months we had been a serious couple, which turned into us remembering how to tell the other what we enjoyed, which turned into exploring to make those things happen until, exhausted, we fell asleep in each other's arms again.

When the sun shone in my eyes, I gently disentangled and made two cups of in-room coffee. I was brushing my teeth while the second cup was brewing. While rinsing my mouth, I felt Suzanne's arms around my waist and her bare breasts and hard nipples on my back.

"Move over, sailor," she said, yawning. "You don't get a monopoly on minty-fresh breath."

I took the coffee back to bed, and a few minutes later, a comfortably naked Suzanne pranced over, took a sip of hers, and without a word of warning, climbed on me, kissed me deeply, her hair falling over my face and shoulders, and guided my hands where she wanted them. She also did things with one of her hands, I couldn't say which one, only an experienced woman would know how to do.

After luxurious showers together, washing each other's backs and nothing else, well, almost nothing else, we laid around in the plush bathrobes, talking more about the evening, the lovemaking, our proposals, the ring, and more about the lovemaking.

"It was special," we laughed together.

There was new underwear for me, and some dainty things for Suzanne.

"I ordered it when I made the reservation," she admitted.

"I love you," I said.

"I love you more," she smiled.

We got dressed in our same clothes, which no one on the day staff had seen, and checked out, then headed into the restaurant where we had a fabulous brunch, famished from all our exercise. During our meal, we talked over plans for our wedding, the guest list, the church, St. Patrick's, of course, the reception, and the honeymoon. I wrote it all on the restaurant's linen napkin, which I paid for, of course.

Chapter 60
Jack

"We need to set up pre-marital counseling," Fr. Terrance told me in the confessional shortly after I confessed Suzanne and my endless and varied lovemaking two months before our wedding.

"I'd tell you to go hell, but that would be inappropriate and rude," I whispered through the screen. "Let's just have a nice little Mass and ceremony and we'll live happily ever after."

"I'll need to check with the archbishop."

"You do, and I'll tell him you did tell everyone what I told you in the confessional."

"That would be a lie, and you know it! This is blackmail."

"You're right, Bro! Gotcha! Just kidding. Now, forget the pre-marital counseling. We're too old. We know more about marriage than any priest in the city. Just reserve the church. Prepare a killer homily, and buy some new garments. Yours are a little ratty. Now give me absolution. My knees ache."

Suzanne and I spent the next month mailing invitations to a small number of friends and family – 300. A number in Europe, including Ireland, many in the Caribbean, most, of course, in New York. We even managed to turn this into "fun" after affixing the stamps. We barely reached the mailbox before the scheduled pickup time. We spent the rest of that afternoon planning our honeymoon, making flight reservations and confirming the outdoor reception venue, which we had reserved the morning after our engagement party.

As most couples do, we spent a lot of time together in the days leading up to the wedding. We were happy and comfortable and excited to see each other and even our fights over wedding cake were minor skirmishes in the scheme of things. We compromised on red velvet (her choice) with chocolate and sour cream frosting (my choice), and promised not to shove pieces into each other's mouths at the cake cutting. The most difficult decision we made was which apartment to keep, but even that was a compromise.

"They're both paid for," Suzanne pointed out, "so the only thing we need to pay are condo fees and taxes, which I can afford for both of us."

"I'm no gigolo," I said, in mock seriousness, "but if you want to brag to your friends that I'm you're kept man, that's not beneath me."

"Why don't I get beneath you and we work this out," she said, throatily, getting off the floor and leading me into the bedroom.

Later, we decided to keep both apartments, and she allowed that, since I had enough money set aside until my 104th year to pay the fees and taxes on my place, I should be allowed to keep it and she would be allowed to brag to her friends that I was her kept man. Marriage is about compromise. So is renewed passion, so before dinner and after my amazingly short recovery time, it was my turn to be beneath her.

Suzanne would not compromise on one tradition, though. Even though her wedding dress was beige because our marriage was her second, she refused to allow me to see her in it prior to the wedding. My daughters and her two college-aged sons had gone shopping with her. My daughters had veto power over each dress. The boys were only allowed final approval. They had made a full day of it.

"No."

"Too skimpy."

"Not skimpy enough."

"Mom, we're hungry. Can we have lunch now?"

"Two more designer shops now that we've eaten, ok?"

"Come closer, Suzanne."

"Ohmygod, Suzanne, it's perfect! Dad will love it! And then he'll cry."

"She's right, Mom. You look great! Now, can we get a beer?"

Finally, after the laughter, the tears and some very important negotiations by Lew with the Department of the Navy and the assistant to the Commandant of the Marine Corps, Capt. Richard O'Riley, resplendent in his dress blues, sword and all, walked her down the aisle with her other two sons on either side. He had surprised her at the rehearsal dinner at Erminia the night before, and to say she erupted in shouts and tears would have been doing an injustice to shouts and tears.

"Suzanne," I had said to her, as she responded to the fifth toast of the evening, "Lew has arranged a special guest in your honor."

On cue, Richard, Jr, dressed in civvies, walked through the kitchen door. Suzanne had dropped her empty wine glass, which her son caught before it crashed to the floor, she screamed, the chair flew back, she cried and ran into his waiting arms and nearly knocked him over. Well, not exactly. It's hard to knock over a battle-hardened Marine, but the illusion was there. He carried her back to the table where someone had pulled up a chair, but before he sat down, he saluted Lew, then man hugged him and sat down.

"I ate in the kitchen, Mom," he told her, "so quit trying to feed me and stop crying. I'll be around for a few days before I ship out to my next billet."

Suzanne had looked across the table at me and mouthed "Thank you. I love you even more!" I just smiled back and mouthed "I love you, too," but pointed at Lew, who had his arms around Doreen.

Suzanne and I went our separate ways after a long, passionate kiss in front of the restaurant, which was simultaneously broken up by our kids, who we each took home with us, with strict orders to get us to the church on time and properly dressed.

St. Patrick's Cathedral had seldom looked so good or had such an ecumenical crowd in attendance. Besides all our kids and other family members, my brother and her three sons were groomsmen, and Suzanne's friends and my daughters were bridesmaids. Everyone else, including Mrs. Steinmetz, was there, with, of all people, her daughter, son-in-law, and granddaughter and her new wife. Lew and Doreen sat together holding hands in the second pew.

"You may stop kissing the bride anytime, Jack," Fr. Terry said quietly to us.

So we kissed a little while longer in defiance, then we squeezed our hands and smiled.

"It is with great pleasure and relief that I present to you Jack Sullivan and Suzanne O'Riley-Sullivan, husband and wife."

We headed down the aisle, giggling like teenagers, arm-in-arm and out of church to the best reception Bobby Flay and Mario Batali had ever jointly catered, at a deep discount because we let them use our reception in their individual promotions, which I wrote, and Suzanne and I appeared in.

Chapter 61
Jack

Suzanne and I had wisely packed our bags before the wedding. The next day, after falling asleep too exhausted to do anything other than cuddle, we awoke well-rested and eager to consummate our marriage. We did so several times in several ways before it was time to shower, dress, order room service and get to JFK for our flight to St. Thomas, our first stop. Then it was a two-hour skiff ride over azure waters to a private island, which we had promised to buy if everything worked out like we hoped it would.

Our cabana is large, but not ostentatiously so. All bedrooms overlook the Caribbean, as does the wrap-around deck. The front steps lead down to the salt-sand beach, where we lay most days after mornings snorkeling or other activities.

This morning I was alone because Suzanne took our outboard to get groceries, mail and, of course, Red Stripe, rum, and tequila.

I heard her soft footsteps in the sand. I know she's not wearing clothes because we never do on this beach – it's one of our unspoken rules. No clothes on the beach. Her shadow covers my eyes.

"There's a letter from your lawyers and another one from your agent."

"What's the one from Lenny say?"

I heard her tear open the envelope.

"It's postmarked five weeks ago. Let's see...Dear Jack and Suzanne, blah, blah, blah...enclosed is your first royalty check. Jack, it's twenty-two thousand!"

"Guess we can eat for another week. What did the lawyers have to say?"

"How did you know I opened it?" she asked, innocently.

"Because you're my wife and you're allowed to open my mail unless it's addressed in a beautiful script and smells of expensive perfume."

"Sorry. The agency's insurance company paid the hostile work environment settlement and after deducting their fees they'll deposit your two-thirds share in our account immediately. That letter was postmarked three weeks ago."

"Rats! We could have been eating beans with our rice and fish heads all this time."

"There's also a newspaper clipping. Sukura Motors named Langston it's new vice president of marketing and sales. He and his sixth wife have moved to Tokyo."

"See, Suzanne, good things do happen to bad people."

"Honey, are we ever going back?"

"Lay down next to me so we can discuss this properly," I said. "Be honest, do you miss the city?"

"Uhm, no," she said, a little too hesitantly, "but I do miss my friends."

"Your work?"

"My agent knows where I am, but I don't want to leave you alone."

"I could stand to be apart for a few hours," I joked. "But honestly, you know you can take a modeling job anytime you want...Miss our kids?"

"How can I?" she said, rising on one elbow to look at me, her tanned breast laying naturally on her arm. "One or two of them sail in here every other week."

"Then let's stay here so we can lounge around on the beach naked all day. We'll own the island once I sell my brownstone and we can stay at your loft when we need to visit the city."

"You are such a dreamer," she laughed, as she put her arms around my neck and kissed me. "We still have to put on clothes when the kids or other family shows up, though."

-THE BEGINNING -

About the Author

Patrick James Brown has written for publication since high school. He is the author of an award-winning one-act play, numerous magazine articles, a non-fiction account of North Dakota's statehood centennial celebration, a plethora of successful advertising and public relations campaigns, a children's book, and his first novel, The Mick. The Rebounders is his second novel. He grew up in Bismarck, North Dakota, lived briefly in Atenas, Costa Rica, and currently lives in Fargo, North Dakota.

Author photo by Mark Anthony,
Visionaries Photography, Moorhead, Minnesota.

www.ingramcontent.com/pod-product-compliance
Lightning Source LLC
Chambersburg PA
CBHW051824020726
47502CB00005B/1613